ALEX MILWAY was born in 1978 in Hereford, England. After finishing art school and spending a number of years in magazine publishing, he finally managed to finish a book. He now lives in London with his girlfriend and a curly-haired cat called Milo.

ISIAH LOVELOCK'S
MANSION

THE OLD TOWN
GENTLEMEN'S CLUB

MERCHANTS' SQUARE

DIRE STREET
PRISON

PIRATE'S WHARF

THE MARSHES

Old Town

THE HARBOR

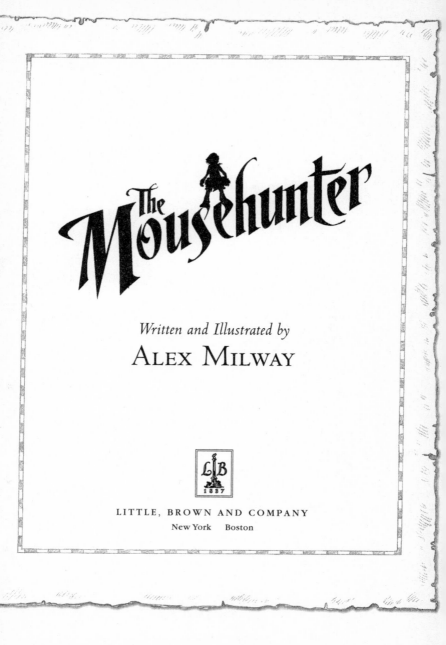

The Mousehunter

Written and Illustrated by

ALEX MILWAY

LITTLE, BROWN AND COMPANY
New York   Boston

Little, Brown and Company

Hachette Book Group USA
237 Park Avenue, New York, NY 10017
Visit our Web site at www.lb-kids.com

First U.S. Edition: February 2009
First published in Great Britain in 2008 by Faber and Faber Limited

ISBN 978-0-316-02454-9

10 9 8 7 6 5 4 3 2 1

RRD-C

Printed in the United States of America

For Katie

A mouse of little consequence
is a rare thing indeed.
Isiah Lovelock

Emiline

Miserley

Scratcher

Drewshank

Spires

Algernon

Mousebeard

Lovelock

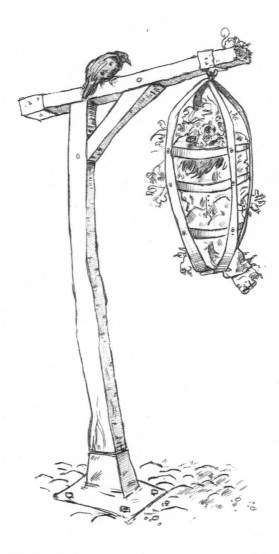

Welcome to Old Town

THE NIGHT HAD BEEN QUIET SO FAR — ONLY THREE bodies to speak of, and none of them carried anything of worth to Mr. Droob. It was a bad night's work if fewer than ten washed ashore, and to bide his time he sat quietly spying the river, rubbing his hands to keep warm.

At the riverside, the Pirate's Wharf gibbet creaked and swayed in the breeze, the last remains of its long-dead pirate struggling to cling to its irons. Mr. Droob watched the thin fog roll off the water, enveloping the dying glow of the street lamps. He saw his assistant leap up to ring the warning bell: another body approached.

Mr. Droob strode down to the river, buttoning his jacket on the way. His assistant waited silently, watching as the body floated nearer. In his arm rested a long hooked pole, and with a looping stretch he dropped it onto the body. It caught at the waist, and he pulled it in.

A quick glance showed clearly that it was the body of a man, and a sailor at that: his blue flared trousers, dirty and torn, and his bloodstained shirt were the clothes of the merchant navy.

With a stomach-churning groan, his assistant took hold of the heavy, lifeless body and dragged it up the bank. With little ceremony he searched the corpse, checking for rich pickings. There seemed nothing of any worth, no pocket watch, knife, or coins, but tied to the man's neck was a small wooden box.

Mr. Droob picked it up and shook it gently. It weighed very little, but there was something inside. Nailed to the box was a metal plate with an inscription, and Mr. Droob's eyes sparkled when he read its words.

"Well, well, well," he said. "What a find . . . what a find indeed!"

The Silver Shark

The Flying Fox

The Mousekeeper

EMILINE ORELIA RACED ACROSS THE HALLWAY TO THE bottom of the grand stairwell. Her rusty mouse-keeper's armor clattered noisily — it was way too big for a twelve-year-old girl — and she clutched it firmly to stop it from falling around her ankles.

Sitting on the bottom step of the stairs, quietly preening itself in a beam of light, was the fearsome Sharpclaw: the very same exotic and supremely expensive mouse that had escaped from the mousery only hours earlier. Not even Emiline had reckoned on its claws being *that* sharp.

Sharpclaws were sneaky and mischievous little devils, but despite being only the size of a hand, absolutely nothing could be left to chance. Emiline's armor covered everything from her shoulders to the tips of her toes, and a pointed helmet covered her face to the bottom of her nose. The only recognizable feature that remained was Emiline's blond hair, which crept out onto her shoulders and curled slightly at the end.

Being a mousekeeper was far from a glamorous job. Emiline had to clean cages, feed the hundreds of mice that lived in her care, and do every other menial task imaginable. She was particularly good at it, though, and showed talents far above her station. It was for this reason that she found herself in her current predicament, armed to the teeth with mousenets, hooks, ropes, and light explosives — anything and everything that could be used to capture the dastardly mouse that was running free.

As she approached, the Sharpclaw continued to clean itself with great attention to detail. Each claw flicked out in turn, receiving a refreshing lick as it sparkled in the light. The mouse let her creep closer and closer without making a move.

Emiline watched and waited, breathing quietly so as

not to alarm it, and when the time was right, she lunged forward and threw out a net. The mouse remained calm, lifted a single claw, and sliced the net to a thousand pieces in a torrent of incredibly quick flicks. It jumped three steps upward and relaxed back onto its haunches, seizing a moment to snarl in her face. It then gave a sharp, shrill squeak and scurried off, just fast enough to keep Emiline slightly out of reach.

Stair after stair, they scrambled their way up. The third-floor landing passed, then the fourth and the fifth. The mouse still hurtled upward, and despite the weighty armor, Emiline kept going. Suddenly, as they reached the sixth floor, the mouse veered off and made a bee-line for the mousery. Her heart sank as she realized the door was open, and the Sharpclaw shot inside and out of sight.

Emiline lit the lamps, provoking a chorus of squeaks and chirrups from the menagerie within. The Howling Scent Mouse started to wail, setting off the Whooping Brown Mouse, who hollered uncontrollably, bringing the Weeping Tearjerker Mouse to tears in a fit of bawling blubber. The noise was deafening.

At least a hundred and fifty different mice lived there, all housed in beautiful cages that mimicked their habitat. It was a collection worth millions, the best in Old Town, and out of the corner of her eye Emiline saw the Sharpclaw. It had caught her attention by jumping up and down, waving its paws high in the air. It wanted her to see it destroy a cage door. The mouse sliced it easily with a flick of a claw, then jumped along and swiped at the next cage, once again waving its paws in the air in a fit of excitement. Emiline screamed for help. The mouse wasn't going to stop there: it was going to set the whole collection free.

She slammed the door shut and called once more. Some of the rarest mice in the world were seeing freedom flash before their eyes. The Sleepy Shorthaired Mouse didn't care to escape, though, and the Nervous Night Mouse of Grin-Grin also faltered in its attempt at freedom, but it was all too clear that most of the occupants of the mousery were scuttling maniacally across the floor. There were big mice, fat mice, six-legged mice, mice with enormous ears, singing mice, skipping mice, rolling mice. The floor had become a swarming carpet of fluffy rodents, and Emiline was in real trouble.

Eventually the mousery door opened behind her and Spires the butler charged into the melee. He took one look at the chaos before him and darted off to collect cages, boxes, and tools. He began to help Emiline gather up all the escapees.

"I'm sure Mr. Lovelock will have a few things to say about this, Emiline," said the butler breathlessly, sweeping up a Lumpy-backed Rock Mouse.

"Well, I'll say a few things to him too, Mr. Spires," she replied. "Who'd have put such a dangerous animal in a rubbish cage?"

Emiline was so annoyed by the butler's tone that she stamped around to the top of the room, picking up a Bangarian Monk Mouse on the way. It was sitting with its head in its hands: an easier catch couldn't be had. Mouse after mouse was seized and returned to its cage; the room became calm. Emiline counted them all. Three were missing, one of them the Sharpclaw. After all that searching she still hadn't found the little monster, and she didn't dare think of the trouble it would cause let loose in the mansion.

⇒ ✳ ⇐

The mouse collection that Emiline looked after belonged to Isiah Lovelock, author of *The Mousehunter's Almanac* and one of the richest collectors in the world. His book had been an overnight success and was now published in every corner of the globe. No other encyclopedia of mice was so well informed about its subject, and every child with dreams of becoming a mousehunter would save their money all year just to buy the latest update. The almanac was a phenomenon, and its wily author knew exactly how to make the most of its worth: toys, puzzles, badges, books — if there was a way to make money out of mice, Isiah Lovelock knew how. He also knew the power money brought to its owner and how to spend it.

Lovelock's mansion was situated on Grandview, the leafy hill that rose high out of Old Town's ancient center. It towered over every other building around and dominated the skyline just as much as Lovelock's wealth gave him power over Old Town's inhabitants. The mansion widened greatly as it rose up into the sky, with many crooked chimney stacks tilting out of its roof at unhappy angles. It leaned heavily to one side, and if the rumors were to be believed, this was due to the huge and ever-growing pile of gold in the attic. Massive wooden props were needed to stop the building from toppling over and were regularly replaced because of the sheer weight they carried.

As an attempt to balance the building, a crude box room was built onto the side of the seventh floor. Unsurprisingly it had little effect, and Isiah Lovelock, seeing no other use for it, deemed it to become the bedroom for his lowliest servant, the mousekeeper.

It was a dowdy room, painted in a light shade of gray, and the only hints of color were made by the damp patches seeping through the walls. With its small arched windows to let in as little light as possible and an awkward, uneven floor, you could be forgiven for thinking that it was purposely built to be horrible. But it was closer to the mousery than the other servants' quarters, so for Emiline it wasn't all bad news.

Apart from a rusty iron bed and a few bookshelves, which carried nothing more than *The Mousehunter's Almanac* and several guides to good mousekeeping, Emiline kept the room fairly empty. There was her cupboard full of protective clothes and, of course, her mouse armor; then there was her chest of mousetraps and mousecatching implements. There were a lot of things mouse-oriented and little else: for someone so dedicated to the task of becoming a mousehunter as Emiline, the normal things in life tended to pass her by.

One thing Emiline did have, however, was her Grey Mouse called Portly. Greys were ordinary mice, of a kind that every child might start their collection with. You could generally teach them a few tricks, nothing too amazing, but Portly was so well trained he could jump through hoops, turn cartwheels, and even bite his name into a lump of cheese. Portly could usually be found perched on Emiline's shoulder — the place where he was most comfortable — but in the ruckus that followed the Sharpclaw's escape, he'd been left behind.

When Emiline trudged into her room, Portly quite rightly took it upon himself to ignore her.

"Portly!" she cajoled for the third time, slumping down onto her bed. The little mouse squeaked grumpily from the top of his wooden mousebox and resolutely faced the wall. Emiline often spent time sitting in her room alone, mainly to stay out of the butler's path, but Portly would always be there to talk to. He could always be counted on as a friend, even though he was just a mouse. When the Whitewater Mouse of Inglenook had careered into the toilet system, it was Emiline who climbed down into the sewers to await its swift deposit from the outlet pipes. When she'd had to wash herself four times so that she could no longer smell the sewage, Portly had been the one she'd complained to. When the Rook-winged Mouse of Scarlet Island made a break from its cage at cleaning time, it was Emiline who had to shimmy up the chimney to stop it from escaping. Once again, it was Portly who listened attentively to her story. Portly had always seemed to understand the lot of a daring young mousekeeper, but not this time.

"Come on, Portly," she asked again. "There'll be some biscuit for you!"

Portly's ears shot to attention, and his little tail curled

upward into a roll. At the crunching sound of Emiline breaking a dry oaten biscuit in two, the Grey Mouse charged to the base of the bed, vanished for a few seconds, and then appeared at Emiline's chin, his nose twitching brightly.

"I had to leave you here, didn't I?" she said gently. "You understand, don't you? That Sharpclaw could have had you for breakfast, and he's still on the loose. If Mr. Lovelock finds out about this, I'm a lost cause!"

Portly sat nibbling at the biscuit. He looked almost ready to forgive her.

"I may be the best mousekeeper in Old Town, but there are plenty more out there who'd jump at the chance to work for Mr. Lovelock. I've got to keep on my toes, Portly. Who knows where that mouse has gone?"

Portly squeaked brightly and ran up and around the back of her neck to hide in her hair. He liked it there, and Emiline stood up and smiled.

From the window, she watched a mist rolling on the road far below, swirling around the orange glow of the oil lamps. As usual, all was quiet. When night fell in Old Town, people rarely ventured out without protection.

Illegal mousetraders walked the streets, selling stolen mice and dealing in banned species. Any innocents who witnessed their activities would often never speak of it again, for illegal traders had the awful habit of setting Red-necked Chomper Mice — who have a particular liking for human tongue — loose on their victims.

During the day these traders would stay out of sight, frequenting the murky mousing taverns and hovels that littered the streets. But once it got dark, the Old Town Guard turned a blind eye to their activities — catching them just wasn't worth their time. Add to these the muggers and rogues who'd rob you faster than you could say Blinking Mouse of Bobo, and it was no wonder decent folk kept indoors.

But as Emiline started to think about going to bed, something caught her eye out on the road. Barely visible through the misty haze, Emiline could just make out the figure of a man. His hunched, shadowy form passed the oil lamp, stopped briefly, and then disappeared from view.

From the hallway, seven floors down, three echoing knocks rang out on the front door. Eventually the butler's footsteps sounded on the stairs and, with a quiet tinkle of a bell, the door creaked open. Emiline's heart began to race. There was only one person who would travel around the city at night by choice; one person even the mousetraders wouldn't touch. It was Mr. Droob, Old Town's Dead Collector.

⇒ ✳ ⇐

"If you could just wait here," said the butler.

"'Course," replied Mr. Droob, clasping the small wooden box in his hands.

He sat down quietly in the ground-floor reception room, his plain brown jacket touching the ground. Isiah Lovelock's name was a welcome find upon the sailor's box. A lousy night had instantly become a lucrative one. But there was something about Lovelock's mansion that made him uneasy. Paintings of far-off lands hung on the walls, and flickering lamps cast twitchy shadows across the floor. Mr. Droob's beady eyes darted nervously around — he was particularly unsettled by a glass case of stuffed Aurora Mice. Their bright colors had faded, but their teeth were bared menacingly.

"Mr. Lovelock will see you now," said the butler, appearing again. His stiff shape made it clear that he didn't care to converse with someone such as a Dead Collector. He ushered Mr. Droob out, then led him to the grand staircase.

The stairs wound up, on and on, until Mr. Droob was directed toward a darkened corridor on the sixth floor. A door at the far end was slightly ajar, and an orange glow leaked into the hallway. Mr. Droob rubbed his hands nervously.

The butler walked ahead and knocked gently on the door.

"Mr. Droob is here to see you, sir," he said, pushing it open and directing the man in.

The room was long and narrow, with one wall covered by a gigantic brown-edged map. A large window was filled with pitch-black night at the farthest end, and in front of this rested Isiah Lovelock, framed by darkness. He was leaning back calmly in a leather armchair — concealed from the waist down by a wide oak desk. A tall plume of smoke drifted upward from the cigarette in his fingers. His emotionless expression — his cold eyes, pale face, and sealed bloodless lips — conveyed a complete lack of interest in the world and in Mr. Droob in particular.

Anyone who didn't know Lovelock might think by his pallor that he didn't get out much, and they'd be right. He rarely ventured out unless on business, and it was noted in the town that he never went farther than the river when he did. This was strange for such a powerful man, but no one in Old Town ever asked questions of Isiah Lovelock.

"I hear you have something of mine," he said abruptly, resting the cigarette on an ashtray on the table.

"I have a box with your name on it," came the reply. Mr. Droob walked closer, his suddenly jelly legs wanting to resist. He stooped over and placed the box on the desk.

Isiah Lovelock craned forward and picked it up. The little box fitted neatly into the palm of his hand, and he shook it gently, feeling a light weight roll inside. A smile crept along his mouth.

"Thank you, Mr. Droob, all seems to be in order. You can leave now."

"But sir, there was a sailor . . . ," stammered Mr. Droob, turning the hat in his hands.

"The sailor was a nobody, a pirate at best. If he had been any better he'd still be alive."

"But for my efforts, sir . . . ," pleaded Mr. Droob.

"Of course. My butler will reimburse you for your time."

Mr. Droob walked reluctantly out of the room, and Spires, who was waiting outside, passed a brown envelope into his hands.

"I think this should be sufficient for your efforts," said the butler, showing Mr. Droob down the stairs.

"I hope I shall find some more things for your master," he replied, flicking greedily through the stack of money that filled the envelope.

The butler smiled. "I very much hope that you won't," he said.

⇒ ✳ ⇐

Squeezed into a secret passageway behind Lovelock's office, Emiline had watched events unfurl through a small slatted air vent. It wasn't the most comfortable of places but had proved a worthwhile venture, as she'd also found one of the escaped mice asleep on a beam. It was a Long-legged River Mouse, a common species, and one of the most pleasing to collectors because of its exceptionally long and elegant legs. Their cages have to be made especially tall to allow for them.

Emiline placed the mouse safely in a mousebox — she always carried one, like any good mouser should — and hung it on her belt. It didn't make any fuss, nestling softly down into the fluffy lining.

Her vision was slightly obscured, but she had a good view of Lovelock's desk. She could see the wooden box clearly. It was a mousebox, just like the one hanging from her waist.

Once the butler and Mr. Droob had left, Lovelock withdrew a small silver knife from his velvet jacket and skewered it carefully into the lid of the box. He twisted it sharply and the lid split open.

His face paled even further. Then he banged the desk violently and slumped into his chair. After a few more moments, Emiline saw his gray spidery fingers re-emerge on the desk and rummage in the box. Lovelock withdrew a small cloth mouse stitched from tatters of old material, and Emiline gasped and covered her mouth. She'd heard of this object many times but never thought she'd ever see one: it was the calling card of the most famous pirate of all. Lovelock pulled a cord to his right and a bell rang out downstairs.

After a minute of waiting, Lovelock's patience withered.

"Spires, blast it, where are you?" he shouted, his words thick with outrage.

Almost immediately, the butler burst through the door, out of breath.

"The pirate's gone one step too far this time," said Lovelock, the cloth mouse swinging ominously from between his fingers. "Who does he think he is?"

"Sir?" said the butler quizzically, breathing heavily.

Lovelock stood up and turned to the window. He tugged sharply at the head of the mouse, and the glass steamed up with the warmth of his breath.

"Head to the harbor and find a vessel under the charge of Captain Devlin Drewshank. Tell him that I wish to speak to him as a matter of urgency."

"But, sir," protested the butler, "the port is the last place I should be visiting at this hour. It's a place for pirates and brigands, not butlers. . . ."

Safe in her hiding place, Emiline jumped with excitement. Captain Drewshank was a celebrity among the mousing community ever since he'd stumbled upon a colony of mice on Moon Island. What business would he have coming to Grandview? Lovelock turned and slammed the desk.

"I have no care for them, and neither should you," he said. "Look at you worrying about such a thing as pirates. You're the butler of Isiah Lovelock! You wear my crest, man. Who would touch you?"

"But, sir . . ."

"Plans are already in motion, Spires, and we must act fast to take advantage. Take my carriage and pay the driver whatever is required. I'm sure you'll make it in one piece."

Spires swallowed. "Yes, sir."

Lovelock raised the tattered cloth mouse and flicked its head sharply, over and over in his hand. It bounced back up time and time again until, in one quick movement, Lovelock grasped the mouse's head and tore it fully from its body. He turned and cast both pieces to the floor, looking at Spires with an intensity the butler had never seen in him before.

"Be sure of it," said Lovelock, "This is the last time Mousebeard gets the better of me."

Emiline shrank back into the passageway, the word *Mousebeard* circling endlessly through her thoughts. He was the pirate of pirates: bigger, nastier, and hairier than any other. Ever since she was tiny she'd heard horrible tales of him and the infamous mice that lived in his beard.

With her heart beating heavily, Emiline checked the mouse in her care. It was snoring sweetly, and making occasional sleepy squeaks. Something exciting was happening — something bigger and greater than anything that normally happened to a mousekeeper. She wanted to be part of it, and from the look on Portly's face as his nose twitched through the vent, he wanted it too.

The Sharpclaw Mouse

THE SHARPCLAW IS ONE OF THE BEST KNOWN AND MOST FEARED OF ALL mice, due to the huge dagger-like claws on its front paws. These claws are almost as long as the mouse itself, and are capable of slicing through wood and metal with effortless ease. The size of its claws doesn't seem to hinder it, however, as the Sharpclaw has evolved strong hind legs to compensate, allowing it to run almost upright.

Throughout history, Sharpclaws have always proved problematic to humans, and the land of their origin — the isle of Umber in the South Seas — is now little more than a barren lump of rock due to the mouse's propensity for destroying anything in its path.

MOUSING NOTES

It takes a particularly strong mousebox or cage to contain a Sharpclaw, and in view of this, only the most fearless of collectors or hunters should attempt to keep or catch one. Due to mousing regulations, the species requires an expensive license to be kept in captivity because of its ferocity. Therefore, Sharpclaws are only suitable for rich collectors with more money than sense.

The Privateer

THE CARRIAGE TRUNDLED ALONG THE TWISTING ALLEYS
and then the roads that led through the marshes
out of Old Town. The fog was thickening, and the
driver followed the glow of lamps for direction.

Mr. Lovelock's butler sat bolt upright, maintaining
his calm demeanor despite the sense of unease growing
in his stomach and the cold air stinging his face. The
harbor was approaching, and there were many places
he'd much rather be. Once the carriage arrived at the
town gates, the driver pulled tight on his horse's reins
and stopped sharply.

"This ain't somewhere I'll be going, sir," he said.

"But I've enough money to pay double for your services, driver. Carry on," said the butler briskly.

The driver leaned forward and peered deeper into the fog. "No. Money's no good to me when I'm dead, sir. You go and I'll await your return," he added, lowering the reins.

The butler sighed and stepped down to the floor. Taking a lamp from the carriage, he held it aloft and stared into the murky gloom. The harbor lay beyond the rusting iron gates before him. A soldier stood upright at their side, his face weakly lit by a lamp attached to a wall behind. He stamped noisily, took hold of the gates, and pushed them open.

The Old Town Gate had stood for a long time, welcoming people to the town, but also keeping any unwanted seadogs at bay. The butler tightened his cloak and pulled his hat down to obscure his eyes. He walked forward as the gates squealed shut behind him.

Through the thick fog, the butler could see the faint swinging lights that sat atop the bows of ships, and he could smell the salty sea more clearly. The dull clanking of buoys and mastbells littered the air like the sound of lost sheep on a mountaintop, and the distant raucous banter of rum-soaked sailors drifted along on the wind.

He gripped the dagger underneath his cloak and walked more quickly.

The ground was of hard cobblestones, and the butler's footsteps rang out rather too loudly. He walked past a number of gloomy buildings, their purpose obscured by the fog, and neared the waterfront. The ships were slightly more visible now, looking like the shadowy forms of a ghostly armada in the distance. He found some steps that took him down to the quayside, and stopped dead at the low sea wall, trying to shield himself from the sea spray that threatened to ruin his immaculately polished shoes. Out on the water, he could see the ominous shadows of bows and masts, their shapes emerging and vanishing with the movement of the fog.

From behind him, he heard footsteps. He turned quickly, thrusting the lamp out. Suddenly a hand grasped his arm and he was bundled to the ground. His lamp flew to the floor and smashed, extinguishing the light immediately.

"Release me!" shouted the butler, struggling, while being pressed against the cobblestones. His glasses eased off his nose — he could just about make them out on the ground in front of him.

"What're you doin' sneaking about by our boat?" snarled a deep, scratchy, seafaring voice.

"I'm looking for Drewshank."

"You're looking for that pirate? What you wanting with him?" said the man, whose hard hobnail boot was stuck firmly in his back.

The butler heard other voices and footsteps approaching.

"I'll ask you once more," he pleaded, "kindly take me to Devlin Drewshank. I'll make sure you're paid well."

"Gold, silver, and gems," said the man, "that's all you folk are about. What d'you reckon, boys, shall we take him to Drewshank?"

The butler was surrounded by dirty feet. If they so much as touched his glasses, his dagger would be put to full use.

"Let's throw him in the briney . . . rob him first, of course," chuckled one voice.

"Nah, let's string 'im up from the yardarm," said another.

"That's a big waste," bantered a third. "Let's eat 'im!"

"That's enough!" boomed a stronger, more assertive voice. The butler felt the weight on his back lighten. "You dirty pirates, treating a nice butler like this."

Mr. Spires was able to stand and pushed himself to his feet, taking his glasses with him. His hat remained on the floor, covered in dirt. He picked it up and made a big point of cleaning it.

"Captain Drewshank?" he asked hopefully. Once his glasses were righted, he was able to size up his thuggish assailants one by one.

"Why, yes it is," replied a man proudly.

Drewshank was tall, with a striking, chiseled face. Dressed in a smart blue uniform, he could pass as a gentleman — at least in the present company. But Drewshank was a privateer, a so-called mercenary for hire, which, according to some, made him just short of being a pirate. With a twinkle in his eye, Drewshank had a huge amount of charm and a good nose for making money.

"And why, sir, have you come to call upon me at this late hour?" he said smoothly.

"My master, Isiah Lovelock, requires your presence."

"Ah! That old rogue, I should have known." Drewshank took the butler by the arm and pulled him free of the rabble. "You'll have to excuse them," he added, "but they help keep unsavory types from the docks. Now, shall we continue this discussion aboard ship?"

"They get more unsavory?" muttered the butler to himself as he followed Drewshank along the quayside.

After a minute's walk, Drewshank halted before his ship, which was resting sideways along a wide wooden pier. Its hull rose a few meters above his head, and its bowsprit shot out like a spear over the quayside. The ship's stern was completely lost to the fog, but orange lights glowed from the cabins and deck, highlighting the ship's beautiful outline and two skeletal masts.

"This is the *Flying Fox*," said Drewshank, looking up proudly. "No doubt you've heard of her."

"Well, no, sir. I tend not to have time for news of the sea," replied Spires.

Drewshank, feeling slightly rebuffed, hastened his walk to the gangplank and stepped on board.

"But the *Flying Fox?*" he continued. "This amazing vessel has sailed the Seventeen Seas, fought among the Espedrills at the War of Angry Neck, and even raced the Diver Mice around Cape Kopper. No finer craft has ever sailed!"

Spires smiled to himself, taking in the details of the ship as he went aboard. It appeared empty of sailors, who were no doubt all in the taverns causing the usual ruckus. He couldn't help but be impressed with the dark-wood deck and golden edging that ran around the hull. Not that he was going to mention it.

"Sir, I apologize for my lack of knowledge regarding your ship, but my master has an excellent understanding of its qualities and those of its captain — which is why I'm here."

Halting with a flourish in front of his cabin door, a proud smile lit up Drewshank's face.

"Of course, I couldn't expect a mere butler to take an interest in the pursuits of gentlemen."

"Not at all. Butlers take a very great interest in gentlemen," replied Spires smoothly. Drewshank's smile vanished.

"So, why did you need my help?" he said pointedly.

Before he could receive an answer, the captain guided Spires into his plush quarters. Oil lamps lit the small cabin, which contained a wide table, a few tall leather-backed chairs, and plenty of mousing trophies. Some decorated cabinets and mirrors were secured to the walls, along with a very indulgent oil painting of Drewshank himself.

"Mr. Lovelock wishes to commission you," said the butler.

"What does he want this time?" Drewshank asked, settling down into the captain's chair.

"I don't know," replied the butler, "but he requests your presence at Grandview immediately."

"Immediately?" exclaimed Drewshank. "A man has to sleep at some point of a night! I'm sorry, but I didn't catch your name?"

"Spires, sir."

"Right then, Spires. Seeing as you're stopping me from falling into my hammock, I suggest you give me good reason to leave my quarters. Nothing to do with him, by any chance?" said Drewshank. He raised an eyebrow and pointed to a poster pinned to the wall. In its center was a sketchy representation of the inimitable Captain Mousebeard, underneath which the caption read:

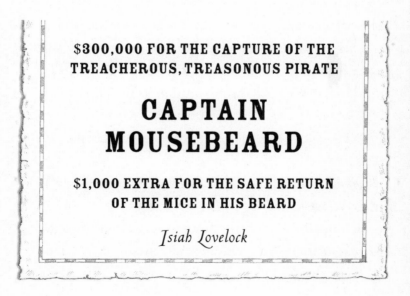

$300,000 FOR THE CAPTURE OF THE
TREACHEROUS, TREASONOUS PIRATE

CAPTAIN
MOUSEBEARD

$1,000 EXTRA FOR THE SAFE RETURN
OF THE MICE IN HIS BEARD

Isiah Lovelock

The butler recognized the poster. They'd been pinned around Old Town, and the frowning, bearded pirate stared out onto every street as though he owned it.

"If it's something to do with him, then I may be interested . . . ," said Drewshank.

"It's a wise presumption," answered the butler, "but I know no more. Our carriage is waiting at the Old Town Gate, to take us there directly. Will you join me?"

The captain lowered his head and scratched it vigorously. After taking a deep breath, he grabbed his gold-braided overcoat from the back of a chair and stood up.

"I hope it's worth my while, Spires. I don't want to be up all night," he said, checking his appearance in a grandiose mirror. He looked good, as usual.

"Very good, sir," said the butler.

⇒ ✳ ⇐

It was early morning by the time Drewshank and the butler left the carriage and entered the mansion. The house was deadly silent; not even a mouse could be heard squeaking from the mousery.

"Please wait here, sir," said Spires as he darted into a

small anteroom, removed his cloak, and tidied himself up. He couldn't be seen looking a mess in front of Mr. Lovelock. After climbing the stairs and speaking briefly to his master, Spires returned, took Drewshank's overcoat, and hung it neatly by the door. They then started the long ascent of the stairs together.

The light still glowed from Lovelock's office, and the butler opened the door and invited Drewshank to sit down. To Drewshank's surprise, Lovelock was elsewhere.

"My master will be with you shortly," said Spires unapologetically, and promptly left the room, closing the door firmly.

The butler reached the top of the stairs and started the long walk down to the kitchen, finding the quiet of the house calming. Mr. Spires was pleased to be back at the mansion. He took a few steps further and the peace was shattered.

"Watch out!" shouted Emiline, charging up from the floor below. Dressed once more in her armor, she clasped a peculiar mouse in her hands. It wriggled and squirmed, sniffing the air all the while through its exceptionally long snout.

"I need to speak with you!" she shouted, breathlessly, while disappearing onto the landing and into the mousery.

"Are all the escaped mice captured, Emiline?" he replied, his tone letting her know that this sort of behavior could not be tolerated in the mansion.

Spires received no reply until a door creaked shut and Emiline appeared once more at the stairs.

"Not quite," she said wearily. "I found that Snorkel Mouse in the bath on the fourth floor, but the Sharpclaw's vanished."

"What did you want to say to me?" asked the butler.

"Who was that man? Was that Captain Drewshank?" quizzed Emiline.

"It was. Why does it concern you?" he replied sternly.

"Mr. Lovelock has a problem with Mousebeard, so he calls for the world-famous Captain Drewshank. It's obvious! And, unlike you, any normal person would be very excited to have him in their home. He caught the first Yellow-nosed Fire Mouse and brought it back to Old Town!"

The butler took Emiline by the arm forcefully and walked her down the stairs.

"Watch the words that come from your mouth, Emiline. This is no place to be talking of Mr. Lovelock and that pirate in such a way. And as for Mr. Drewshank and his overblown tales of mousehunting derring-do, well, you'd do best to keep away from types like him."

"Mr. Spires, you're so old and fusty. For anyone who knows anything about mice, he is as much of a legend as Mr. Lovelock. To sail and hunt mice with Captain Drewshank would be a dream come true," she said.

"Emiline, he'd never take a mousekeeper like you. You're too young."

"Too young? At least I can see past the end of my nose!"

The butler let her go and continued down the staircase alone.

"Go to bed," he said firmly, pushing his glasses up his nose.

But going to bed was the last thing she meant to do.

❧ ❋ ❧

Drewshank looked around Lovelock's office impatiently, his legs crossed and his fingers tapping at the chair. It had been several minutes since the butler had left him on his own, and he was finding it intensely boring and irritating. He had spent most of the time studying the map of mousetrading routes that covered the wall, wondering if he could learn any secrets about the great man's latest investments around the Seventeen Seas. He'd learned nothing new, or at least nothing of any importance.

Drewshank had had dealings with Lovelock before; many of them were quite dangerous tasks, such as transporting an expensive mouse around the world, or guarding a hideously large amount of money on its route to a fellow mouse collector.

Sometimes their business relationship held benefits for both parties. It was upon Lovelock's request that he'd taken part in the Green Island Mousehunting Expedition, where he accidentally discovered the Spiny Rock Mouse by sitting on it. (He never let on that he required surgery in order to remove the rodent.) For his contribution to mousing Drewshank had received a plaque at the Mousehunters' Lodge — a fine honor indeed — and Lovelock became the first person to get the new breed of mouse in his collection.

But this was the first time Isiah Lovelock had called him to his mansion; these sorts of undertaking were usually set in motion at dimly lit coffeehouses or in the genteel parlors of the Old Town Gentlemen's Club at Isiah's invitation.

Eventually, Lovelock entered the room and shut the door. Drewshank sat a little straighter in his chair while Lovelock walked slowly around to his desk and sat down.

"Ah! Captain Drewshank," he said, a slight tiredness in his voice, "you must excuse me for calling you here at such an unseemly hour, but I need you to set sail at the first opportunity. There's no time to waste."

Drewshank sat back and flicked a speck of mouse hair from his knee.

"I don't know if that's possible at such short notice. And if it were, I'd need supplies and more crew, Mr. Lovelock," said Drewshank.

Lovelock's face barely flickered: "I've already contacted

the relevant people, and supplies to last three months will be at the harbor first thing tomorrow. I've taken the chance to hire more men for your voyage, and also ordered six of the most powerful cannons in Old Town — these are being taken to your ship as we speak."

"You're not one to be underestimated, Mr. Lovelock."

Lovelock's stare only hardened. "I'll tell you in no uncertain terms, if you complete this task then I'll make you the richest and most famous privateer that ever lived."

Drewshank's eyes glazed over for a moment, and then he shifted in his seat. He'd be damned if he'd roll over for Lovelock quite so quickly.

"I must admit, you've got me interested, but you'll need to give me more information to persuade me. For a start, why are you so impatient to send me off tomorrow?"

Lovelock walked to the map. He pointed to Hamlyn, a port nestled on a small rocky island just two days' sailing from Old Town.

"My merchant ship, the *Lady Caroline*, was attacked and sunk in the seas north of Hamlyn. That infernal pirate Mousebeard was involved, and I want you to see to it that he never sails again."

Drewshank noted that Lovelock's breathing had hastened slightly, and a tinge of color appeared in his cheeks. The captain raised an eyebrow. "That's no small task, Isiah," he said. "But I see you've upped the reward for his capture."

"You've noticed my posters then?"

"I haven't met a sailor who doesn't have one pinned to his hammock posts. Everyone in Old Town dreams of catching him."

Lovelock smiled thinly. "There's a lot of talk of catching Mousebeard in the taverns, but so far I've not seen one captain so much as point his ship in the right direction, let alone put up a fight. Why, if I was younger I'd go myself. . . ."

Lovelock's hand tensed and he clenched the jacket over his chest. He gripped the desk with his other hand and gazed at its surface: "And with *Lady Caroline* now resting on the ocean floor, I'm going to have to take the mouse by the whiskers, so to speak."

He turned to Drewshank. "I want you to hunt him

down," he said forcefully. "You so often claim you're the best there is, captain, so prove it — I'll pay for whatever you need. That reward will be mere pennies compared to what I will give you if you succeed. Are you up to it?"

Drewshank's head was suddenly filled with all the terrifying stories that had been told of the pirate; tales of incredible sea battles, horrific torture, and senseless murder. But his head had never bettered his heart when it came to making decisions, and Lovelock's final challenge roused him. He smoothed his hair and stood up.

"You ask a lot, but you ask the right man, Lovelock. Mousebeard's *Silver Shark* will be no match for my ship!"

"That's the kind of talk I need to hear. There's another small thing I ask of you though. . . ."

"Hmmm . . . What is it?"

"I need him brought back to Old Town alive. The *Lady Caroline* was carrying something exceptionally important. Mousebeard is certain to have it, and I want it back."

Drewshank sat down again. "I should have known there would be some funny business involved," he muttered.

"What's that?" said Lovelock sharply.

"I asked what this exceptionally important thing might be."

"You don't need to know, Drewshank. . . ."

"So it's one of your more secret investments that you'd rather were kept quiet, is it, Isiah?"

"You could not overestimate its importance, captain," said Lovelock, deadly serious. It was clear he did not appreciate Drewshank's insinuation.

"But you put this most important thing in the care of those fools on the *Lady Caroline*?" said Drewshank. "If you'd asked me to transport it in the first place, you wouldn't have had half this trouble!"

"Very true, captain. But here I am now, asking for your help, and prepared to pay you a fortune for it."

Drewshank smiled and straightened his collar.

"A fortune?"

"Enough to see you wealthy for the rest of your days . . ."

"Hundreds of thousands?"

"At the very least . . ."

Lovelock sat down in his chair and took a large bank

draft from the drawer of his desk. He scribbled an amount across its center and signed it in his beautifully styled handwriting before sliding it over the desk to Drewshank.

Drewshank pulled himself up in the chair again and caught sight of the vast number that Lovelock had written.

"How about this as a prepayment?" said Lovelock.

Drewshank couldn't withhold a smile from his face.

"Seeing as the money's right, what can I do but accept? It's a deal," he said. "I look forward to bringing home the mighty Mousebeard. All those stories about him will be nothing compared to the one of his capture."

"I admire your confidence, Captain Drewshank," said Lovelock, without returning his smile. "Now I have a lot resting on this voyage. I imagine Mousebeard will have at least a week's sailing on you, so to get you up to speed, your first port of call should be Hamlyn. Visit the old Mouse Trading Center near the docks; there you'll find Lady Pettifogger — I believe you've had dealings in the past?"

Drewshank's face turned a light shade of pink, but he embraced his embarrassment.

"Beatrice Pettifogger . . . ," said Drewshank, with distant memories flashing before his eyes, "now there's someone a wiser man would try desperately to avoid."

This time Lovelock allowed a smile to appear. "I know she'd be delighted to see you again, captain," he said.

"Delighted? I'll make sure I look my best then."

Drewshank unclasped a button at the top of his jacket and felt better prepared for it.

"We'll set sail at high tide tomorrow morning," he said determinedly. "At full sail, with the wind behind us, we'll make Hamlyn in good time. My crew will relish the challenge."

"I knew you'd be the man for the job, Drewshank," said Lovelock. "I'll come to the harbor in the morning to see that all things are in order."

"Excellent," said Drewshank. "Till tomorrow then."

He rose from the chair and flicked his hair back. Drewshank was a man of many qualities, not least in his role as captain of the *Flying Fox*, but he did like to make a grand exit. He swirled on the spot and left the room.

"Till tomorrow . . . ," replied Lovelock.

Outside the office, Drewshank met the butler. He was carrying coffee, but the captain resisted its delicious aroma. Instead he carried on down the stairs, collected his long overcoat, and left the mansion.

As he made his way to the carriage at the roadside, he couldn't stop thinking about the journey before him. Catching Mousebeard would make him truly famous and rich beyond his wildest dreams. Because his mind was filled with thoughts of gold, he barely took note when a quiet tearing sound emanated from below the seat he was seated upon.

Something had sneaked into the carriage with him; something small and furry with terribly sharp claws.

The Messenger Mouse

BELONGING TO THE GENUS OF AVIAN MICE, WHICH INCLUDE SUCH PRIZE *specimens as the Red-winged Onloko, the Messenger Mouse has been utilized throughout the past two centuries for the delivery of letters and important information. These small winged mice have an average wingspan of just under half a meter and are capable of traveling hundreds of miles in one flight. Using a particularly keen sense of smell, these light-bodied rodents can be trained to pinpoint specific destinations.*

Originally discovered on the island of Wihan at the edge of the Cold Sea, Messenger Mice were so rare that only the Official Postal Service was sanctioned to use them. However, after a successful breeding program, it is thought that almost two-thirds of the population of Midena now keep a Messenger Mouse among their collection.

MOUSING NOTES

Messenger Mice are best kept outdoors in good-sized pens, where they have the freedom to stretch their wings. If you feel like spoiling a Messenger Mouse, keep an eye out for Frizzle Worms — a delicacy that they seem to rate very highly.

Running Away

A T THE BREAK OF DAY, THE OVERNIGHT FOG HAD cleared and the harbor was bustling with life. Taverns opened their doors and numerous stalls popped up at its outer edges, providing a bright backdrop to the salesmen and sailors who muscled their way along the cobblestones. Fishermen hurried along in their knee-high rubber boots, trying to avoid the reeking, troublesome seadogs making their way back to ship after a night of hard drinking. People of all colors and creeds mingled at the docks, and by day it was an exciting place to be.

With the arrival of ships throughout the night, news had come flooding in of an unusual weather front off the coast of Hamlyn. Three vessels had vanished at sea during the night, and after the sinking of the *Lady Caroline* in recent days, it did little to settle sailors' nerves. Not only was Mousebeard in the vicinity, but a treacherous storm threatened their livelihood.

Needless to say, voyages were being diverted or canceled to avoid the menace. Drewshank, however, had no such option.

"Bring all the gunpowder aboard!" he shouted briskly to a hairy sailor on the quayside. Drewshank had gotten little sleep the previous night, but he would make sure the ship left on time.

"Aye, sir!" replied the sailor as he ticked off an entry on a piece of notepaper. Drewshank walked the ship and checked on all the crew: carpenters chipped away on the gun deck, making space for the new cannons; pigs and cows were herded below; sailors climbed the lofty masts with Rigger Mice in tow and mended any broken stitching on the sails.

Captain Drewshank oversaw all these movements and repairs along with his burly right-hand man, Mr. Fenwick. It was a massive undertaking, for the *Flying Fox* had to be fully prepared to face such an enemy as Mousebeard. High tide was in a few hours, and they had to depart on time so as not to come aground in the shallow route to the sea.

As he went to check food supplies in the mess, a young boy approached. His clothes were far too big for him and he'd tied the trousers into large knots at the ankles to stop him from tripping over. His dark scruffy hair hung limply, and he looked like he'd had a very trying morning.

"Mr. Piper," said Drewshank, "how are things belowdecks? Have you gotten rid of that troublesome mouse yet?"

Mr. Piper, or Scratcher, as he was familiarly known, was only ten years old, and was the *Flying Fox*'s mousekeeper. Never a boy of great natural ability, Scratcher always had to work hard to get anywhere, but he did a good job of caring for all the nautical working mice that were needed aboard ship.

"Captain, he just keeps escaping," he said breathlessly.

"He's torn hammocks and sliced crates clean open. A pound of hardtack's been devoured too. There are crumbs everywhere!"

"This won't do, Mr. Piper," replied Drewshank.

"I'm trying my hardest, sir," the boy said, stooping to catch a breath. "It's as though he knows every move I make."

"There's no time for this. We simply can't set sail with him onboard. The *Fox* will soon be looking holier than Reverend Doyly."

Scratcher stepped back to attention. "Yessir," he replied snappily.

"As wily as he may be, he's only a Sharpclaw," said Drewshank. "Admittedly his claws are the size of daggers, but come on! Exert yourself!"

"But, sir . . . ," insisted Scratcher, "I'm only a mouse-keeper! I'm not trained for this sort of thing. He cuts through my nets and traps. There's nothing that can capture him."

Drewshank stuttered. Despite his bravado, he had no idea how to catch the mouse. Still, it would be a stout challenge for the boy.

"Outwit it!" he barked.

"Yes, sir!" replied Scratcher meekly. The boy brushed aside his hair, clenched his fists, and stormed off below-decks.

"Useless boy," tutted Drewshank unfairly.

⇒ ❋ ⇐

When the rising sun hit the window of Emiline's room, she rose wearily from her bed. Her mouse Portly greeted her with a few high-pitched squeaks, and she wished him a good morning in reply.

The previous night Emiline had made a decision. Whatever else had come to pass by lunchtime, one thing was certain: she was going to be on Drewshank's ship as it sailed toward Hamlyn. She'd heard the conversation between Isiah Lovelock and Captain Drewshank, and she suddenly knew her future lay outside of a towering mansion in the heart of Old Town. There were bigger and better things for her in this world.

Her bags were already packed. That easy task had been seen to the previous night, but now came the hard part: she had to leave the mansion without being heard.

Emiline picked up Portly's small travel box and slung it over her back along with her shoulder bag. This carried few things but *The Mousehunter's Almanac*, numerous traps, tools, and a few clothes.

She tiptoed through her door, shut it quietly, and told Portly not to squeak. As well trained as he was, he did like to squeak whenever possible. Stepping lightly down each stair, she tried to make as little noise as the creaky floorboards allowed. When she reached the third floor, where one of the windows opened onto the flying-mouse pen at the rear of the mansion, she stopped to look out. As she'd hoped, the butler was outside readying messages, tying them into thin leather harnesses that sit on a mouse's back. This was one of his early-morning duties, along with collecting the papers and getting Mr. Lovelock ready for the day. He appeared to enjoy this task though, and took great pleasure in letting the mice fly out into the sky.

Of all the mice capable of flight, the most useful was the Red-winged Onloko Mouse. Its long feathered wings, which far outstretched its body, allowed it to fly for days on end without rest, and Mr. Spires was preparing two of these for a long-distance haul. Emiline never quite knew whom Mr. Spires sent messages to — she assumed they concerned Mr. Lovelock's activities, as his mousetrading empire stretched across the whole globe.

Without the butler around to worry about, she continued steadily to the ground floor and detached the tinkling bell from the front door. It took a great amount of courage to open it onto the street, but eventually she walked out into the gloriously bright day.

The mist had cleared from the previous night and it was perfect weather for sailing. A breeze brushed against her face, and the fresh air filled her lungs. From the doorstep there was a clear view of the harbor, and she could see the brightly decorated masts of the *Flying Fox.* She had no time to rest. High tide would be upon them soon, so she took one last look at the mansion and ran off down Grandview.

⇒ ✳ ⇐

Luckily for Emiline, the winding roads and pokey alleyways were quiet. It was a lot darker and dingier in the main town than at Grandview: creaking, ancient buildings rose up wherever there was the slightest bit of space, and sunlight struggled to reach the ground. Without the small river of bright blue sky that raced above her, Emiline would have found it hard to believe it was daytime. Some shop fronts and street-facing windows were still shuttered, but she could smell the potent scent of baking bread breaking free of the buildings.

The route opened out into Merchants' Square, and Emiline stopped to check that Portly was coping with the ride. Thankfully, he'd tied his tail tight around a post within his box and was trying to sleep out the journey. It had been a long time since she'd been to this part of the city, and she was blinded by the light reflecting off the grand white marble buildings at the square's edges. This was the historical heart of Old Town, playing host to the world-famous Mousetrading Hall — its glowing walls bulging with the weight of its own history. Alongside stood the stately Town Hall, where the first Mousetrading laws were passed, and then at the far corner of the square stood Old Rodent's Academy — the greatest school of mouse learning in the whole of Midena. Its tall pillars and thick oak doors put Emiline's decrepit

Fluffbin's School of Mousekeeping to shame. But this wasn't the time for sightseeing. Emiline closed Portly's box and set off again, flying across the square and back into the winding alleys. With the city rushing past, she felt a little tug as everything that had ever played a part in her life was being left behind.

Eventually, the streets stopped dead, and the glistening marshy fields spread out in front of her. She was on the short road to the harbor, which ended with the town wall and the Old Town Gate, and high on the horizon was the wide expanse of the sea.

She could already hear voices from the docks. Seagulls filled the sky, and the masts of countless ships bobbed gently over the top of the wall. Emiline felt the nerves tingling through her body.

She continued to the Old Town Gate and stood for a moment in thrall to the sight. Sailors and traders were bustling about everywhere; boats of all shapes and sizes rose from the sea. And standing high up above all other masts were the flags she'd seen from Grandview. There was the *Flying Fox,* the largest ship at port, and it looked wonderful.

"You heading through, miss?" asked the soldier on guard. "Or you just come for the view?"

Emiline was taken by surprise, but she gathered together all her confidence.

"Going through," she said, pointing to the harbor.

The soldier looked her up and down, and then moved to the gate.

"Right you are, miss," he said, and let her through.

Emiline ran forward without hesitation. She slipped into the moving crowd, darting back and forth to avoid planks, crates, and all sorts of objects that all were carried at her head height.

Drewshank's ship was even more magnificent up close and in the splendid light of day. It was made of a radiant dark brown wood, which twinkled with the water's reflection. Beautiful decorative golden mice embellished the cabin windows, and the top of the bow was edged with golden wings. The detail was so well carved that the angry mousehead that adorned the bow looked as though it might jump down and run at you. The gun deck, highlighted by a band of lighter wood running along the hull, rested much higher than Emiline's head, and each cannon protruded forth from its metal cover. The *Flying Fox*'s sails were wrapped and sagging gently, while colored flags fluttered in the breeze from above the crow's nest. It was everything Emiline hoped it would be, and yet something strange was going on.

The ship was quiet, and there was no movement upon deck. She approached its mooring and realized all its sailors were on the quayside, watching excitedly for something to happen aboard.

"What's going on?" she asked, trying to get the attention of a tall red-cheeked sailor.

"Go away!" he replied harshly.

"Excuse me, sir!" she said defiantly. "Would you please tell me what's happening!"

The sailor turned round and peered down at her. He had piercing, aggressive eyes, and he took hold of her forcefully.

"There's a Sharpclaw onboard, causin' havoc. Will that do ya?" he said angrily.

"A Sharpclaw?" she gasped.

Suddenly, the crowd stirred and cheered, and the sailor turned back to the ship. A fully armored figure had come charging onto deck, spear in hand. Whoever it was wasn't very tall, and Emiline figured it must be a mousekeeper. She barged her way to the front of the crowd to try and see better.

The mousekeeper stopped dead in his tracks and raised his spear to strike. He thrust it down, and as the spike vanished from view the Sharpclaw jumped high into the air, its gleaming, menacing claws primed and ready for a strike. It landed feet first back onto the spear and then sliced down with its claws, shearing the weapon in two.

The crowd hushed. The mousekeeper jumped backward, and the Sharpclaw dropped out of sight. Emiline crept along the sea wall. She eventually reached the gangplank and saw Captain Drewshank resting against a pile of chests, his hand placed on his head in frustration.

"Captain Drewshank!" said Emiline confidently. Although she was nervous about approaching the man, this was no time for her to give in to nerves. "I can catch that Sharpclaw," she said proudly. "Let me help out that mousekeeper you've got onboard!"

Drewshank looked at Emiline. It was clear he was unimpressed with her stature.

"That boy needs a challenge like this from time to time," he said. "I doubt a small girl like you can help."

The crowd cheered and started to laugh. Drewshank and Emiline turned to watch a hanging bag of sand fall from the masts and hit the mousekeeper full on the head.

"Gah!" shouted Drewshank. He sensed the crew were enjoying the situation too much. And at this rate the ship could never be ready to sail at high tide.

"Captain Drewshank!" said Emiline with exasperation. "He's useless!"

Drewshank's nerve broke.

"Oh, go on!" he muttered. "You couldn't do much worse. . . ."

Emiline jumped up immediately and passed Drewshank her shoulder bag and Portly's box. He unwittingly accepted them, and let her onto the ship.

All the sailors cheered as if another gladiator had entered the arena. Emiline was a little concerned about her lack of armor, but she paced over to the stunned mouse-keeper and checked if he was okay. He seemed to be breathing all right, and he started to stir as she tapped him on the shoulder.

"Excuse me," she asked, "can I borrow your helmet?"

Before he could give an answer, she'd yanked it free of the boy's head.

Emiline looked around her and spotted the mouse descending the mast. Once she'd spotted its extraordinarily long talons, she knew it was the escaped mouse from Lovelock's collection. That was the only Sharpclaw in Old Town — somehow it must have hitched a lift with Drewshank.

"Come here!" she said, creeping up to the mast. The Sharpclaw leaped to the ground and scurried to the top of a wooden trunk. It appeared to recognize Emiline, and stopped to stare at her.

"I'll get you, mouse!" she declared. While holding the helmet in one hand, she loosened a net from her belt and held it out at the ready. She knew the net couldn't hold the mouse, but as she slung it out, and the Sharpclaw reared and slashed violently with its claws, the one thing it wasn't expecting was a solid iron helmet to come plummeting down on top of it.

She immediately jumped onto the trunk and knelt firmly upon the helmet and the restless, wriggling mouse beneath. It was scratching frantically at its sides, but at least for the moment it was secure.

The crowd roared from the quayside, and Captain Drewshank charged onto deck.

"Fantastic! I thought we'd be stuck here for days!" he bellowed, and returned her bag and mouse box. "What's your name?"

"Emiline," she replied proudly, clearly struggling to maintain her hold on the jostling helmet.

"Do you have much planned for the months ahead?" he asked hopefully.

"Not that I know of," she said, "and yes, I'd love to sail with you!"

Drewshank laughed.

"Of course! You can teach Mr. Piper here a thing or two!"

Scratcher had risen gently to his feet and was standing unsteadily. He looked thoroughly depressed.

"Ah! Mr. Piper," cheered Drewshank, "meet Emiline. She'll show you how to catch mice!"

Emiline saw him attempt a smile, but only manage a small grimace. He looked quite friendly, she thought, if a touch helpless. Drewshank called the sailors to get on with their jobs and ordered Scratcher to fetch the strongest iron-lined chest he could find. He duly returned with a battered old box the length of his arm, and after he squirted a dash of Knockout Spirit under the helmet, the Sharpclaw fell gently to sleep. Emiline cautiously pulled the creature out and secured it in the chest, ready for returning to Lovelock's collection.

"Well done, Emiline," said Scratcher sourly, at the least trying a little to be friendly.

"Easy when you know how," she said, sliding from the trunk and returning his helmet. "I'll help you learn, if you like?"

"I suppose," replied the boy quietly.

From the edge of the ship, Emiline heard a familiar voice.

"Drewshank!" it called. "How is everything? Ready to sail?"

The captain turned and greeted Isiah Lovelock and his butler as they stepped onboard. They'd been watching Emiline's display of mousehunting from the quayside and had remained unseen up to now. It was such a rare occurrence to see Isiah Lovelock that all the crew stopped in their tracks to get a look.

"Is that Isiah Lovelock?" asked Scratcher, his jaw thoroughly dropped.

Emiline was about to reply when something odd happened. Lovelock took a few more steps along the deck and then suddenly stopped, clutching his chest. His head bent over, and his hand clung to his knee to stop from toppling over. He looked to be in pain, breathing heavily, struggling for air. His butler rushed to his side.

"Are you all right, sir?" asked Spires, uncertain as to what had happened.

"Yes, I'll be fine," replied Lovelock. "Just an old war wound playing up. Come on, let's carry on. We'll not stay long. . . ."

He put a handkerchief to his mouth, and his pain seemed to subside, but he held his chest and made only a few more steps onto the boat before halting.

"Drewshank!" he called, punching out the words breathlessly. "How is everything? Ready to sail?"

"Back on course, thankfully, due to this mouser," he replied. "Are you all right?"

Lovelock raised one hand in acknowledgment, stretching himself upright. His breathing continued to be forced.

"Ah, Emiline," said Mr. Spires. "We'd wondered where you'd gone to."

Emiline walked closer and nodded to her employer. Drewshank's face looked puzzled.

"You know each other?" he asked.

"She works for me. Emiline's my mousekeeper," replied Lovelock, leaning against the rigging to steady himself.

"She's only a mere mousekeeper?" asked Drewshank. "Her title sells her short — she could be a mousehunter with those abilities!"

"You have your bag and your mouse there, Emiline," quizzed the butler. "You weren't planning on running away?"

Emiline's face started to glow red.

"Captain Drewshank has asked me to sail with him," she said rather sheepishly.

"No. There's no way you can leave Mr. Lovelock's service, Emiline," said the butler firmly.

"Spires!" snapped Lovelock, authoritatively. "Let me decide these matters."

The butler fell silent.

"She has too much spirit at times, but Emiline is certainly one of the best mousekeepers around," he said. "Yet if she thinks she would do better onboard this ship than in my employment, then maybe I should let her go."

"Emiline could be of great worth to us," added Drewshank.

"Fine. So be it. Spires, arrange for the employment of a new mousekeeper. It's good to have a change once in a while."

"Yes, sir!" he choked.

"Now, Drewshank, show me that things are in order," said Lovelock. He took the captain aside and made for the quayside once more. The butler remained with Emiline and seized the chance to talk to her.

"Emiline, this voyage isn't safe!" he said worriedly. "You know exactly where it might lead, and with all these pirates!"

Emiline smiled.

"They're not pirates, Mr. Spires, and this could be everything I ever dreamed of."

"Very well . . . ," he said, delving deep inside his cloak, ". . . then take this. It might help keep you safe, and if you ever come face-to-face with that godforsaken Mousebeard, don't be afraid to put it in him."

The butler withdrew a sheathed dagger and passed it to Emiline. It was an ornate, ancient object, with a lumpy red handle. When Emiline pulled it from its casing, a magnificent etched silver blade was revealed. Emiline couldn't take her eyes off it.

"Like I said, if you come across danger, don't shy from using it."

Emiline held it up in her hand, letting its surface sparkle and fizz in the light.

Spires cast a glance at his master and then back to the mousekeeper.

"You take care now, Emiline," he said finally, and clutched her shoulder in a rare moment of affection.

"Of course I will!" she replied, reassuring him with a smile and placing the dagger into her bag.

Spires nodded, and went to join Lovelock and Drewshank. The ship was crawling with sailors once more. In a few hours Emiline would be leaving Old Town for the first time in her life, and sailing with none other than Devlin Drewshank. It had been an exciting day already and it wasn't yet lunchtime.

"Come on," called Scratcher, restlessly, "I'll show you to our quarters."

The Rigger Mouse

THIS WONDERFULLY USEFUL MOUSE ORIGINATED IN THE FORESTS OF THE *Northern Peninsula and is now found on sailing ships the world over. In the wild, Rigger Mice live high up in Alberry trees and use their dexterous claws to construct networks of walkways and nests using the sinews of plants and leaves. This habit so intrigued the first human settlers that they sought to utilize it onboard their shipping vessels. Rigger Mice soon became famous for making the strongest rope in the world.*

    When first put to use, Rigger Mice were set free on a ship's mast with the right materials, and their vine-like constructions were cut down and used as rigging. However, it was found that Rigger Mice had an acute knowledge of the strengths and weaknesses of rope, so a mousing school was created to train them further. It is now common to find these mice working alongside sailors all over the rigging — from securing loosened stitching in the sails to mending frayed and aging stretches of rope.

MOUSING NOTES
Rigger Mice can prove faithful companions and willing workers, although they've been noticed to suffer from extreme lethargy after long voyages. Mousekeepers must ensure that their daily schedule includes time for meals and rest periods.

The Flying Fox

OLD TOWN LOOKED VERY SMALL TO EMILINE AS THE *Flying Fox* left the calm harbor and sailed onto the open sea. She peered over the ship's side and reveled in the fine spray that passed over her face. The jagged rooftops of the mansions on Grandview were becoming a distant blur, and as the sails filled, they sped away at an even greater rate of knots.

Portly sat on her shoulder, breathing in the unusually fresh air in spadefuls. It seemed the trend was to have pet mice onboard ship. Emiline had always thought parrots to be the pets of sailors, but times were obviously changing, and the mouse had taken over. She was pleased Portly would at least be able to make a few new friends on ship, and they could maybe teach him a trick or two.

The ship was alive with sailors and mice, all harmoniously busy with one job or another. Rigger Mice were running up and down the masts tending to the ropes and sails, and every half hour, at the sound of a whistle, a sailor would cast a Knot Mouse overboard to judge the speed of the ship. It was very different from the quiet and subdued nature of Lovelock's mansion.

"Emiline!" called Scratcher, breaking into her thoughts. "The captain wants a word with you."

Scratcher seemed a little flustered. The ship's cook had been moaning at him because an angry Messenger Mouse had broken loose and was causing havoc in the mess.

"Have I done anything wrong?" asked Emiline, feeling a little nervous.

"No, I doubt it," said the boy grudgingly; "he loves you at the moment."

Scratcher directed her to Drewshank's quarters and ran off again, apologizing for being in a rush. Standing silently in front of the cabin door, Emiline bit her lip and knocked tentatively. She heard a few footsteps, then the door swung wide.

"Ah! The expert mousekeeper," announced Drewshank. "How are you?"

"Very well," she replied, suddenly feeling a little uncertain about addressing the captain. She looked around at the ornate and slightly overdecorated cabin. The painting of Drewshank almost took her breath away.

"Excellent . . . So then, your role aboard ship!" said the captain. "Being your first voyage on the *Flying Fox*, there are certain things you must get to grips with, and a day in the crow's nest is one of them. I take it you're not afraid of heights?"

"No! Of course not! But won't I be helping your other mousekeeper, sir?"

"Oh, at some point I'm sure, but being onboard ship requires a lot more than just dealing with mice. You must be a sailor too!"

Emiline had never considered herself sailor material, but in life you had to give everything a chance. As long as she didn't have to sing any shanties, she thought she'd be able to cope.

Drewshank passed her a small silver telescope.

"This will be your eyes for the day, Emiline. We've heard that there's some bad weather in the vicinity, and that could be the end for all of us. Keep a good watch today, and tomorrow you can learn how to swab the decks."

Emiline's heart sank.

"Swab the decks? Sir . . ."

"And then maybe we'll get you to do an inventory of every sailor's mouse on board. These pets are getting out of control!"

Drewshank stepped closer and lowered himself to talk to Emiline eye to eye.

"I'll let you into a little secret here . . . I saw a Four-bellied Mouse hanging from the rum storage rafters yesterday — and you know what a thirst they can have. We'd be out of grog in days. I admit, it's a good mouse for a sailor to be seen with, but they must be kept in check."

"Aye, sir," said Emiline, unwittingly falling into sailor-speak.

"Excellent. Well then, I suggest you go and find my

first mate Fenwick. He'll show you how to get settled in the crow's nest."

"Aye, sir," she replied once more, and trudged slowly to the door, telescope in hand.

"That's a very fine mouse on your shoulder, by the way," added Drewshank. "I once had a Grey myself. Scruples was its name — was always stealing cheese."

"Thank you, captain," said Emiline, leaving the cabin. Portly squeaked *thank you* too, in his own little way.

➵ ✳ ➴

"Are you Mr. Fenwick?" asked Emiline. A sweat-soaked stocky man with a well-tanned face and shaved head stared back at her. He was wearing a dirty white shirt with rolled-up sleeves, and his long cotton trousers sat bulging over a pair of enormous boots that had seen better days.

"Aye. That's me," he said in a thick country accent while wiping the sweat from his never-ending brow. An equally beefy Brown Mouse looked questioningly at Emiline from his shoulder.

"Captain Drewshank told me to find you."

"Ah! Now I understand why you look like a girl! You're that Sharpclaw catcher!" he said excitedly.

Fenwick seemed truly overjoyed at her arrival. She forced a smile and decided to return any pleasantries that might come her way.

"Right," said Fenwick, "I'll be lookin' after you while onboard. Any problems, turn to me. Scratcher will be a great help as well, I'll bet. But don't you be bothering the captain unless he asks for it!"

Emiline agreed and waited patiently for Fenwick to tell her what to do next.

"Right," he said finally, scratching his chest, his mind seemingly taken by a hundred and one other tasks. "What d'you think of Trumper?"

He picked up his Brown Mouse and held it in front of Emiline. The mouse smiled and twitched its whiskers while letting out a small fart. A pungent eggy smell filled the area, causing Fenwick to blush.

"He does that quite a lot," said Fenwick apologetically.

"That's nothing; I've known a lot worse from the

Stinky Blowhorn Mice we had at home," offered Emiline. She thought Trumper was rather overweight in truth, but it looked like a friendly enough animal — and besides, Portly himself could be said to have a little pot belly, but Emiline was quite oblivious to it. At the sight of the mouse, Portly scuttled down her arm and came to a rest in her hand, forcing Emiline to introduce him too.

"And this is Portly. . . ."

Fenwick looked impressed.

"Look at him! He's very fine indeed."

Emiline started to worry that Portly's head would grow too large if he received any more praise this morning.

"Greys and Browns get on well, so I've heard," said Fenwick, allowing Trumper and Portly to sniff each other's nose. Emiline tickled Trumper, then returned Portly to her shoulder.

"I'm supposed to be on watch from the crow's nest," said Emiline, pushing things along.

"Ah, right! Of course. This way, then!"

Fenwick led Emiline to the base of the main mast and rigging. He leaned back, looking up to the crow's nest, and his mouse did the same.

"Just climb up and you'll get there," he explained. "And if you need any help, just shout. Your watch will last until midnight, but you'll get some grub halfway through your shift. Scratcher will bring it up for you."

"That sounds fabulous," said Emiline, and she started to climb slowly.

"Keep an eye out for Chervil!" he shouted. "We haven't seen him in days, but I'm sure he's just been hidin' while at port!"

"I'll keep an eye out," she said, not knowing who he was talking about. A twelve-hour shift would seem like forever, she thought, but at least she had Portly to keep her company.

Fenwick waited for Emiline to reach the crow's nest safely and then returned to his duties. As Drewshank's first mate he did a lot more than he probably ought — it wasn't that the captain was particularly lazy or useless, more that he needed the occasional extra bit of help. But Fenwick was more than happy with the way things were: it was Devlin Drewshank after all, and who wouldn't have wanted to be his right-hand man?

Emiline found it hard climbing the rigging, and was exhausted by the time she'd reached the crow's nest. She pulled herself over the wooden side and dropped to its floor. Seated on a ledge just in front of her was an enormous golden-brown cat. He sat like a king: upright and commanding, and his eyes bored right into Emiline's.

"Meeooww," he said languidly.

Portly quickly shuffled into Emiline's hair, and peeked out nervously.

"Hello," replied Emiline softly, and stretched out to stroke the cat's long curly fur. The cat accepted the fuss and blinked slowly in appreciation.

"Must be Chervil," said Emiline to Portly, trying to calm him. "I couldn't think of a better place to hide than up here."

The cat blinked slowly and turned to look out to sea. From where he was sitting, he could see over the side of the crow's nest and had a terrific view of all the gulls swooping into the ship's wake.

"I see," said Emiline, "not only a good hiding place

but a wonderful vantage point too! But he doesn't seem at all bothered with you, Portly, so I shouldn't worry."

The mouse crept out from her hair and leaped onto the wooden side. The view was spectacular, and Emiline lifted her telescope and peered through. She was, after all, supposed to be on watch.

⇒ ❋ ⇐

Hours drifted by so slowly that Emiline struggled to keep her eyes open. Ever since Old Town had vanished from the horizon, all that she'd seen was sea; mile after mile of open water to the horizon. The wind had kept up strong, and they were making good progress, but it was so boring.

Chervil had long since fallen asleep at Emiline's side, and Portly had even found him quite agreeable to lie against, sleeping among his dense, warm fur. The two of them were breathing deeply in unison, and it made it even harder for Emiline to keep her eyes open.

The bright morning had faded into an overcast afternoon, with gray clouds speckling the otherwise white sky. The weather seemed to be turning for the worse, and as dusk approached, Emiline heard her name called from below. It was Scratcher, and he was making his way precariously up the rigging with a steaming tin of food in one hand.

"Time for some grub!" he shouted. He finally emerged over the top of the nest and dropped down next to Emiline. A wonderful smell of warm beef broth arrived with him.

"It seems like I've been here for days," said Emiline.

Scratcher stared at Emiline for a while before replying. It was unusual to have someone close to his own age onboard, and a girl at that.

"You're halfway through now," he said, regaining his voice. "It's dull at first, but you get used to it. And you've found Chervil! That'll please everyone."

Emiline took the food graciously and scooped the broth into her mouth with a large clump of bread that Scratcher brought out from his pocket. It was delicious, and tore Emiline's thoughts from the monotony of being lookout.

"So did you always want to be a mousekeeper?"

"Of course," she replied, lingering over another mouthful of food, "but I'll soon be a mousehunter!"

"You — a mousehunter?"

"I'll be the youngest the world's ever seen," she replied with the utmost sincerity. "I'll pass the tests, catch the mice . . . become the most famous mousehunter there is."

"I'll believe it when I see it," laughed Scratcher.

"Don't you want to be a mousehunter?" asked Emiline, somewhat bewildered by the boy's attitude. Portly had stirred from his sleep, and was sniffing the air, wondering what smelled so nice.

"I'm a good mousekeeper, but my skills leave me when it comes to catching the darn things. I know my limits."

"That's the wimpiest thing I've ever heard! You can be whatever you want. Look at Portly here; he's just a Grey, but he's as clever as any Bojimbo Conjuring Mouse!"

"Well, maybe," stuttered Scratcher. He took hold of the rigging and nervously kicked his ankles. "I think I should be getting back now," he said. "I have the Messenger Mice cages to clean."

"Suit yourself," muttered Emiline, and she returned to her food. Despite him being slightly underwhelming, she couldn't help liking Scratcher, and his brief company had been a relief.

Chervil had woken with the commotion, and had also started taking an interest in Emiline's dinner. With the two animals now craving something to eat, Emiline distributed her leftovers between them. Food was the best thing to lift spirits after all, and they sat contentedly as the sky faded into darkness.

The gloomy conditions turned even gloomier when Emiline felt a faint drizzle start to fall, and she tightened her coat to stop the chill from creeping in. Unlike normal cats, Chervil seemed to revel in the dim light and damp conditions, and sat upright again to keep watch.

While peering through the telescope into near darkness, Emiline heard movements on deck, and leaned over the nest to see small lamps being lit. The sailors were readying the ship for the long dark night ahead; the day-shift mice were put to rest while the Night-light Mice were brought out to illuminate the deck. Emiline watched a young sailor place some Listener Mice at the bow.

"Ingenious," murmured Emiline, realizing they were there to warn of oncoming ships: there really was no mouse put to waste onboard ship.

Emiline felt a soft prodding on her arm, and saw Chervil was trying to get her attention. On the horizon she saw a quick burst of lightning connect the sky and sea. It lit up huge brooding clouds rising up into the heavens. A low grumble of thunder traveled over the waves, and immediately a bell rang out from the deck.

"Drop the sails, storm front ahead!" shouted Fenwick. Drewshank appeared on deck and started to pace up and down, his striking form lit up by the lamplight, even from such a distance.

"Hold tight, men!" he shouted. "We'll keep sure and let this one pass!" Hearty calls of "yessir" rang out all over the ship.

Emiline watched the lightning draw nearer while the thunder grew louder. It was a strange sensation, being able to see the storm approach. The waves were growing with each minute, lifting the ship up and down like a slowed-down rollercoaster. The sky above darkened further with the massive spread of clouds chasing toward them. The air crackled.

"It's almost upon us," called out Drewshank. "Only those sailors needed remain on deck. The storm will be quite a ride!"

Fenwick came to his side and shoved a rope into his hand. Other sailors had already strung out lifelines across the deck, but the first mate always looked after his captain.

"Hold tight yourself, sir!" he said, doing his best to make Drewshank safe. He then walked to the main mast and shouted up to the crow's nest.

"Get yourself down, Emiline! No place for you in a storm!"

Emiline heard his cry and waved back in response. But as she tried to pick up Chervil, the boat tilted onto its side. She realized the waters ahead had switched direction, and the course of the ship was shifting. It was being drawn slowly onward against its will, and against the direction of the wind.

Drewshank called out more orders. Emiline picked up

Chervil and made for the edge of the crow's nest to climb down. In the darkness, the descent looked much farther than it had previously. She lifted her legs over the side and caught a foothold. Chervil let out an angry meow and his movements stopped dead — his eyes staring out to the sea.

Emiline looked cautiously over her shoulder, and gradually it became clear: the frothing, swirling water was vanishing into a deepening twisting circle. This was much more than a freak storm. She threw herself and Chervil back into the crow's nest, stretched out to grab the bell, and rang with all her might.

"Captain Drewshank!" she shouted as loud as she could. "Whirlpool dead ahead!"

On deck, Drewshank heard her words and then saw it for himself. The whirlpool, emerging from the darkness, was at least double the length of the ship and growing, sucking them ever closer with its overwhelming power.

"Get the sails set! We need the wind!" ordered Drewshank sharply. He threw his rope to the ground and ran to the rigging. Mr. Fenwick beat a course to the wheel and aided the helmsman. Now all the sailors had seen the whirlpool, and were calling orders down the line. The clatter of trapdoors signaled the arrival of the rest of the crew from below deck.

"We need those sails, men!" Drewshank shouted once more.

The rigging was soon awash with sailors and mice. They worked frantically, knowing their time was short.

"Hard to starboard!" shouted Drewshank, his voice almost breaking. The ship lurched in the water as the helmsman turned the wheel forcefully with the help of Fenwick. Sailors grabbed hold of anything secured to the deck as it rose sideways. Emiline tumbled in the crow's nest, her heart pounding hard in her throat; Chervil fell down on top of her; Portly scratched his way urgently into her jacket. There was no way she could safely climb down now. The rain battered her face as the wind blew it whichever way it pleased.

Emiline hurriedly searched for a rope and eventually found a piece wrapped around the crow's nest that was secured to the rigging. She was scared, but she calmly tied the rope to her waist and fitted it around Chervil's belly. She could feel herself tilting over and clutched the crow's nest as tightly as she could. The sailors on the rigging struggled to keep hold, grabbing the ropes for dear life as the mast neared horizontal with the sea. Waves crashed onto the deck. The *Flying Fox* fought against the whirlpool and eventually righted in the water, but the circular waves were stronger, pulling the ship closer.

Drewshank gripped the side of the ship and looked hard into the whirlpool. The black heart of its pull looked closer to hell than anything he'd ever seen. His fingers dug in, and he twisted his leg three times around a guide rope. The noise was terrific, whooshing and gushing with such force that he struggled to think straight. He thought desperately about what to do.

And then he saw a sharp streak of silver bolt through the darkness. He rubbed his eyes, unsure of what he'd seen. An immense roar tore through the air, and the swirling water blasted upward into columns of jet black before cascading down onto the *Flying Fox.* A huge silver-bodied serpent reared up like an angry cobra from the whirlpool. Its pointed, skeletal head roared ferociously before scything downward and cutting the sea in two. Two jets of pure white steam blasted from its nostrils as it twisted back into the air, its pulsating scaly body thrashing around violently. It was too dark to see the monster's full extent as it rose high in the air above the ship, but there was no missing the glistening tentacles jutting out from its mouth and its burning, bright red eyes.

Everyone onboard froze. The sea monster was the mythical Grak, and that meant one thing: certain death for them all.

The Elephant Mouse

THE ELEPHANT MOUSE IS THE LARGEST MOUSE DEEMED SUITABLE FOR *keeping in a collection by the International Mousehunting Federation. This thick-limbed, big-eared, and long-nosed rodent can grow to a meter in height and is often house-trained like a dog. Elephant Mice are generally docile creatures and make suitable family pets — unlike some of the more fancy collectible mice — but they have difficulty climbing stairs, so this should be taken into account when getting one for your home.*

MOUSING NOTES

Elephant Mice have few specialist requirements, and as long as they have a nice warm bed made of straw, they can make wonderful pets in any home.

The Giant's Reach

"READY THOSE CANNONS!" SCREAMED DREWSHANK AS the Grak's head lowered and eyed its prey. Drewshank thrived in times of danger, his blood raging through his body, and he waited impatiently for his sailors to take their positions.

The whirlpool subsided as the Grak circled menacingly in the air, but the waves were growing by the second. "Hold firm!" shouted Drewshank, and the monster's mighty, ugly head shot down and drove straight into the hull, knocking the ship sideways. Sailors went flying about the deck. The ship groaned as it keeled over, but it was a tough vessel. It rode the tumbling waves and righted jerkily. Drewshank took a breath, and watched as the Grak twisted below into the circling waves. He caught glimpses of its silver scaly body, but he waited. And waited. And then, the water broke.

"Fire!" he bellowed, his veins almost exploding from his neck.

The starboard cannons unleashed their fury. The Grak pulled up, its serpentine body twisting like a tornado in the air, and the shots vanished into darkness, consumed by the tempestuous sea.

"Fire!" he shouted again. Once more the cannons fired, sending clouds of smoke into the air. This time some of the shots hit the target. The monster let out a deafening scream and careered back into the water, vanishing from sight. The sailors cheered loudly. If anything, though, the sea became even more ferocious. The waves rose up again like an impenetrable black wall around the ship.

"Ready the cannons!" ordered Drewshank, wiping his drenched hair out of his eyes. He stood firm, but all he could hear was the raging water smashing at the ship's hull. With a screeching wail, the Grak burst out of the sea once more.

"Fire!"

The monster cried out as the cannonballs struck with deadly accuracy, but it powered forward with such force it hit the side of the vessel and lifted it clear of the sea. Drewshank crashed to the floor.

The *Flying Fox* was truly flying for the first time as it sped awkwardly through the air. The sailors hung on with all their might, but some lost their grip, tumbling into the deafening roar of the sea.

The ship smashed back onto the water and twisted into a huge wave, its bow slicing keenly through into the pitch black of the sea. Ice-cold water flew over the deck and the *Flying Fox* was sucked into the deep. Towers of bubbles rose up around the hull and shot off in trails behind the ship. Every sailor's lungs soon reached bursting point, but they held on, and the sea started to lift them. The ship was being forced up and up by the air trapped in the hull, the pressure becoming almost unbearable until finally it was catapulted clear into the air.

The *Flying Fox* landed back on the sea like a skimming stone, skipping twice before coming to rest on calmer waters. Drewshank gasped for air, just as every other sailor did. He found his footing and stood up uneasily. He surveyed the black waters ahead but could see no sign of the Grak or the whirlpool.

"Water's breakin' in below!" shouted Fenwick, who was drenched to the core.

Drewshank looked around at the wreck that had become his ship. Water sloshed back and forth over the deck, and crates and splintered wood lay strewn everywhere. Torn sails snapped in the wind.

"Fix the leaks, men," ordered Drewshank. "Assess the damage and get the cannons ready again."

He looked into the distance and his heart dropped. The Grak was spiraling out of the sea once more and it was coming at them.

"That monster's not done yet!" he shouted.

The crew braced themselves for another onslaught. Screaming loudly, the monster dropped and shot straight at them like a torpedo, sending water and snorts of steam blasting out into the air. The cannons fired out, but the Grak's huge form lifted into the air and continued to rise until its scaly body was directly above them.

But it didn't attack. The air was immediately filled

with more ear-piercing cries. Drewshank turned to follow its course and witnessed a second awesome Grak rise out of the sea a few hundred meters behind them.

"Of all the luck in the world . . . ," gasped the captain. "We're done for!"

The two monsters veered upward to where they clashed high above the masts. Their jaws crunched into each other's skulls, and they twisted away together, tumbling downward just clear of the ship, until they punched into the water in a writhing mess.

As the two Graks submerged, a wave swelled, caught hold of the *Flying Fox,* and drove it high up and far out across the sea. Drewshank's sailor's legs were trusty, and had served him well in the past, but that was the last straw. His chest convulsed and he was sick on the floor.

Drewshank righted himself and wiped his mouth sheepishly.

"Find some sails!" he shouted queasily to what remained of his crew. "There must be something left hanging from those masts! Get us out of here!"

Tired sailors unhooked themselves from their posts and surveyed the damage.

"Captain!"

Drewshank heard a shout. It was Scratcher, his face blackened with soot and tears. He was holding a taut thin rope over the side of the ship — it was the remainder of the rigging from a broken mast, and something was attached to its end, dragging in the water.

Drewshank and Fenwick ran over. During the battle they'd forgotten entirely about Emiline. They looked desperately to the dark sea and saw the battered remains of the crow's nest floating along at the end of Scratcher's rope. Fenwick took hold of it, and the two of them pulled as hard as they could against the waves. As the crow's nest neared, they could just make out a body drifting behind. Emiline's small mouse was sitting on her chest, and Chervil was paddling frantically behind.

⇒ ❋ ⇐

Lord Battersby watched the storm from his apartment window. Standing stock upright in his light-gray navy uniform, he rubbed his hands against one another with worry. The port of Hamlyn was taking a battering.

In charge of the Old Town Guard's navy, Battersby

was a man of great power. He was tall and broad, and had a strikingly strong and imposing chin.

"I wouldn't wish to be out in this," he said darkly, watching the ships rise and fall in the docks, ten-foot waves crashing at their hulls. "It could ruin our plans if the *Flying Fox* fails to arrive."

Lady Pettifogger approached Battersby, her diminutive size making him look like a giant. She was beautiful — she knew it too. She held a scarf loosely in her hands, and she played with it casually as lightning cracked outside and lit up the port.

"Drewshank has a solid ship. He'll make it through," she said confidently. "Don't worry yourself."

Lord Battersby looked pensively at her. "There's a lot riding on that trumped-up privateer — too much if you ask me, Beatrice. We should never have agreed to all this so willingly. There must have been an easier way?"

Lady Pettifogger shook her head slowly, gave a sultry smile, and placed her hand on Battersby's solid back.

"Lovelock knows what he's doing, Alexander. Besides, Mousebeard never runs from a fight, and I'm sure he knows there's a ship on his tail by now."

"I hope you're right," he said sternly.

Battersby picked up a glass of wine and gulped it down. The storm was intensifying, making the window shutters rattle.

"I'm just not cut out for all this plotting and scheming," he said, placing his hand on the wall. "Put me on a warship any day."

He looked down at Lady Pettifogger and she smiled again, her enchanting green eyes flickering in the lamplight.

"It won't be long now, Alexander. You have a whole fleet awaiting your command at Eiderbeck. You'll soon get the battles you crave. . . ."

Hearing these words calmed Lord Battersby, and he placed his arm around Lady Pettifogger awkwardly. His shoulders lowered and a wry smile formed on his face, showing the lines of age around his eyes.

"And then the fun will really begin. . . ."

⇒ ✳ ⇐

When the mist had cleared from Emiline's eyes, she felt a sharp pain at the top of her head. There was a lump the size of an egg under her hair, and she pressed it gently, wincing with pain all the while. Her body ached with tiredness. She was lying on a bed in a strange and unfamiliar room. The walls were blue but slightly moldy, and there was a strange smell all around.

A draught was fluttering the moth-eaten curtain, and the dying rays of sun filtered into the room. At the end of her bed sat Chervil, the ship's cat, and his forthright stare turned to a slight curled smile as he saw Emiline rise.

"Hello!" she said gruffly. She was surprised at how dry her throat was. Portly scuttled up onto her shoulder, ran under her hair, and squeaked.

And then Emiline remembered the sight of the mast tumbling below her. She remembered hitting the cold water, seeing the black murky deep consume her, and then no more. She was alive, at least, but she'd like to know where she was.

Pulling herself up further, she looked out of the cob-webbed window and saw a bustling sea front and harbor. There were street vendors and sailors everywhere — although judging by their colorful but dirty clothes, they were more likely pirates. Mouse traders and boat-builders all jostled for attention in the last minutes of the day, and it set her mind racing. For a moment it even stopped her head from hurting.

Emiline impatiently unlatched the window and leaned out to get a better view. The salty air filled her lungs, the caws of seagulls filled her ears and she got a much clearer idea of where she was. Unlike Old Town, the houses were relatively low and squat, and they were all uniformly constructed of gray, yellowing stone. They varied little in scale as they rose up both sides of the harbor, but their higgledy-piggledy arrangement created a shimmering patchwork in the dying rays of the sun. It definitely wasn't Emiline's home city, and it dawned on her that they must have reached Hamlyn.

Emiline would have been surprised if she had known how much this strange place was related to Old Town. Hamlyn was a noisy place, full of tight alleyways and rough-and-ready taverns. Such an unruly place showed few signs of riches and wealth, but, unknown to Emiline, her old master held a great influence over it. Hamlyn had been linked to Old Town for many years, serving as a useful outpost and stopping point for trading and naval ships en route to other lands in the Great Sea. As such, its population consisted of pirates, privateers, and old seahands wanting a rest from the sailing life. Old Town paid little attention to its lawlessness and the black-market dealings that took place there, simply because it liked to use Hamlyn for its own means whenever the need arose. The Old Town Guard rarely interfered, and this proved beneficial for all parties, including Isiah Lovelock, who had two Mouse Trading Centers on the island. Without the gaze of the authorities, his empire had full control over its trade in mice.

Emiline stepped off the bed, battling the dizziness that threatened to send her back under its covers. She picked up her bag and mousing belt that lay beside her, opened the creaky wooden door, and found herself in an uneven wood-timbered corridor. She could hear laughter and cheering from the floor below, but her attention was taken by a huge mouse plodding toward her. It was almost waist-height, with thick tree-trunk legs and ears that drooped down to the floor. It looked like an Elephant Mouse, but Emiline had only ever seen one in *The Mousehunter's Almanac* before. They weren't your typical everyday mouse, and Emiline was taken aback by how friendly it seemed.

The mouse made a deep, gravelly yelp of a squeak as it approached and stopped in front of her, nudging her leg with its side. Upon its back was a tray carrying a glass of water, and Emiline took it and drank deeply, as she was so thirsty. The mouse squeaked again and wandered off happily. If everywhere outside Old Town was this wonderful, thought Emiline, leaving Lovelock's mansion was the best thing she'd ever done.

She followed the Elephant Mouse as it lolloped along and eventually reached a narrow staircase that led to where all the noise was coming from. She watched it turn sideways in the staircase so that it wedged itself firmly between walls, and then it clomped downward one front and back leg at a time.

At the bottom of the stairs, the expansive room that emerged before Emiline's eyes was filled with bearded sailors and laughing women. Tables stretched around the room, with tall candles flickering at their centers, smoke lilting up into the rafters above.

At these tables, people were playing games with their pet mice on their shoulders. Dice and small mouse counters were being thrown on checkered boards, and any scraps of food or coins that landed on the floor were quickly collected by Scavenger Mice, who always found a happy home in Mousing Taverns. Hamlyn's potent Pipsqueak Beer was swilling over tables and down throats at an alarming rate, and the atmosphere was one of slight chaos. It was an inn — a dark, rowdy, pirate- and mouse-infested watering hole — and Emiline loved it.

"Emiline!" shouted Scratcher, jumping up and running over to her. "You're awake! It's been days!"

"Days?" Emiline questioned.

Scratcher took her glass and dragged her to a table where Drewshank, Fenwick, and a number of other sailors were standing and smiling ecstatically. Their clothes were looking a bit battered since the last time she saw them, and some of the men carried cuts and bruises on their face. Drewshank, however, looked as snappy as ever.

"A welcome sight!" said Drewshank happily, beckoning Emiline to take a seat.

"Elbert!" shouted Fenwick to the bar boy, as Emiline sat beside him. "A pint of Pipsqueak for our brave mousekeeper here!"

He placed his hand on her shoulder and smiled cheerfully as he drank from a huge tankard of his own. His mouse sat languidly on the table, and Portly scurried across to greet it. Trumper burped a squeak of greeting, leading Fenwick to apologize for letting him sip his beer.

"It's good to see you back in the land of the living," said Drewshank. "Nothing has ever wrenched Chervil from the ship before, but he wouldn't leave your side. I guess he's pleased you saved his life, as we all are, and we have to be thankful for small mercies."

Emiline looked puzzled.

"We lost many men to the Grak — eaten whole or swallowed by the deep. I even received a cut across my eyebrow! You were lucky, Emiline!" Drewshank stared mournfully into his beer, then banged the table. "What Long-eared Mice came to be doing in the sea off Hamlyn is a question I want answered."

"Wouldn't surprise me," said Fenwick, "if it were that Mousebeard who put 'em there."

The table immediately went silent.

"You could be right," added Drewshank. "Not only cannons lie in our path, but angry sea monsters."

Emiline's mind wandered again at the thought of Mousebeard and the Grak. She remembered being terrified as a child at the entry in *The Mousehunter's Almanac* about Long-eared Mice, and how they turned into sea monsters when they came into contact with salt water. As she was reliving her horrific experience once more, a voice pierced the din and brought her back to the real world.

"Is she awake? Is she alive?" it shouted. A short man came barging through the room, barely able to see above the shouting people and tables. He was dressed in neat, yet oil-splattered, work clothes, and his little face was almost covered by enormous round glasses.

"Ah! She made it, Drewshank, I knew she would! I told you that potion would do the job!"

The man took Emiline's hand and shook it vigorously, all the while inspecting her for any continuing signs of damage.

"I'm Algernon Mountjack!" he said brightly, perching

on the end of the bench next to her. "Welcome to the Giant's Reach — the best inn in Hamlyn!"

Drewshank cut in, fearing the short man's gusto might overwhelm Emiline.

"Thank you, Algernon, it seems your cure worked wonders! That Fire Mouse spit really does make good medicine," he said.

Emiline and Scratcher both felt suddenly sick.

"But I told you it would! Now, Emiline," Algernon said, in his supercharged manner, "I hear you're a famous mousekeeper, and I think I like you already. If you have time I'll show you my workshop. I'm currently working on a rocket-powered attachment for my Whale Mouse. I think you might be interested? Yes?"

"I'm sure she'd love to see it," said Drewshank firmly, "but I think she might like a bit of quiet now."

"Ah, of course," said Algernon. "I'll look forward to taking you round."

"That would be perfect," said Emiline cheerfully.

"Yes, it would," he replied. "You'll find me behind the bar when you're ready. Oh yes, one more thing. That

Beatrice Pettifogger was asking after you, Drewshank. Said she had something for you."

Before Drewshank could utter a reply, Algernon had shot off at a cracking pace, picking up a few glasses on the way. His excitable manner could be as infuriating as it was endearing.

"Is that *Lady* Pettifogger?" asked Fenwick, slightly concerned.

"I'm afraid it is," said Drewshank, sighing. "I suppose I should go and grace her with my presence. There's only so long I can put it off."

He huffed and rose slowly from the table.

"She's probably only got a bundle of trouble for you, sir!" said Fenwick.

"I know . . . ," the captain replied regretfully. "I'll be careful. Could you return to the *Fox* and check that the repairs are coming along all right? See if you can find any more sailors to join the crew too. As you know, we're a bit thin on the ground."

"Aye, sir," he replied, "but what about Emiline here? Can't leave her with old Algernon — he's a nut!"

"She'll be fine if Scratcher stays."

Drewshank patted the boy on the back. "I'll return to pay Algernon for the room, and get you two and Chervil at the same time. Get as much rest as you can, Emiline; if the ship's in order we'll be off as soon as we can, and I'll need you to be at your best."

Everyone stood up and left the two mousekeepers to themselves.

"How's your head?" asked Scratcher, watching Emiline take Portly from her shoulder.

"It's all right," she replied, "but we should go and visit Algernon's workshop. Can you see him?"

"But the captain told you to get rest!"

"Don't be boring." She sighed, rolling her eyes. "Where's your sense of adventure?"

It was clear that Emiline's injuries were healing quickly.

The Sylakia Mouse

RECOGNIZED AS THE FIRST HUMAN-DESIGNED MOUSE (ITS NAME DERIVES *from the ancient Andirian word sylak, meaning "to build,") the Sylakia was conceived and bred with one purpose in mind — money. A hybrid of numerous stout-bodied mice, it was initially deemed exceptionally useful for factories, where it was kept to run on treadmills to power machinery.*

Notable for its thick legs and high arching back, the Sylakia has since become a cause célèbre for Old Town, where it was first bred. Now known to suffer from a peculiar strain of arthritis in its tiny joints, the Sylakia feels immense pain from a young age. Unfortunately, the protracted breeding process that resulted in the Sylakia also bred out most vocal capacity, so the animal had little way of showing its suffering throughout the long hours it worked. However, after nearly sixty years of use by the populace, the Mouse Liberation Front highlighted the Sylakia's cause, and it is now banned from any workplace.

MOUSING NOTES

An unusual mouse to find in any collection these days. For better or worse, the Sylakia is a vanishing breed.

Algernon

DREWSHANK RANG THE BELL OF THE MOUSE TRADING Center and peered through the small glass panel of the door. The old, battered building slotted perfectly between two smarter houses overlooking the harbor. It was tiny, and a lot less grand than he'd expected. There were no windows at its front, just a sign nailed onto the limpet-riddled stone wall, with MICE FOR TRADE painted in big swirling letters. It looked a most unfriendly place, not at all suited for showing off expensive rare mice. Drewshank wondered why anyone would ever visit it. It was certainly nothing like the one in Old Town, nor even the gleaming new Umberto's Trading Center situated farther up the road.

He pulled his jacket tighter around his chest and patted down his hair. Eventually a light came on and the door opened.

"Devlin Drewshank. Come on in, it's been a while."

Lady Pettifogger stood in the dimly lit entrance, her sharp beauty radiating like a beacon. She beckoned him into the room and shut the door, taking time to bolt numerous locks on the inside. Her long brown hair lilted softly over her shoulders, and Drewshank, unusually, felt nervous. There was something about Beatrice Pettifogger that had always made him uneasy.

The room he'd entered smelled of washed floors and disinfectant, and could easily have been mistaken for a doctor's office.

"Never one to rush, were you?" she said playfully.

"To this shoddy building?" he said sarcastically. "Or to you? Seeing you again has made me realize why I wanted to stay away in the first place."

"Devlin!" she tutted. "After all we've been through!"

"I'm here for business only, Beatrice," he said seriously.

"It's just been so long since I last saw you," she said,

taking Drewshank through to the next room, which was much larger and lit by flickering gas lamps. "I've missed seeing your face. And before you make any more nasty comments about my home, Isiah likes to keep it like this for a reason."

"A reason?" queried Drewshank.

"Obviously, it's not a reason we freely talk about, Devlin."

Her voice dropped to a hush and she placed a finger over her lips. "We'd best be quiet in here. These are all the mice that aren't for sale, and they are so easily woken. They do make such a racket when they're awake!"

Drewshank suddenly realized the room was filled with cages of all sizes, and within them were mice of all kinds. He'd been too preoccupied with Beatrice to notice before, but now he realized there were also metal bolted doors on each wall, and some even had bars protecting their circular windows. The Trading Center spread out much more than its small front let on.

"So you still have a thing against mice . . . ," he said.

"Such smelly little creatures. But Isiah does like me to be in charge here. He says I have a knack for spotting good breeding, and on that point I'd have to agree. We're currently involved in Snapper Mice breeding trials. . . ."

"Breeding trials?" queried Drewshank, his voice squeaking like a mouse.

". . . and, funnily enough, I do quite like to see the results," she added.

"The results?" queried Drewshank once more. He received no reply; instead Lady Pettifogger took a sharp turn onto a staircase and led the way upward.

As usual, Lady Pettifogger was dressed provocatively, in a flowing yet well-fitting red dress, and Drewshank looked on gloomily as she vanished upstairs. He had a terrible feeling that the evening was going to end badly.

"I knew Mousebeard would be an offer you couldn't refuse," she said knowingly, opening a door to a glowing orange room, filled with the warmth of a roaring fire. She showed him to a chair and poured him a glass of wine.

"We'd have been closer to our goal too, but you can't account for sea monsters," he said, sitting down in an upright and slightly guarded manner. He knew better than to trust her.

"I take it that the ship's still in one piece?" she said, hopefully.

"Just about," he replied. "We're lucky the shipwrights work quickly here in Hamlyn."

"It's amazing what a bunch of pirates can achieve when they put their skills to something useful," she said. "They also make very good spies."

Lady Pettifogger took a folded map from a tabletop, and passed it to Drewshank. "Without them we wouldn't have this!"

Drewshank unraveled the browning parchment; it was hand-drawn, and a detailed chart of the seas that surrounded Old Town and Hamlyn, as well as many far-off lands. Islands were sprinkled over it like lily pads, and in the top corner was a wide red circle, scratched into the map in what looked like blood.

"As you know, Lovelock has many contacts around the Great Sea and beyond. We've noted every attack Mousebeard's made in the past few months and plotted them on the map with tiny black mice. We believe that the pirate's hideout is located at the far reaches of the Cold Sea, somewhere in that red circle on the map. It's beyond his usual hunting ground, but we don't know the exact coordinates. It is said that he hides on an island so tall and impenetrable that no one has ever been able to scale the cliffs that lift it into the sky. If you do come across his lair, you may have to find a way past such obstacles if you're to capture him."

Drewshank looked a little amazed by Lady Pettifogger's information.

"So, our target is simply the Cold Sea? Beatrice, I'd have thought your spies would come up with more than this!" he said.

"Oh come on! You're the best captain there is, Devlin. If you head north and use the map and your wits, you'll surely succeed."

"Well, that's not in doubt; like you say, I am one of the greatest privateers who ever lived! But even so, Lovelock seemed to think that you had *useful* information for me!"

Lady Pettifogger leaned toward Drewshank, who shuffled back further into his chair.

"This is Mousebeard we're talking about, Devlin," she

said, smiling sweetly and holding her arms out. "I've told you all the knowledge that we have. . . ."

She paused for a second then spoke softly, ". . . You know I don't want to see you getting hurt for our sake — you're much too special."

Drewshank struggled not to be charmed by her. But he ignored her outstretched arms and looked at her with what he hoped was his least handsome expression.

"If I die, Beatrice, you can be sure it won't be for you. I foolishly tried once before, and all it got me was three years in the clink," he said.

"Captain Drewshank!" exclaimed Beatrice, playfully.

"Three years of breaking up mouse biscuit, dressed in godawful prison attire . . ." Drewshank's eyes clouded over, remembering the rotten smell of mouse food as though it were still lingering in his clothes.

Lady Pettifogger reached over and touched his knee softly, and Drewshank had to suppress a horrible feeling of joy.

"It was such a long time ago," she pleaded. "You never used to be one for grudges. . . ."

Drewshank took that as his cue to make a move. He stood up without a second thought.

"And I hear you've now become close friends with that Lord Bumblebee, or whatever his name is," he said.

"Devlin, you know perfectly well that it's Lord Battersby!"

Drewshank's eyes made brief contact with the Lady's, and he suddenly remembered how they reminded him of his first pet mouse. He kicked himself — he was thinking kindly of Lady Pettifogger — and looked away as fast as he could.

"Well I don't particularly care," he said grumpily, "so you might as well stop trying to sweet-talk me."

"I was doing no such thing!"

She made one more attempt to get closer, holding out her arm to touch him, but Drewshank smiled knowingly and stepped away.

"I think I should be going," he said. "Your spell is already taking effect."

Lady Pettifogger laughed. "Those days have long passed, Devlin. I've changed — Battersby's been good for me."

"I don't believe that for one minute, Beatrice. And Battersby's a thug. A pompous, proud military man, with no other talent except waging war," he said, making a move for the door. He finished his drink and returned the glass to Lady Pettifogger. She stretched up her hand for him to kiss, but Drewshank declined.

"As much as I'd like my heart torn in two again, I'd rather not have it happen this evening," he said, and made his way out without looking back.

Once the outside door slammed shut, a concealed door opened in the bookcase behind Beatrice Pettifogger. Lord Battersby stepped out angrily.

"Me? A thug?" he exclaimed. "Drewshank was always a fool and a damned fop, and I'm pleased to see nothing's changed."

"He's no fool, Alexander," said Lady Pettifogger. "You do yourself a disservice by thinking it."

"You still hold a soft spot for him. . . ."

"No!" she said firmly, approaching him and stroking the war medals on his chest, "but he doesn't deserve the fate you've lined up for him."

"He's a cocky you-know-what, and it's all for the

good of Old Town, Beatrice! If we're going to return our fair city to its past glory, then it's something that has to happen."

"You're right, of course," she said quietly. "I'll send a message to Isiah, he'll be pleased to hear things are going to plan."

"Oh, he will indeed. Drewshank was a terrific choice of mine, don't you think?"

Lady Pettifogger smiled briefly.

"Of course, Alexander. He'll see it through to the bitter end, too. Just like you, his pride will allow for nothing less."

※

"From what I heard, it's been quite a week for Grak attacks," said Algernon as Scratcher and Emiline followed him up the stairs to his workshop in the roof. "At some point, I'd be very interested in hearing of your encounter." He turned, leaned toward Emiline, and peered over the rim of his glasses.

"These creatures become monsters when humans meddle with them," he added, suddenly becoming serious. "Two Grak incidents in the Great Sea in the space of a week is no coincidence!"

Algernon continued to the top of the stairs, where they reached a dead end. He pushed aside a dirty painting of a yellow, flea-ridden mouse to reveal a hidden lever, and he pulled it violently. With a click and a thud, a trapdoor dropped open above them and a ladder slid down.

"Go on," he said, and ushered them hastily upward.

Emiline and Scratcher clambered up onto the floor above them into darkness. They heard the trapdoor close behind them; light and the sound of squeaking mice filled the room.

The mousekeepers gasped as the workshop revealed itself before them. It was a mass of copper pipes, machinery, and flashing numbered dials; shelves were filled with books and instruments, and the walls covered in pictures of whales, mice, and islands. Algernon was always one to experiment with the latest technology, and the workshop was gently lit not by gas lamps but by the cool glow of electric bulbs.

Scratcher's eye was taken by a clockwork metallic

globe that was ticking madly on a little table. He went over a little fearfully and picked it up, and watched the islands and countries spin around.

"What does it do?" he asked, but Algernon didn't hear. He was whistling strangely.

At his call, a band of brown Boffin Mice scurried across the floor. Emiline clapped her hands with excitement — she'd never seen any up close before. It's easy to identify them because of the white ring of fur around each of their eyes and their two sticky-out teeth. If you saw them at a distance, you could almost swear they were wearing glasses.

"Ah, watch out for them," Algernon said as the mice ran up the wall to a small ledge. "I call this my Marvellous Mouse Machine, although the name's open to discussion." Emiline noted that every time Algernon spoke, it was as though his mind was already racing ahead onto the next sentence.

"What Marvelous Mouse Machine?" asked Scratcher.

"You'll see!" laughed Algernon.

The Boffin Mice ran up to a shiny metal panel and pressed some buttons, one at a time, until a huge crack sounded through the workshop and a large portion of the roof folded inward. The night-time sky opened up above them and half of a gigantic gleaming copper telescope slipped gracefully downward into the room, with its small eyepiece stopping just in front of Algernon's face.

"There we go, take a look through here," he said excitedly.

Emiline took hold and peered into the telescope. Her heart skipped a beat as she realized she was looking at a far-off shore, lit by the moon. In the blue light she could make out a creature moving slowly, and it eventually dawned on her that it was a Giant Himolo Mouse, its body taller than the trees.

"It's a Giant Mouse!" she said excitedly. "But they're extinct?"

"A Giant Mouse?" interrupted Scratcher. He nudged Emiline out of the way and looked for himself. "Wow," he breathed.

"Isn't it marvelous," chuckled Algernon. "You can see all sorts of mice through there if you look hard enough! There's a special setting just for mice — you could look at buildings or stars if you'd rather, but who'd want to do that?"

Emiline couldn't believe it. "But why don't you tell people about the Himolo Mouse! This is the greatest discovery in years!" she said.

"Oh no! No, never. As soon as one of those rich mouse collectors who only care about money got their grubby mitts on it . . . well I wouldn't like to think about it."

Algernon gestured to the mice, who raced onto the telescope and pressed a few more buttons along its side. It creaked and twisted, and gently rose back into the roof, closing off the hole to the sky at the same time.

Portly had become very excited by Algernon's Boffin Mice, and he slipped out from Emiline's hair and climbed to the top of her head to get a better view.

"You're not bored with all this, are you?" Algernon asked, while his hands scoured the surface of the table for something interesting.

"Not at all!" declared Emiline. "Portly here seems very impressed."

"Ah! What a splendid Grey!" said Algernon, taking a

moment to see Emiline's mouse. Portly's ears shot to attention.

Suddenly remembering his role as host, Algernon rushed to find two little wooden stools among the debris of his workshop. He brushed a mess of twinkling objects off one, and they burst open with tremendous flashes of light as they hit the floor.

"Oh, sorry!" said Algernon absently.

Emiline took her hands from her eyes and sat down next to Scratcher. Opposite them, Algernon looked serious once more.

"So then," he asked, "you're sailing with the dashing Captain Drewshank."

Emiline blushed slightly. "I couldn't think of anything better," she said excitedly.

"And I hear you're out to capture Mousebeard — old Drewshank never takes the easy life, does he?"

"I know he'll find him," added Scratcher.

"He will? Mousebeard's name strikes fear into the hearts of sailors for good reason, you know!" said Algernon seriously. "For one thing, he's supposed to take immense pleasure in tying up his prisoners and feeding them, one limb at a time, to Short-fanged Sea Mice. I doubt he's a man who'll give up easily. . . ."

"Drewshank can do anything when he puts his mind to it," said Scratcher confidently.

"Yes, maybe you're right. He certainly survived that sea monster. But you two should take extra care of yourselves. Good mousekeepers are a dying breed in these lands."

"We'll be fine, Algernon," replied the boy. "We've survived the Grak — what worse thing can come at us?"

"That's all true, Mr. Scratcher, but never believe you're past the worst when you're at sea. It has a terrible way of surprising you when you least expect it!"

He turned to look at Emiline.

"And you know how the Grak became Grak, don't you?"

"Yes . . . ," said Emiline.

"Well, have you asked yourselves who dropped the Long-eared Mice in the water in the first place?"

"Drewshank thinks Mousebeard could have been involved," said Scratcher eagerly.

"Hmmm," replied Algernon.

"You don't . . . ," Emiline was about to ask a further

question, but was interrupted by Scratcher, who had taken to nosing around the workshop. He came to a stop in front of a dusty old photograph.

"Who's this?" he asked, looking at the three people standing on top of a mountain. One was far shorter than the others, yet he looked the most happy as he held a particularly fine Triplehorn Mouse. Its head was as large as a fist just so that it could carry the three hefty horns.

"Oh, that was me a long time ago," said Algernon, "back in the days when I went mousehunting. What a mouse that was — only the second to be found on the island of Dundinia. That's Isiah Lovelock in the middle. He's now rich and famous, having written that fascinating book."

"Isiah Lovelock? He has the best mouse collection in the world," said Emiline. "I was his mousekeeper."

"Ah! I should have known. He always could tell a good mouser," said Algernon, who went and reacquainted himself with the photograph. "We don't get on too well these days; he's grown a little too big for his boots — thinking he can run the mousetrading world and all. He thinks he owns us all sometimes. You're wrong about his collection though."

"I am?" said Emiline, greatly surprised.

"Mousebeard the pirate has the greatest collection. But I wouldn't tell that to Lovelock . . . ," he added with glee.

"Mousebeard?" choked Scratcher and Emiline together.

"Oh yes, everyone knows that!" Algernon said, matter-of-factly.

"Who's the other person in the picture then?" said Emiline, greatly intrigued.

"He was a good friend of ours. We lost him while on a voyage to an island a long way from here. Jonathan Harworth was his name."

"What happened?" asked Scratcher.

Algernon looked slightly put out when he heard Scratcher's question, and he rustled his hair and walked back to his table.

"Something rather horrible, and I don't care to go into detail," he said. "It was a long time ago now. . . ."

Scratcher tried to delve deeper. "What was it?" he asked.

Algernon closed his eyes and thought hard.

"Young man," he finally said to the boy, "in this world everyone harbors a secret; some people even have two. Isiah Lovelock probably has at least three, and I don't doubt that Mousebeard has near five. But I'm not going to say anything more on the subject."

Emiline considered quizzing him more, but thought better of it. Algernon remained quiet for a few moments while he picked up and arranged some papers. He wasn't one to be still for long, however.

"Aha!" he said, suddenly jumping into life and running to a large tank of water. "Yes, yes, yes!" he exclaimed. "I remember why I invited you up here! My rocket-powered Whale Mouse attachment."

Emiline looked on in bewilderment as Algernon opened a sliding door into the tank. In a burst of bubbles, a bloated Whale Mouse shot into view, with a small gushing metal attachment on its back.

"With the aid of my invention, this little mouse can

swim at the equivalent mouse speed of eighty miles an hour. I've yet to find a good use for it, but the mouse seems incredibly pleased."

Leading out from the tank was a large glass tube that traveled around the room. Algernon lifted a lever, another door in the tank slid across, and the streamlined yet rotund mouse shot out into the tube. He happily powered around it, without a care in the world, making three passes of Emiline in the space of only a few seconds.

Emiline stared in amazement. On top of her head, Portly was looking on, incredibly jealous.

"He'll be zooming around there for hours now," Algernon said excitedly. As he spoke, a bell rang from near the trapdoor.

"Oh no! That's young Elbert downstairs, calling for assistance," he said. "I'm sorry to cut short this delightful discussion, but we'd best head down now. Maybe we can do it again soon? There's plenty more things for me to show you!"

Scratcher and Emiline agreed and made their way

back downstairs. Algernon sealed his workshop shut and charged off, waving goodbye as he passed them.

Among the rabble in the inn sat Drewshank. He was relaxing quietly in a booth to himself, supping from a bottle of Blind Mice Beer. Chervil was curled up tightly on the table in front of him, and he greeted the young mousekeepers as they entered the room. He was quite subdued after his visit to the Mouse Trading Center.

"So you've visited Algernon's workshop," he said, his voice tired.

"It's amazing!" proclaimed Scratcher, idly stroking Chervil's head.

"He's certainly a character," Drewshank replied, sipping some beer.

"How was Lady Pettifogger?" asked Emiline, sensing that something had occurred.

"Same as she ever was," he said, in an unusually downbeat manner. "And that worries me. Something doesn't sit right with all this business. I've been caught out by her before, and I'm starting to smell something terribly whiffy about this whole mission."

"That'll be the Elephant Mice," said Scratcher, as one of the huge mice passed by with beers on its back.

"Maybe," grumbled Drewshank. "There's definitely some stinking mice involved in all this, of that we can be dead sure, but I wish I knew what they were. Still, I shouldn't burden you with these things . . . just keep your eyes and ears open. Lovelock and Pettifogger are tricky customers with cronies everywhere. I just know something's up, but I can't tell what."

⇒ ✳ ⇐

The sun broke the top of the horizon, casting a bright red glow across the tall rock of Hamlyn. From the *Flying Fox*, Drewshank watched the morning light hit the buildings rising up all over it like the spines on a porcupine.

On the quayside, the sellers and fishermen were already sorting out their stands, and sailors were loosening their boat moorings as Drewshank oversaw the last of the supplies arriving on deck. He was anxious about the journey ahead, but he was determined, as ever, to see his commission through.

Drewshank and Fenwick had come to the conclusion that they should take a course north, just as Lady Pettifogger had suggested, but they had nothing more than the map to go on.

"Mildred!" he shouted, stepping down onto the quayside.

A thin boy with strawlike hair approached, carrying a long stick with a dried fish attached to its end. His head was covered by an ill-fitting helmet that was the uniform of a Weather Teller. More commonly referred to as fish danglers, Weather Tellers were found at every port, standing quietly day after day ready to reveal the weather forecast with the help of a dried fish. Weather telling was regarded as a noble trade by sailors the world over, as the specially prepared fish were usually very reliable.

"Yes, Mr. Drewshanks," he replied keenly, ever getting his name wrong.

"Any news on the weather?"

"Of course, Mr. Drewshanks, but you won't like it!"

"I won't?"

"Fog, sir," said the Weather Teller sternly, looking intently at the fish on the end of his rod. "It's twisting slightly to the left, see."

Drewshank felt his heart sink.

"And occasional squalls to the north," he added.

"Thanks, Mildred," said Drewshank in exasperation, as he returned to the ship. "Those fish . . . they ever get it wrong?"

"No, Mr. Drewshanks. Only if they run out of salt, but my fish was freshly salted only yesterday."

"Oh well," replied Drewshank finally, "I suppose it could be worse."

"Yes, sir . . . ," called the Weather Teller. "Take care, sir!"

Ten minutes later, a loud whistle blew and the *Flying Fox*'s gangplank slid onto deck. Four small paddleboats, waiting for the word from the captain, let their oars hit the water and took the strain. Ropes lifted from the water and the *Flying Fox* gradually pulled away from its berth in tow.

Aboard ship, it would have seemed that no one on the mainland was concerned about their voyage, but that could not have been further from the truth. Lord Battersby stood by his window and watched the *Flying Fox,* charting its course out to sea. He held detailed notes of the gun placements before him; his spies had done a good job at checking out the *Flying Fox* and its crew. He knew exactly what it was capable of.

And at the other end of the harbor, Algernon had taken no rest that night and watched the *Flying Fox*'s departure through his telescope. He then promptly scribbled a note in his indecipherable hand, and readied a Messenger Mouse for flight.

It was safe to say that, unknown to Captain Drewshank and his crew, their actions were being watched very closely indeed.

The Moose Mouse

A VERY FUNNY-LOOKING MOUSE, SO NAMED BECAUSE OF ITS PECULIAR *brown furry ears that resemble antlers. The Moose Mouse lives in herds and is known to make an annual mass migration from the east coast of Sintruvia to the west, crossing great streams and puddles on the way. It is a mouse capable of withstanding great hardship and surviving in very difficult conditions.*

MOUSING NOTES

Not a mouse for anyone with a small home. In larger collections, Moose Mice have been best cared for in huge rooms, with a great mixture of terrains.

The Creeping Fog

THE *FLYING FOX*'S DEPARTURE FROM HAMLYN FELT VERY different from leaving Old Town. It was a brave sailor who chose to sail against Mousebeard, and Drewshank had found it impossible to recruit fresh blood. His crew were already stretched to the limit: everyone was now working to breaking point, including Emiline, who found herself following out other sailors' orders more often than she cared for.

She swabbed the decks, mended rope, helped the cook wash the dishes, and kept regular lookout from the crow's nest; she had become the general drudge, regularly attending to Fenwick, who also had to see to ten jobs at once.

Scratcher found himself doing more than usual as well, but it felt right to play a more prominent role on ship. If anything he found it made people respect him more, and that was always welcome. He'd been given a rough ride by the crew ever since he folded under the might of the Sharpclaw, but he tried not to let it get to him.

The *Flying Fox* sailed northward for what seemed like days and days to Emiline. The weather remained fine, and the sea unusually clear of vessels, due in no small part to the continuing threat of Grak attacks. So when, on the eighth day of sailing, a mysterious fog appeared on the horizon behind the ship, Captain Drewshank paid more attention than usual.

Fogs were of particular danger at sea because they blinded the vessel. They could send a ship off course easily, and even lure it to the rocks. And this fog seemed to be gaining on the *Flying Fox*.

"That's no normal bit of weather," said Fenwick. "With things as they are, we shouldn't be having no fog."

He was standing in Drewshank's cabin, peering out of the windows that looked out over the stern.

"I think we should make every effort to avoid it,"

replied the captain grimly, remembering the words of the Weather Teller. Lady Pettifogger's map was spread out in front of him, with the *Flying Fox*'s current course plotted over it in bright pins. A cluster of black mice was drawn on the map right where they were heading.

"It's going to be tricky enough finding that pirate as it is without us getting lost in fog as well," said Drewshank.

"Aye, sir. We don't need to take any more risks just yet!"

"Quite right," said Drewshank. "We'll soon be in Mousebeard territory, so we need to be on full guard. Give the order to get a move on."

Mr. Fenwick snapped to attention and made his way onto deck, passing Emiline on the way. She was holding a Brown-nosed Gruffler Mouse in her hands, and it was wriggling all over the place. Grufflers were angry mice, with dark gray fur and a tendency to cause mischief.

"Is that a Gruffler?" asked Fenwick before shouting out his orders at the top of his voice. The ship turned a little, and a great whooshing noise filled the air as every sail caught the wind fully, pushing the *Flying Fox* faster through the waves.

"He's been biting through ropes," said Emiline with

frustration. "I'm going to have to lock him up now, and we just don't have the space for him."

"These pets can get a bit out of control," said Fenwick, his eyes watching the actions of his crew. "Have you seen this fog?"

Emiline looked to the horizon at where the first mate was pointing and saw a mass of gray, obscuring the break between the sea and sky.

"That's trouble brewing, that is," he said, his mouse appearing at his shoulder. "I ain't never seen a fog like it. Looks like it's comin' right at us."

The Gruffler Mouse decided that was the moment it was going to bite Emiline, and with a frustrated wriggle it clamped its sharp teeth around her finger.

"Grrrrouch!" she yelped, and tore the mouse off her hand and held it aloft, its legs dangling helplessly.

"I see you've got problems enough of your own," he said, smiling.

"It's never-ending, sir," she replied.

"Aye, that can be the way of sailing sometimes. We're making good progress now though."

Scratcher called out from the other end of the deck,

and Emiline made her leave with the mouse in tow. He was carrying a small cage, and he opened its door so that Emiline could deposit the Gruffler. It was only just big enough for it, but until they could get a bigger one sorted, it would have to do.

"Have you heard about this fog?" said Scratcher excitedly, bolting the cage door.

"Fenwick says it's trouble," replied Emiline.

"All the sailors down below are talking about it like it's a ghost or demon or something. They all say it's bad news. . . ."

"It's just a fog!" said Emiline. "We get them all the time in Old Town."

"But this one's coming after us. They think it might be a ghost ship."

"Sailors are crazy. . . ."

"But I've seen one before . . . ," butted in Scratcher defensively.

"When?"

"A year ago, just off the coast of the Western Isles. It had three masts and tatty sails, but it shot through the water like a rocket!"

Emiline looked to the fog.

"Well, I'll believe it when I see it," she said, folding her arms.

⇒ ✳ ⇐

For two hours they sailed with the wind behind them, but it all proved to be fruitless: the fog continued to give chase, and was now catching up with them.

"It's no good," said Drewshank to his crew who had massed on the top deck; "we can't outrun it. Whatever it is that pursues us, the only course of action is to batten down the hatches and face it head-on. Tie up the sails, and weigh anchor. We shall sit here, swords drawn."

"But, cap'n," asked a sailor with a huge bustle of hair, "what if there's an ambush waiting in the middle of it? Or a ghost ship out to spook some unsuspecting vessel like ours?"

The huddle of sailors all responded with nervous chatter and mutterings of "Mousebeard." Superstition ran deep among the crew of the *Flying Fox*, and after the Grak attack, nerves were a little shaky.

"We will get through this!" said Drewshank strongly.

"Nothing will get the better of the *Flying Fox*, but I believe we're best off fighting whatever it is head-on."

"So stand firm at your posts," said Mr. Fenwick. "We'll take more measures once the fog's upon us."

"Aye, sir!" shouted the sailors.

"See!" said Scratcher to Emiline. "I'm not the only one who believes in ghost ships!"

"You're all mad!" she returned, then headed off below deck.

By dusk the fog was so close that the sea behind them was completely hidden. Emiline and Scratcher had fed all the mice onboard and were collecting the Watcher Mice from the bowsprit. Apart from a host of armed sailors standing on guard, most people were now below deck.

"I've never seen anything like it," said Scratcher, placing a mouse into a wooden box full of straw. "It's as though it's bewitched."

"I agree that there are odd things at sea," replied Emiline, "but I certainly don't believe in bewitched fogs. How can a fog be bewitched?"

Emiline let loose three Night-light Mice from a

mousebox, their eyes beaming like torches, and then she leaned over the edge of the ship. The fog was creeping closer, and she watched the wisps of gray claw their way across the water. It would only be minutes before the ship was completely enshrouded in darkness.

Fenwick shouted out: "Everyone inside or below deck if you're not on guard!"

It had been decided that patrols would take it in turns to keep watch on deck, but for safety, everyone else had to remain below in their quarters.

Scratcher made his way to the trapdoor, and stopped for Emiline.

"Come on, what are you doing?" he said.

Emiline was itching to see what the fog was like close up. She wanted to touch it and feel what it was made of.

"You go on, I'll follow," she replied confidently. Scratcher didn't bother to speak. He simply raised his hand in annoyance and left Emiline to her own devices.

The fog inched closer and finally touched the side of the ship. Within minutes it had spread over the top deck. Emiline stood by the open trapdoor and let the fog swirl around her. It was cold and damp, but it had a strangely sweet smell, like that of fragrant burning wood. Fogs don't normally smell sweet, she thought.

"In you come," ordered Fenwick, and Emiline felt a hand take hold of her ankle and tug it gently.

"All right!" she replied, pulling the wooden trapdoor over her head.

⇒ ❋ ⇐

A loud banging on the door woke Algernon from his dreams of machines and mice.

"Who is it?" he shouted sleepily. Swinging himself out of bed, Algernon opened the window onto the chilly night. He slipped his glasses over his nose and finally saw who was making the racket. A band of soldiers were huddled around his door, swords and rifles held at the ready.

"Algernon Mountjack," ordered a soldier, "on the orders of the Mayor of Hamlyn, open your door. You are under arrest for conspiring against the state. As of now, your premises are under the control of the Hamlyn Guard."

Algernon jumped back from the window and composed

himself. He ticked all the mental notes off one at a time in his brain: he liked to prepare for instances such as these, but they would always surprise you no matter how ready you were. He slipped on his shoes and overcoat, picked up his goggles and leather hat, and bundled down the stairs at breakneck speed.

Once more the soldiers rapped on the door.

"Right, break it in!"

Algernon sped through to the bar, avoiding the two sleeping Elephant Mice not far from the doorway. He patted his pockets with his palms, and found them empty.

"Gah! Keys . . . ," he muttered to himself. "Keys . . . where are you?"

He kicked a load of crates out of the way and pushed aside some empty beer glasses. His keys were nowhere to be seen.

"Come on, I need you!" he growled.

The front door banged as the soldiers made their first hit. It shuddered and cracked, but nothing gave. Inn doors, particularly in Hamlyn, were always sturdily built for fear of rowdy pirates breaking in.

Algernon scampered around, scouring one surface after another, and then his thoughts turned a corner and he remembered exactly where he'd put them. He jumped up onto the bar and grabbed the key chain from a peg high up on the wall.

"Aha!" he cried as the front door was rammed again; this time its top twisted inward and the hinges buckled and snapped. Algernon jumped to the floor and budged a rusty old beer pump on the bar with his elbow. Sweat was dripping from his forehead and stinging his eyes. As the front door finally smashed open with a third and final bang, a trapdoor dropped down right before Algernon's feet, revealing a twisting staircase.

"Get him!" ordered an officer in the doorway as five of his men ran past him into the Giant's Reach. The Elephant Mice didn't take kindly to noisy strangers and shook themselves frustratedly from their sleep. They made angry low-pitched squeaks and charged toward the oncoming soldiers, hitting two men squarely and painfully in the kneecaps.

Algernon rushed down the steps and reached a round wooden door. He took out the key chain and selected a little bronze key, placed it in the lock, and twisted it. His arm jolted as it failed to open.

"Damn things!" he cursed, removing it and checking that it was the right one. It was, he was certain of it, and he tried again. He heard a gunshot, a loud wail, and a thud on the floor above. His heart seized — the soldiers had killed one of his Elephant Mice. He hit the door with his hand in anger.

"There he is!" shouted a soldier, appearing through the trapdoor. The man fired a reckless shot downward, and Algernon ducked as it flashed off the wall to his side. He twisted the key again.

"Don't kill him just yet!" shouted another soldier. "We want him for questioning!"

The key clunked as it spun around. Algernon sighed with relief. He pulled open the door just as another bullet bounced off the wall above him.

"Stop right there!" ordered a soldier, running down the stairs.

Algernon jumped through the door and locked it shut. He stopped to catch his breath in the darkness, hearing gunshots cracking into the door behind. Placing his hand to his right, he yanked a metal lever and three lamps fizzled into life nearby. As their glow grew stronger, a wonderful sight greeted him. A narrow underground river surged through the cave on its way out to sea, with the sparkling water reflecting off the twisted stalactites. Resting on the water, calmly bobbing up and down, was his favorite invention. It was his splendid small copper submarine — a more rounded and perfectly designed craft you couldn't find.

Algernon rushed over to his pride and joy, and grabbed hold of the metallic ladder that was attached to the sub's side. He cranked the wheel that unlocked the entry hatch and waited a few moments before it popped and swung upward. A bright light beamed out.

With a huge bang the door to the cave exploded and smoke rose into the air. Algernon jumped frantically into the submarine.

"Fire at will, men! Don't let him escape!" shouted the officer.

Algernon's heart leaped as he settled down into the cockpit; it was so exciting to be heading out to sea. He secured the hatch above him and flicked the power switch. Lights lit up all over the dashboard, and the engine kicked in with a mild grumbling splutter.

The submarine started to sink, and despite the constant sound of bullets chiming on the body of the submarine, Algernon settled himself comfortably into the pilot's seat. At his call, three of his highly trained Boffin Mice appeared from a pipe near his head, and made themselves comfortable on his shoulder.

Through the small glass window, Algernon watched the water rise up and over the vessel. He tightened his hat, lowered his goggles, and with a push of the gear stick, his submarine rocketed off into the deep.

⇒ ✳ ⇐

On the *Flying Fox*, sailors sat huddled on the lower decks with their weapons in hand. The fog continued to surround the vessel, and it completely obscured any view from the portholes.

Emiline waited with Scratcher in their quarters, mouse cages filling every conceivable space, and candles dimly lighting the interior. She was trying to make Portly jump over a makeshift hurdle, but he was showing no interest in obliging. He'd been acting oddly since the fog had appeared, and Emiline was concerned.

"He doesn't seem himself," said Scratcher, clearing condensation from a steamed-up porthole.

"I think he might be a bit seasick," replied Emiline, tempting her mouse with a slice of nutty cheese.

"I noticed some of the Messengers were under the weather too," added Scratcher, "but I reckon it's this fog that's got them down."

Emiline changed the subject. "I never asked you why you were called Scratcher. It seems a funny name."

"Ah . . . ," he replied reluctantly, "I knew you'd ask that at some point."

"Well?"

"Well, on my first voyage with Drewshank we were transporting a cargo of Scruffy Mice. . . ."

"You caught lice!" interrupted Emiline, and Scratcher was immediately embarrassed.

"I was scratching for weeks. . . ."

Emiline laughed out loud, causing her friend to blush terribly.

"You learn from your mistakes," he added quietly.

Portly suddenly looked to the porthole, then lay down and covered his ears.

"What was that?" asked Emiline, gently stroking the mouse. Scratcher placed his ear to the window.

"I can hear something," he said.

Emiline looked confused.

"Listen!" he said.

The whistling wind was carrying another noise altogether. It was faint, but growing louder all the time.

"What is it?" asked Emiline, a worried expression falling over her face. She could now hear it too: it sounded like the haunted wailing of a hundred lost babies, and it was terrifying.

Portly rose with a start and scurried straight up Emiline's arm to hide under her hair. The wailing grew louder and louder, forcing the mousekeepers to shield their ears with their hands. Above the din, they heard the ship's bell ring out from top deck to summon everyone with their weapons.

Emiline rushed to look out of the porthole with Scratcher, but they still couldn't see anything.

"We'd best go!" he shouted. "Do you have a weapon?"

Emiline pulled out her dagger, and Scratcher nodded in approval. Once he'd secured a thin sword to his belt they left the cabin, their hearts beating fast.

A messy procession of sailors wound its way up through the decks and out into the dense fog. Everyone had an idea about what was making the awful noise, and sailors were muttering curses under their breath. Captain Drewshank stood alert in the open, his sword drawn at the ready. Mr. Fenwick was nearby, and he gave the crew orders to position themselves at the edges of the ship to halt anyone trying to get onboard.

It was almost impossible to see through the misty darkness, but the Night-light Mice dotted around the deck provided some points of reference. The wailing continued, and Emiline took a place at the stern, her dagger clasped tightly. Every member of the crew was alert, hoping to catch a glimpse of what was out there.

Within minutes it sounded as though the ear-piercing noise was upon them. Nerves were taut, and everyone gasped as the gray murky night instantly became darker. Emiline's insides went into freefall. Like the passing of a cloud in front of the moon, an immense black mass was drawing up alongside the *Flying Fox*. Despite the fog, everyone could make out its shape — it was a ship, of that there was no doubt. The *Flying Fox* started to rock on the water, and the sailors gripped their weapons firmly.

"Ready yourselves!" shouted Fenwick, his cry echoing out into the night.

"Stand firm," ordered Drewshank, marching through his crew to the ship's side. The lamps fizzled out; the wind picked up; everyone grew even more nervous as they looked around themselves blindly. Night-light Mice started to run around deck in a crazed fashion, the light from their eyes making little impact in the fog.

Emiline felt a hand on her shoulder. She jumped.

"Are you all right?" asked Scratcher, his voice struggling to be heard above the din.

"Never been better . . . ," she replied. "Are they going to come onboard?"

"If it's a ghost ship, there won't be anyone. . . ."

Emiline huffed. The fog was cold and she was now shivering.

"It's not a ghost ship!" she barked, squeezing her grip on the dagger.

"Hold your positions, men!" shouted Drewshank.

Emiline still couldn't see a thing, but she felt a change in the air. The wailing was gradually getting quieter.

"It's moving on," she whispered to herself.

They listened intently as the wailing moved farther away, drifting off into the night. As the noise subsided, Emiline heard the unsettled mutterings of the other sailors. The wind eased, and after a short while it all fell silent but for the soft lapping of water at the ship's hull. Drewshank's crew started to relax, and lamps were lit once again. To everyone's surprise, the fog was clearing and they could see the moon and stars shining down on them.

"Captain!" shouted Fenwick.

Drewshank walked over to his first mate, who was pointing at a small object hanging from the main mast.

"I think you should see this," he added.

The captain looked up to see a thin rope hanging down. A noose had been tied at the end and a cloth mouse was dangling from it limply by its head.

"Mousebeard . . . and the *Silver Shark*," said Drewshank grimly.

The Magnetical Mouse

THE MAGNETICAL MOUSE HAS A BULLETLIKE NOSE THAT ALWAYS POINTS DUE north. No matter what the mouse is doing, whether it's eating or casually cleaning a paw, its nose will purposefully remain pointing in the same direction. The Magnetical Mouse's nose is so precise that every shipping vessel in Midena is now required to keep one by law.

You can also find them in the collections of mountain climbers and explorers. Originating from the volcanic regions of Crimsonia, it is believed that a particularly strong presence of metal in the topsoil of the land alters the Magnetical Mouse's composition, rendering it magnetic from birth. Scientific attempts to breed the mouse outside this area have resulted in healthy mice, but all without the magnetic ability.

MOUSING NOTES

A rather grumpy mouse by nature, possibly because it's thought to suffer regularly from headaches due to its magnetic nose. Mousing regulations state they must be housed in a wooden structure, as metallic cages have been known to irritate them.

The Silver Shark

WITH THE AID OF THE MOONLIT NIGHT, THE *FLYING Fox* followed the course of the fog so as not to lose the dreaded pirate. Under full sail it had kept close to its quarry, if not managing to steal any ground, but Drewshank was beginning to wonder which ship was the real prey now.

At first light, Drewshank appeared from his cabin, wrapped up in a leather waterproof jacket. He was holding a Magnetical Mouse in his hands, and its nose was firmly twisting to the left and looked rather awkward. Whenever you're at sea you can't get a more trustworthy implement for finding your bearings than a Magnetical Mouse. As Drewshank neared the bow, whichever way he turned, the mouse's nose never strayed from due north, and it was getting very annoyed because of it.

"Judging by our coordinates and Pettifogger's map, sir," said Fenwick, joining the captain, "we're approaching the point most sailors believe Winter Vale to be — though not many have ever entered or come out alive. Mousebeard's hideout is thought to be beyond, on the other side."

"Do we follow, Fenwick? We want to find Mousebeard, but this way he has us exactly where he wants us." Drewshank scratched his chin thoughtfully.

Fenwick paused and looked at the horizon. The air had grown considerably colder.

"You want my honest opinion, sir?" he asked.

"Of course . . ."

"Well then . . . ," he breathed out heavily, "it feels like a trap. But it could take days to find both him and his hideout if we don't carry on. The map shows the other side of the valley opening out into a massive landlocked sea — and to me that sounds like the perfect place for a pirate to hide."

Drewshank nodded slowly and chewed the inside of his cheek.

"This is all very sinister, but we came here to capture him, didn't we? Maybe not quite in this way, but it was our definite intention from the start."

Drewshank placed the Magnetical Mouse into a mousebox clipped to his waist and locked the lid.

"Hell, we've got the firepower — let's prepare the ship and be ready for him."

Mr. Fenwick puffed out his chest.

"Aye, sir!" he said, and proceeded to order the crew to sail straight on.

The morning couldn't have come sooner for the crew. They'd been spooked by the appearance of the *Silver Shark,* and couldn't see how the pirate had managed to get onboard or how he'd conjured up such a mysterious fog. Everyone took some solace from the warmth of the sun, although it did nothing to clear the fog that they chased, which remained like a cocoon around Mouse-beard's distant ship.

While Emiline was cleaning the Messenger Mice cages with Scratcher, Mr. Fenwick called for them. Something had been spotted in the sky, and he needed their help. The mousekeepers rushed up to the deck and found the captain and Fenwick craning their necks upward.

"Ah, Emiline!" said Drewshank. "Keep it quiet, but how are you with mouse spotting?"

Emiline was a little confused, but she felt confident enough in her knowledge of mice.

"Not bad," she replied, somewhat modestly.

Sheltered from other sailors' view by the bulk of Fenwick, Drewshank held a telescope to her eye and directed her to a black speck on the horizon.

"What's your expert opinion?" he asked.

Through the crystal-clear lens, Emiline focused in on a flying mouse. Its wings were huge and densely covered in pale white feathers. Its small body hung gracefully between them, with four feet hanging beneath, but when she looked at its head she instantly pulled away from the telescope. She glanced at Scratcher, who was itching to have a look. He could tell by the look on her face something was wrong.

Emiline raised the telescope again and took another look to be sure. The mouse's soft gray body faded into white at the nose, and its short black whiskers burst out-ward. But she couldn't make out any eyes.

The Mousehunter's Almanac had only a brief entry on this mouse, but most people who'd read it remember it vividly. And Emiline, of course, knew full well what it was.

"It's an Omen Mouse," she whispered, knowing exactly what a sighting of the mouse would do to the crew.

Drewshank nodded his head wearily.

"This voyage just takes the biscuit. It's a good thing I'm not superstitious, eh?" he said. "Still, keep it secret. Don't tell a soul."

The captain stomped off to his quarters, leaving Fen-wick with Scratcher and Emiline.

"Yer both youngsters," said Fenwick, feeling quite im-portant, "but when you're on ship and been on a few voyages, seeing a blind Omen Mouse flying alongside means only one thing — the ship's headin' for the bot-tom of the sea. I'm sure you understand what the sight-ing would do to the crew."

Scratcher stood quietly, and nodded.

"Apart from the captain, we're a superstitious lot on the *Flying Fox*," added Fenwick, "so the longer we can keep it under wraps, the better. Drewshank will do what he can though, I'm sure."

"You have our word," said Emiline.

"Good," replied Fenwick. "Now I've got to go and help Mr. Stringhopper tie up some barrels."

The mousekeepers returned to their duties, but Scratcher was visibly shaken by the sight of the Omen Mouse.

"Don't worry about it," said Emiline, patting him on the back. "Drewshank's good at getting out of trouble. I read that he fell from a crow's nest once, and the only thing that saved him was his expensive Toulouse Mousace bell-bottoms. The extra-flared legs snagged on a mast hook and stopped him from hitting the deck."

Scratcher let a smile slip out.

"And he's never bought anything but designer sailor-wear since! I tell you, that man can get out of anything."

⇒ ✳ ⇐

The *Flying Fox* followed the fog for three days, continually sailing north. The temperature had fallen considerably over the past week as they crossed into the Cold

Sea, and on the day they spotted granite snow-capped mountains lifting out of the sea, an icy wind rushed through the ship's sails.

"Land ahoy!" shouted a sailor from the crow's nest. The crew all appeared on deck to get a good view. In spite of its clear beauty, the way ahead looked daunting and inhospitable.

Fenwick stood at the ship's side and pointed to a break in the mountains straight ahead.

"There she goes, captain," he said as Drewshank walked up to him and pulled his jacket tighter around his chest.

"The fog's disappeared into it?" he asked.

"Aye, sir. Watched it creep in myself. Mousebeard's in there somewhere!"

Drewshank nodded firmly.

"Then we go after him, Fenwick. . . ."

"Aye, sir."

They reached the opening of the valley and were dwarfed by the sloping cliffs on either side. The water grew calmer, but a fine flurry of snow had started to fall.

Standing out on top deck, taking a well-earned rest

from sewing together mouse blankets, Emiline was trying to get used to the cold. She stood wrapped in many layers of clothes, and with a thick fluffy hat covering her ears, marveling at the beauty around her. The ship had sailed through the channel in the mountains to where it joined a wide river, and Emiline gazed in awe at the jagged rocky outcrops careering out of the water on both sides, each one covered with spiky green trees. Through the light snow that drifted on the wind, she could hear the cries of the Howling Moon Mice that inhabited the land.

The temperature had dropped even further, and thin icicles were now forming from every overhang on deck. Emiline tried desperately not to shiver, but the biting winds permeated even the densest of vests. As for Portly, he'd had enough of the cold. Taking Chervil's lead he'd made a nice bed for himself, along with Trumper and a number of other mice, in Drewshank's cabin. The unlikely group huddled together happily, and despite the captain's initial protestations about his quarters being overrun, they were left alone.

For two hours, the *Flying Fox* negotiated all the twists

and turns of the Vale. The farther it sailed, the higher the land grew, until they were completely surrounded by breathtaking mountains on every side, with black clouds scudding across their peaks. Eventually the ship reached a sharp turn, with a noticeable drop in the river. The current suddenly slowed, and gradually changed directions. Uncertain of what was to come, Drewshank called the crew to assume battle positions.

The *Flying Fox* followed a more gradual bend, and the seemingly endless horizon appeared as the mountains grew smaller and the land sloped off into the water. In the far distance was a peculiarly tall island that rocketed into the sky out of the sea, with clifflike rocky sides forming an impenetrable defense. A strange mist rested at its top, shivering the sky above it like a heat haze.

"Well, well . . . ," said Drewshank. He'd heard many rumors as to what Mousebeard's hideout looked like, but now, he realized, he was actually witnessing it. But he didn't have time to marvel for long.

"Captain!" shouted Fenwick, from the bow. "Look!"

Drewshank's eyes lowered to sea level. He swallowed a long, heavy gulp. Sailing at full pelt toward them was the

Silver Shark. Never before had he seen such a sight. It was made of sparkling metal and glowed like a shooting star coursing across the waves. Taut puffed-out sails were driving it hard toward the *Flying Fox,* and painted prominently on its bow was a frightening shark's head with gleaming silver teeth that shot forward and cut the water into slices. To make matters worse, four immense cannons were aimed directly at them from its bow. Drewshank had expected an ambush, but nothing could have prepared him for this. He quickly calculated how much time they had. Though traveling at terrific speed, the *Silver Shark* was still too far off to unleash its cannons.

"Hard to port!" shouted Drewshank, racing to his post at the helm. Shouts and orders broke out across the *Flying Fox,* and sailors rushed back and forth frantically. The *Flying Fox* turned sharply in the water and revealed its starboard arsenal.

"Ready the broadside!" shouted Drewshank, and the sailors on the gun deck jumped into action.

Scratcher heard the orders, and suddenly found himself on the front line in the gun deck. His heart was racing as he rushed to the ship's magazine to distribute gunpowder. Barrels were piled up to the ceiling, and a small shaft of light shone through from an adjacent cabin. He unlatched the mouse cage and waited a moment as a line of very well-behaved Powder Mice queued up in front of him. He picked one up and filled its leather backpack with gunpowder.

"Emiline!" he shouted.

She appeared in an instant and threw off her thick coat.

"It's Mousebeard!" she cried excitedly.

"I know. And I need your help," he said with unusual force. "I need you to help me fill up all the Powder Mice's holders. They'll do the rest. . . ."

Emiline was surprised at Scratcher's tone of voice. She saw that he'd been in battle before; he knew what it was like. There was no time for niceties.

Scratcher used an odd-shaped jug to fill up the mouse's gunpowder holder and then, after tying the holder's top to stop any spillage, he placed it gently on the floor.

"Be careful with the mice as you put them down — it's dodgy stuff, gunpowder."

Emiline watched the mouse run away to the cannons. She quickly picked one up and copied Scratcher. Before long all the mice were filled up and rushing away to the gunners to be of assistance.

"What now?" she asked.

"Return to the top deck, you'll be safer up there for the moment. I'll call you again if I need any more help."

Emiline agreed, and ran off. As she reached the stairs, the ship shook with the sound of a huge explosion. The *Silver Shark* had let rip its guns, and had hit its target. A cannonball shot through the lower deck sending sharp splinters of wood everywhere. The gunners cried out and scattered.

Plumes of smoke filled the air in front of the *Silver Shark* but within seconds it had burst through and was visible again.

"Fire!" shouted Drewshank as the target appeared.

The *Flying Fox* rocked back in the water as its cannons fired. Acrid smoke engulfed it. Cannonballs smashed straight into the oncoming warship, ripping holes through its sails. Its metal body provided an impenetrable defense though, and as the *Flying Fox* continued to fire, any shots that hit the hull merely left round, bulging dents.

Emiline appeared on deck in time to see the smoke lifting and the *Silver Shark* turning in the water only two hundred meters away to reveal its mighty broadside above them. It was clearly the equal of the *Flying Fox,* and because of its high sides, no sailors could be seen on the deck. It was a mighty vessel, thought Emiline, suddenly realizing the fearful position they were in.

A torrent of explosions rocketed out from the *Silver Shark* once more, and smoke filled the air. This time they hit the target even harder. With a deafening explosion, the starboard side of the *Flying Fox* burst into flames, and screams of terror rang out from the gun deck.

Emiline was thrown to the floor. Horrible thoughts filled her head.

"Scratcher!" she shouted. She ran back to the stairs and jumped down. There was scalding smoke flowing everywhere and it made her eyes sting. It was hot; so terribly hot, and she felt very scared, but she had to find

Scratcher. Amongst the noise and blackness she heard orders shouted. Her eyes caught glimpses of action, broken up by the swirling smoke; she could make out sailors grabbing buckets and struggling to dampen the fire that threatened to take hold. There was panic all around, but nowhere could she see her friend.

She called out Scratcher's name, pushing past a bloodied sailor crouching on the floor. Powder Mice were still running back and forth, always strong and sure. Suddenly a thought came to her: the mousery.

Back on the top deck, smoke was billowing from the trapdoors. Mr. Fenwick ordered the helm to turn the ship for another attack. The *Flying Fox* lurched in the water — taking such a tight turn was always a risk — but it soon righted and rallied for a second offensive.

Drewshank tried to take stock of the situation. He peered around the ship from the poop deck, the smoke now so thick and heavy that it made seeing very difficult. He could tell his sails were still intact, but the fire burning below was lapping over the starboard side.

"How are our cannons?" he shouted out, catching

sight of the *Silver Shark* through the smoke. It was turning as well, readying itself for another attack.

"We're running low on gunners," called out a sailor, "but we're good for another round!"

"Excellent!" shouted Drewshank. He raced to the side of the ship and looked out to where he thought the *Silver Shark* would be. He heard shouts from below deck; it was unbearable not knowing how his crew were managing, but he could only hope they were keeping on top of the fire. He had to bide his time, wait for the right moment, then strike.

Emiline shifted through the blackened corridors, dodging bodies at every step until she reached the mousery.

"Scratcher!" she called out in desperation. Some mice had been freed, but there were full cages remaining. And there was still no sign of her friend.

Emiline picked up all the mice she could hold and charged back down the passageways. It was hopeless looking for anything in the smoke-filled darkness. After reaching the stairs, she pelted up into the light and heard Drewshank call out an order.

"Aim for the sails and masts, men!" he shouted heartily. "Fire!"

The *Flying Fox* jolted once more and Emiline's footing gave way. She dropped the mice cages awkwardly and the doors snapped open. She tried to steady herself as the scared mice rushed for cover.

The *Silver Shark* took direct hits on its main sail, and the mast creaked and toppled with a great crash. Drewshank was covered with gun smoke once more, but he felt the *Silver Shark* must still be within reach. He called out for his cannons to fire yet again.

As if in response to his words, the guns on the *Silver Shark* boomed out and tore into the hull of the *Flying Fox*.

Emiline heard cannonballs whizz overhead and scorch straight through the sails and masts. She dropped to the deck for cover as bits of wood and material rained to the floor.

"Emiline? Is that you?" said a voice from the trapdoor.

Emiline looked up, and there, emerging from the smoke, was Scratcher, running up the stairs.

"Scratcher!" she cried happily.

The boy's face and body were blackened with soot and his arms fit to burst with mice cages. Emiline got to her feet and reached out to help him bring them to the deck.

"Be careful up here," he said, as he vanished below to bring some more cages.

"I will!" she shouted out.

Mr. Fenwick rushed to Drewshank's side.

"Cap'n, our gun deck's in tatters," he said ominously. "The fire is under control, but we're good for nothing now. . . . We should get out of here or stand and fight with our swords."

Drewshank looked out to sea through the clouds of dark gray smoke.

"I can't see a way out of this," he said. "They'll know we're in trouble and will want to finish us. How are the crew?"

"They're all right, sir. We've got heavy casualties, but everyone who's left's ready for the battle."

Drewshank paced back and forth.

"Well, there's no going back now. We've come this far. . . . Line the deck with sailors, get them armed and ready," he said rousingly. "We'll not go down without a fight!"

Drewshank steeled himself and withdrew the sword from its sheath. Setting an example, he stood tall before the oncoming menace.

Scratcher appeared once more with cages and dropped them to the deck in exhaustion. He closed his eyes and let out a stifled cough.

"You okay?" asked Emiline.

"Mmmm," he groaned. "It's horrible down there."

"You know," said Emiline, "you were quite impressive earlier. You really were. . . ."

The smoke was lifting slowly, and Scratcher sat up and smiled. For a moment he forgot about the horrors of the gun deck and felt almost happy.

"Arm yourselves!" shouted Fenwick as he rushed across the deck. He passed Emiline and Scratcher and stopped for a second.

"Everything all right?" he asked, patting Scratcher on the shoulder. "We ain't out of it yet, so find yourself a weapon and be ready."

With that he upped and left, and Scratcher sighed, unclasping the sword from his belt.

"I'd like a rest," he said, gripping the sword tight.

"And me," replied Emiline, removing the dagger from her belt. As soon as she saw it again she remembered the words of the butler and felt her energy stirring.

"Face to face with Mousebeard . . . ," she said bravely. "This could be it. . . ."

"Maybe," he replied, pulling himself to his feet. "The pirate's supposed to take kindly to mousers, though."

"Let's hope so," said Emiline, lifting herself up too.

The mousekeepers stood side by side. The sound of cannons had ceased, and all that could be heard was the cracking of warping wood and snarling fire.

Drewshank stood waiting for sight of the *Silver Shark.* He'd walked to a group of battle-weary sailors and stood amongst them — each and every one looking out feverishly onto the smoke-filled sea. Drewshank could feel the ship drifting and being buffeted by the water's push and pull. The *Silver Shark* was approaching.

"Ready, men!" he ordered as a flash of silver flickered

through the smoke. The *Silver Shark* was only meters away. The hulls collided, scraping forcefully together with a deafening screech.

"Brace yourselves!" shouted Drewshank.

The *Flying Fox* shook violently, creaking and growling as if in pain as the *Silver Shark* muscled its way alongside. Everyone could see Mousebeard's ship in all its glory: with tall sides rising at least two meters over the *Flying Fox*'s deck, and seemingly bulletproof metal plating running along its length, it showed little sign of the battle it had just encountered.

"It looks so unreal," said Emiline. Scratcher gaped as he looked the craft up and down. The ship was so well protected by its metal shield that he couldn't see inside, and moreover there was no sign of any pirate.

"It's incredible," he muttered. Both ships were eerily silent. Drewshank walked back and forth in front of his crew, his eyes never leaving the *Silver Shark.* Still they waited.

"Show yourself!" barked Drewshank, finally breaking the silence, his hair shaking with the words. There was no reply.

Fenwick joined him at the ship's side.

"They're playing games with us," he grumbled.

Suddenly, a series of short blasts burst out from the *Silver Shark,* and spear-tipped grappling hooks pierced the hull of Drewshank's ship and pulled it closer until the two hulls were only meters apart. Emiline felt the hairs rise on the back of her neck. She lifted her weapon in response, and watched as the rest of the crew did the same.

"Here they come," said Scratcher.

With a clunk and clatter, the part of the *Silver Shark's* side immediately above them collapsed down into a series of long iron-lined gangplanks, landing with a bang onto the *Flying Fox.*

Drewshank walked to the edge of the deck, and stepped upon a gangplank. He could see onto the *Silver Shark,* but the deck appeared empty. He made a move to progress further, when an incredibly loud voice boomed out.

"Why do you insist upon chasing us to your death!"

Drewshank jumped slightly. He hadn't expected this sort of a greeting, but he stood firm, thought awhile, and then replied in the most confident voice he could muster.

"We've come for Captain Mousebeard on the order of Isiah Lovelock," he said boldly.

"And who might you be?" replied the voice.

Drewshank looked briefly to his crew, who were spread out behind him.

"Captain Drewshank of the *Flying Fox,* of course!"

"Aha," said the voice, "So then, Captain Drewshank, of the, well, shall we say *Sinking Fox.* Would you mind if we came aboard?"

With those words, a horde of armed pirates dressed in a uniform of stiff jackets and breeches charged out of the ship and ran down the gangplanks, their long swords slicing the air.

"Let's have 'em!" bellowed Fenwick, pulling his captain behind him and a wall of sailors. Sword and steel clanged and chimed as the first wave hit. Shouts and screams filled the air.

Scratcher and Emiline watched on from behind the defenders. The crew were all around them awaiting their chance to fight, but as a continual stream of pirates charged out onto the *Flying Fox*, it was clear that the battle had left them horribly outnumbered.

"They just keep coming," said Emiline. "What can we do?"

"We'd not stand a chance against them, Emiline," replied Scratcher, watching pirates and sailors fight each other to the death. He could see Mr. Fenwick standing tall above the crowd and defending Drewshank heroically.

"Our time will come," he said assuredly. Small puffs of smoke continued to drift out around their legs from the open trapdoor nearby, and the mice in cages at their feet were squeaking in terror.

"Hold them back!" shouted Drewshank, now standing on a crate and getting a view of the fight as it continued. He rallied his crew, who were fighting valiantly.

Another wave of pirates ran down the gangplanks and hurtled into the crowd. Scratcher saw them charge, and he grabbed Emiline's arm: one of the attackers had broken through and was running at them. The man was skinny and roughly shaven, and he was swinging a rusty, jagged cutlass over his head. In two seconds he'd be upon them.

Emiline froze — she didn't know what to do. Scratcher thought fast and jumped out to swing at him with his sword. The pirate pushed aside the boy's attack easily and bundled him to the floor. He stopped and looked frighteningly at Emiline.

"What's in there?" he sneered, glancing to the ground where the cages of mice lay. "You have mice? Ha! Mousebeard will be pleased." He grabbed at Emiline, his hands clawing for her neck, but a spark fired her from the inside, and she darted under his arm, striking him with her dagger.

The man howled in pain, and made an even more determined effort to grab her. Once more he lunged, but this time Scratcher pushed his sword up from where he lay on the floor, and it was over as quickly as it had begun.

Emiline watched as the man's body slumped to the floor. For a split second, the world around her fell completely silent as she realized what they'd done.

"Is he dead?" asked Scratcher tentatively.

She nudged the body with her foot.

"I think so," she said, her legs and arms trembling. The pirate didn't move. "We've killed him. . . ."

She suddenly felt like being sick.

"Come on," said Scratcher, "we can't hang around."

"Of course," she said dully as a roar went up from the attackers — Drewshank had been cornered.

"Lower your weapons!" he shouted to his crew, his hand and sword raised in the air. A stocky pirate whose sword and body was twice the size of his own had trapped him. The few surviving crew members, including Fenwick, whose shirt was in bloody tatters, ceased fighting immediately. Their shoulders slumped.

"Drewshank!" whispered Emiline, under her breath.

Mousebeard's pirates rounded on everyone and tied their wrists together before shoving them to the ground in a huddle. Emiline and Scratcher stayed close, and as the attackers took away their weapons and possessions, they tried to resist, but it was futile; their arms were bound and they too dropped to the floor.

The noise died down, leaving the groans of the injured

sailors among the smoke. Only Drewshank remained on his feet. A deep laugh filled the air and everyone turned to look at the *Silver Shark.* Against the light smoke drifting up from the *Flying Fox* stood the demonic figure of Mousebeard, who was laughing from his ship's deck. As more smoke cleared, Emiline saw his immense beard was writhing at the sides of his face and below his tricorn hat. In all the noise and pandemonium, no one had realized that Mousebeard himself had been watching the fight.

"Lovelock's a fool," Mousebeard boomed. His face was shadowed by the cold sun, but the sight of his huge form — at least the width of two normal men — sent daggers of fear into the hearts of his prisoners. His chest was firmly pushed out to the width of his bulging belly, secured in place within a woollen gray jacket by metal mouse-skull clasps. A wide leather strap crossed his chest diagonally down to his waist, with three pistols attached to its front, and after taking two long steps down the gangplank, he unfurled his wide spade-like hands and gripped the majestic silver cutlasses that hung at his side.

"Imagine sending out a mere paddleboat to capture me!" he boomed again, withdrawing the cutlasses and thrusting them into the air.

Drewshank reeled.

"You're a coward, standing up there!" he shouted back angrily. A pirate kicked him in the guts as a reply. He put up no resistance, as his heart was sinking further and further with each second, and he felt broken. He slumped to the floor wearily.

"Coward?" spat Mousebeard, his beard twisting and snapping as he spoke. "You don't have a clue, captain."

He turned and made his way back up the gangplank to his ship. Halting on the edge of the deck, he turned to his men on the *Flying Fox.*

"Collect up their mice, weapons, and any booty you can find before we sink this hulk," he added in his grizzly voice, "then bring them aboard. They should all fit snugly in the brig."

Then he disappeared from view. Pirates shifted on deck, pushing bodies around as they searched for any rich pickings. With tears in his eyes, Drewshank watched them move like scavengers among his fallen crew.

"How has this happened?" he murmured. "Devlin Drewshank, the great Devlin Drewshank. Captured by a pirate . . ."

He sat wondering, sifting things through his mind. This was the famous Mousebeard he'd come after. Not even all the powerful navies in the world had so far been able to catch him, and yet his foolish arrogance and the temptation of riches had fooled him into believing he was good enough — what *had* he been thinking?

His arm was tugged by a pirate, and he rose to his feet to have his arms bound.

"Lovelock . . . ," he cursed. Lovelock was a shrewd man, he thought. He would have known Mousebeard was out of a privateer's reach, even if it was someone as famous and dashing as himself. What had he achieved other than simply holding up the pirate's passage?

Drewshank instinctively looked out toward Mousebeard's island hideout and beyond. Something strange was spreading out along the horizon behind the island. A faint, broken line stretched across the sea, approaching stealthily. He resisted a pirate's pull on his arms to look longer. And then it hit him.

Drewshank laughed; quietly at first, just a few chuckles — and then a full belly laugh. His remaining crew couldn't understand what had gotten into him.

"Mousebeard!" shouted Drewshank.

The pirate appeared once more on deck.

"What is it?" he hammered back.

Drewshank tried to direct the pirate's attention with a nod of his head.

"It would appear that we've both been fooled, and you've fallen into a very big trap," replied Drewshank.

Mousebeard looked out over the water. It soon became clear that the line consisted of sailing ships — their white, full sails now visible above the gray, choppy sea. The pirate hurriedly pulled out a short black telescope from his pocket and, looking through, saw an armada of at least forty warships of all shapes and sizes approaching with speed. Mousebeard quickly turned to look at Winter Vale past the *Flying Fox,* and saw even more ships emerge. There was only one navy that could muster such a force, and that was the Old Town Guard, led by Lord Battersby. The final piece of the trap had fallen into place.

"May the Spirit Mice rain fire on you, Lovelock," growled Mousebeard.

"The *Flying Fox* was just the lure," said Drewshank bitterly. "Mere bait for your *Silver Shark*."

"Get the prisoners onboard and scuttle their ship," shouted Mousebeard, angrily. "We have little time. Crank up the mist generator and get us out of here."

The Powder Mouse

ORIGINALLY KNOWN AS THE RUNNER MOUSE OF CRESTFALL ISLAND, THIS *mouse has for years been specially trained by the navy to carry gunpowder between cannons aboard warships. It is a particularly steady runner, capable of sprinting without wavering or tripping. The Powder Mouse has played key roles in many of the great sea battles, and Captain John Blouseworthy of the battleship* Intrepid *claimed that without them he would have lost the battle of Cape Crank during the Third War of Midena.*

Because most of its life is spent in close proximity to cannons, the Powder Mouse is unfortunately susceptible to deafness at an early age. It is a sad affair, but at the age of two, all Powder Mice are retired and sent to Mouser Retirement Homes for ex-service mice, where they are cared for into their old age.

MOUSING NOTES

It can be kept very happily in a collection, as long as it has plenty of space to run around in. The Powder Mouse can also be employed in the home, where it's very useful for passing salt and pepper between guests at dinner parties.

Mousebeard

A THIN MIST WAS LILTING UPWARD ROUND THE SIDES OF the *Silver Shark,* and Mousebeard ground his teeth frustratedly. His main mast had fallen and the Old Town Navy was closing in. His eyes flickered with bitter thoughts, mulling over his predicament, while he clenched his hairy, muscular hands behind his back.

"Miserley?" he barked, his eyebrows dipping while he scratched his black beard, deftly avoiding the small mice that lived within its mess.

"Come on, where are you?" he shouted once more, his temper fraying.

Eventually a girl with long dark-brown hair appeared, her eyes sparkling mischievously. On her shoulder sat a peculiar mouse with brown fur and dark rings under its eyes. It had two earrings in one of its tufted ears, and its black eyes twinkled.

"About time too," said the pirate, staring at his wayward mousekeeper. "Send a mouse to Ogruk; we'll be needing his services."

Miserley remained relaxed.

"I already have done so," she said, clutching the daggers that hung from her belt.

"Of course you have," grumbled Mousebeard, who was getting tired of her cleverness. "You'd better go and make yourself useful somewhere else, then."

Miserley rolled her eyes, let out a very loud huff, and marched off, leaving the pirate alone on the bridge. Through the gathering mist the burning *Flying Fox* was creaking and lurching in its death throes. Mousebeard watched as his pirates grabbed their last haul of booty, returned to the *Silver Shark*, and raised the gangplanks. Small explosions went off within the condemned vessel, blasting its hull to smithereens and sending it straight to the ocean floor.

"What are you waiting for!" he shouted. His men rushed to their posts and climbed the rigging. "Head to the island! We'll seek safety in its shadow."

"Sir?" queried a pirate from high up on the mast. "But there's no way out from there without Ogruk. . . ."

"Do as I say!" snapped Mousebeard. "The navy is still far enough away, and the *Shark* can take a hit or two. What are you all? Men or mice?"

With a flurry of activity, the remaining sails opened and they set off through the thickening mist.

"All these boats just for us?" said Mousebeard. "Isiah must be up to something . . . I'm not usually this important to him."

"Aye, captain," said Scragneck, appearing from below deck and taking his place at Mousebeard's side. "They set us up good 'n' proper. But we won't go down easily."

Scragneck was Mousebeard's first mate and a nasty customer. He had a shaved, scarred head, and lacked most of his front teeth; they had been lost to the ravages of fighting and the rotting quality of sugary Rodent Rum. He had no respect for life and not one good bone in his body, but Mousebeard saw his presence as a necessity for maintaining order onboard.

"We won't go down at all, if I know Isiah," said Mousebeard. "He won't want me dead now. He'll want to hang us all from the highest gallows for everyone in Old Town to see. And he definitely won't leave without his precious mice."

"They were a rum catch for sure," added Scragneck, "for they're the prettiest things I ever seen. But if it comes to it, nuthin' would please me more than to take the drop beside you, cap'n."

"Kind words indeed — especially from such a wretched mouth as yours. But even the will of Isiah Lovelock won't get me in the gibbet, you can be sure of that."

"That's pirate talk all right," said Scragneck, cackling to himself. His sinewy body was sickly compared to the bulk of Mousebeard, but the first mate's scheming and treacherous disposition made him the equal on many other counts.

"We'll need more than talk against those ironclads.

Let's give them something to think about, eh? Order our gunners to send a few flaming presents to our friends out there before the mist consumes us all."

"I'd be overjoyed to, captain," replied Scragneck.

⇒ ✳ ⇐

Imprisoned in the hold at the lowest reaches of the *Silver Shark*, the remaining crew of the *Flying Fox* were chained together in a space barely big enough for them all. Boxed into the narrowing bow of the ship, with a locked iron grille rising from floor to ceiling in front of them, there was no opportunity for escape. It was dark and dank so far down below the water level, and with each breath the prisoners could taste the age-old smell of sweat and grime. The only light came from two small oil lamps glowing at the base of the stairs to the higher deck, their flames perfectly still.

There were only ten sailors left, including Emiline and Scratcher, and the mood was anything but happy. As the sound of cannonfire rumbled around them, they thought of their lost crewmates.

"It's my fault," said Drewshank. "But I'll get us out of here, I promise you."

"Don't be stupid," announced Fenwick; "we all knew what we were getting ourselves into. Besides, that was the whole of the Old Town Navy and then some. There's more goin' on here than we know. . . ."

"It's all to do with Lovelock, I know it is," grumbled Drewshank.

"To warrant those huge warships — sea-borne fire-brands, mortar vessels, and ironclad destroyers. It must be somethin' special, and I wouldn't want to be on the receiving end of it!"

"As much as I hate to say it, we're going to be," replied the captain, "unless Mousebeard has something extraordinary up his sleeve. Whatever it was that he stole from the *Lady Caroline*, it was certainly important."

"But, cap'n," said Fenwick, "if they attack the *Silver Shark*, she won't stand a chance. And we'll be as much use as caged Messenger Mice down here."

Fenwick looked up abruptly — he could hear footsteps, and suddenly a guard stormed down the stairs.

"Shut up your chatter!" he shouted, marching to the

bars and shoving a long pike into the gaps. The prisoners sat quietly.

"Any more gassing and I'll poke your eyes out!" he growled, turning his back and leaving once more. He stopped at the base of the stairs, took one last look at the prisoners, and ran upward.

"There must be a way out," whispered Scratcher as the guard vanished out of sight. "Maybe there's some way we can let the navy know we're onboard? They might go easy on us?"

Drewshank shook his head. "I doubt they'd be much interested in us," he said. "I fear we're of no importance to anyone anymore, and the *Flying Fox* is sinking as we speak."

Emiline was picking at the tight cuffs clamped to her wrists.

"I can't get these things off!" she said angrily.

"If they're built like the rest of the ship, there's not much that'll damage them," said Drewshank. "Don't waste your energy."

"But they're digging in," she moaned. Emiline wasn't one to go on about things, but she was worried. She hadn't seen Portly since they were sailing through Winter Vale, and she was desperate to know what had happened to him.

"Just take it easy," pleaded Scratcher.

At those words the guard came crashing down the stairs again.

"I told you!" he shouted. "Shut up!"

He thrust his pike right at Emiline. The speared end was only inches from her nose when a smile broke across her face.

Portly had always been a mouse of great character — a good deal above what his breeding as a lowly Grey Mouse should have allowed — and he always showed excellent initiative. Emiline was only slightly surprised, therefore, when his little head poked out from behind the guard's foot.

"Sorry," she said weakly, repressing a giggle.

"You're on thin ground, girl!" snapped the pirate, withdrawing his weapon slowly. He surveyed all the prisoners.

"This is your last warning!" he said, hitting the end of his pike on the floor for effect.

Emiline couldn't help but smile again.

The guard gave a disgruntled sigh and made his leave again. Portly darted from behind his foot, scampered over to the wall, and squeaked. By now all the prisoners had seen Emiline's mouse and felt a sudden relief. This was made even greater by seeing a column of assorted mice racing down the stairs to join Portly. They were pet mice from the *Flying Fox,* as well as a few Messenger Mice and an occasional Powder Mouse that had survived the battle.

One by one they scampered through the prison bars, and Portly scurried up to Emiline to squeak hello before gesturing to another mouse. A very odd-looking creature then ran to her: it had a thick mane of red fur around its neck, and from its mouth protruded an array of tiny, razor-sharp teeth.

The little mouse jumped at Emiline's wrists and started to chew at the metal clasps. Burning hot filings flashed out of its mouth like a welder's torch, and within no time the bindings were broken and clunked to the floor. To Emiline, the mouse looked like a Steel Jaw from the far-off Isle of Launay, but she'd have to check it in *The Mousehunter's Almanac* to be sure. It was an odd mouse to have kept as a pet, though, she thought.

The sprightly mouse proceeded to bite through the other prisoners' bonds, grinding down each one in turn. No one had expected such a turn of events, and then, quietly skipping up to their prison, came another.

"Chervil!" cheered Fenwick, watching the cat brush his long curly fur languidly against the bars. Seated on his back was a Creeper Mouse, who jumped off and shuffled through to Drewshank with a great big steel key in its mouth. Creeper Mice were well known for their exceptional stealth abilities, and were often employed by the army for secret spylike activities. It had obviously stolen it from one of the guards with the help of the ship's cat.

"Meeoow!" said Chervil happily.

"Well I never!" declared Drewshank, and he took the key carefully from the mouse's tiny mouth. He stared out through the bars to see that the coast was clear.

"Anyone for a jailbreak?" he said, putting the key in the lock at the side of the barred grille. With a loud *clank* it unlocked. Despite Drewshank's best efforts to move it quietly, the grille swung noisily upward, with rusty chains rising and falling at its edges. He cursed.

"Why don't they oil these things?" he moaned. "Hide yourselves!"

The prisoners ducked into the shadows. Drewshank jumped out, walked to the stairwell at the center of the deck, and raised his fists. With loud crashing footsteps, the guard came quickly down the stairs, his pike protruding out in front of him.

"What are you —"

Before the guard could finish his words, Drewshank pulled at the end of his pike and pushed him heavily to the floor. The man landed on his back and cried out for help, but Fenwick grabbed him and knocked him out. He dragged his body out of sight, but there was another voice now heading their way.

Drewshank took the pike and stood ready. Eventually, a girl of Emiline's age appeared. It was Miserley, her jacket pinned tight around her by her mousehunting belt. She looked around feverishly, turning back and forth, sending her hair drifting out and over her face.

Drewshank dropped the pike and grabbed her arms,

pulling them tightly behind her back. She wriggled fiercely, kicking her heels into his shins with all her might.

"Get off me!" she shouted, twisting sharply and hitting Drewshank firmly in the stomach. The captain folded in two, stunned by the strength of the girl, and before he could react, Miserley had broken free of his grip and kicked him to the ground. She flicked her hair to the side and snatched the daggers from her belt.

"Any more fun and games?" she asked, looking for signs of the other prisoners.

Her mouse appeared from under her hair and looked around. Acting as another pair of eyes for Miserley, it darted its beady eyes about.

Seeing Drewshank begin to move, she grabbed his head by the hair and thrust the dagger up to the front of his throat. Drewshank choked, as he felt the cold steel blade against his skin.

"I'll kill him!" she shouted, dragging Drewshank a short distance so that her back was against the stairwell. "One little slice and your precious captain will die, so show yourselves and get back behind those bars!"

Emiline turned to Scratcher from behind a wooden crate.

"D-do as she says," spluttered Drewshank. His crew reluctantly stepped out of hiding, and slowly crept into the center of the deck.

"Back behind the bars!" she yelled.

The crew put their hands in the air and idled back into the prison.

"Throw me the key!" she demanded, staring at the prisoners. Drewshank placed his hand into his pocket and let the key fall to the floor.

"Now stand up!" she ordered. The captain lifted himself slowly, and the dagger dropped from his throat to reappear at his back.

Miserley walked him to the prison area and shoved him in while pulling down the chains that lowered the iron grille.

"You almost got me there, Drewshank," she said triumphantly, "but you just don't have what it takes."

She looked at the grouped prisoners, and counted them with a nod for each. Once she'd reached the end, she shook her head and mumbled something to herself.

She counted again, and suddenly a look of horror crossed her face.

"Where's the boy and girl?" she demanded, her eyes shooting around the room. Scratcher and Emiline were nowhere to be seen.

"Where are the mousekeepers?" she shouted once more. The prisoners remained silent.

Miserley glanced around the prison deck hopelessly. It was true; Emiline and Scratcher had escaped from right under her nose.

"Guards!" called Miserley. Two pirates rushed to the hold.

"Don't let the prisoners escape," she said angrily, "or I'll see to it that you're hung out on the yard arm!"

❧ ✳ ❧

Emiline clung to a wooden wall in the middle of the *Silver Shark*'s gun deck, letting each breath slip out as quietly as possible. She was hidden in darkness between thick iron joists, occasional shafts of light flickering across her face with the bobbing movement of the ship. Excitable pirates were everywhere, charging this way and that with cannonballs held firmly in their hands. A line of armored Powder Mice were racing along with them.

Pyramids of cannonballs were built up alongside the guns, which numbered at least fifteen on each side of the ship. Through the wide hatches that opened for the cannons, Emiline could see nothing due to the mist.

It had shocked Emiline to find that there was a girl like herself onboard. She'd spotted the mousebox around her belt, sitting alongside other mousehunting implements, and realized she too was a mousekeeper. The mousekeeper of a pirate: for some reason, Emiline felt slightly jealous.

Scratcher darted up beside her, and slid to a halt.

"I can't see a clear route out," he said worriedly. "Pirates everywhere!"

"What can we do then?" whispered Emiline.

A huge blast hit the side of the *Silver Shark*, punching it over onto its side for a brief second. A terrific whooshing noise followed, and through the gun hatches Emiline saw the unmistakable glow of scorching fire burning the mist away. The navy was upon them.

Pirates were suddenly all around the mousekeepers,

tending to the cannons and oblivious to their presence. Within seconds the first volley of cannonfire had been let loose from the gundeck. The smell of battle soon filled the deck, and smoke started to fog the air. The guns fired again.

"Let's make our move," declared Emiline. She grabbed Scratcher's wrist and ran out of hiding. Darting in and out of shadows, desperately avoiding anyone's sight — as well as the paths of the scurrying Powder Mice — they found a passageway at the stern with stairs leading to the top deck. A metal-edged window threw light over their dirty faces, making them blink and withdraw from the brightness.

The *Silver Shark* was moving fast in the water, but through the fading mist and smoke, it was clear that the navy had surrounded the vessel. Warships stretched out for as far as the eye could see. Puffs of smoke were flashing out of the ships as their bombardment grew stronger.

"They're rubbish shots!" said Scratcher, noticing that few were hitting the ship.

"They won't want to hurt us too badly," explained

Emiline. "Mousebeard has something precious of Love-lock's."

Over the deafening noise of cannonfire, Scratcher heard something boom even louder.

"Did you hear that?"

"What?"

Emiline listened harder. The noise boomed out again, rippling the sea and the ships upon it.

"What on earth is that?" she exclaimed.

Cannons on all sides stopped firing. The window went dark, while outside, the sailors watched a shadow spread across the sea and navy.

"Look!" said Scratcher, tapping Emiline on the arm.

His attention had turned to the stairs, where they could just make out a mouse that sat sniffing the air.

"That's a Ring-eyed Brown," said Emiline, with authority. "And it's even got pirate earrings too!"

Another loud boom shook the whole ship, and the mouse fled.

"What's happening?" said Scratcher, looking anxiously at Emiline, but she had fallen to the floor.

From the top deck they heard Mousebeard call out: "Just in time, Ogruk! Once again I am indebted to you!"

Scratcher heard a loud gushing noise, and suddenly the ship jerked upward, rocketing into the air. The force pulled him down too.

"What is it?" yelled Emiline. Eventually the force subsided, and they felt the ship bobbing up and down, as though on softly rolling waves.

They stood up uneasily and dusted themselves down. For a moment all was calm. And then blades appeared at their necks.

"So here you are, Blonde," said Miserley, holding Emiline tightly with her mouse squeaking loudly in her ear. "I can always rely on Weazle here to find escaped prisoners!"

"Make one move and I'll cut ya in two," said Scragneck, his sword primed and ready at Scratcher's jugular. "I think it's time we taught you both a lesson."

The Dung Mouse

NOT A PRETTY CREATURE, THE DUNG MOUSE HAS SHAGGY BROWN FUR, *and a long tail that wags constantly. The animal does very little other than defecate, hence its name (although it does eat and sleep occasionally), and is very smelly.*

Not an animal to be disregarded, however; its dung has proved extremely useful as a source of renewable natural energy. Once dried, the dung can be burned as a solid fuel — which produces very little odor — and is used in fireplaces and kitchens all over Midena.

MOUSING NOTES

Dung Mice can become violent if their routines are broken, or if they're provoked. However, as long as they're kept in a spacious pen that's regularly attended to and cleaned, these animals can play a beneficial role in any home.

Giant Island

"A GIANT!" SHOUTED LORD BATTERSBY INCREDULOUSLY from the bridge of his warship, the *Stonebreaker*.

"He's got to be a leftover from the old continents, sir," said Lieutenant Smedley nervously, looking up at the incredible creature, whose head threatened to touch the clouds in the sky. There was a clear tremor in his very posh voice. "There's a few who still roam these lands, but we had no idea there was one in that old volcano, *and* in cahoots with the pirate."

"Don't you think that you should have found out about this earlier?" said Battersby. "I hadn't reckoned on dealing with a mythical creature!"

"Sorry, sir," replied Smedley. They watched the giant

stoop before them and, with one of his huge hands, cup the *Silver Shark* to lift it high out of the water. Then he turned and strode back toward the towering island in the middle of the sea. Each footstep the giant took in the water sent huge bulging waves rippling out, spreading the navy farther and farther apart.

"But he's harmless enough, though, I assure you," whined Smedley. He watched Ogruk stride farther away, and the boat lifted and dropped awfully. "Giants will go out of their way to avoid hurting anything. That's what the history books tell us. . . ."

Battersby clutched a wooden rail to stop his legs falling away.

"History books!" he yelled. "That giant could flick us to kingdom come!"

He wiped his brow.

"Tell the commanders to ready their vessels! Send them to the island, prime the firebrands, and direct the mortars to the cliffs. It looks like a siege is the only way. Let's hope Mousebeard's giant doesn't get in our way again."

"Of course, sir!"

"And release the Messenger Mice," he added. "I expect at least one pirate will not be wholly trustworthy and true to Mousebeard's cause. That's all it will take to get us the mice!"

"Yes, sir!"

"Oh, and Smedley," said Battersby calmly, "if we lose Mousebeard because of this accursed giant, I'll be sure to send you to the Mouse Mines of Minsu!"

⇒ ✳ ⇐

The giant clambered over the cliffs in two massive steps and dropped down into a lost world so green and lush that it looked completely out of place in the icy climate of the Cold Sea. Shafts of steam rose into the sky from the bustling forest floor, and flying mice zigzagged through the air, taking full advantage of the warm currents to stay airborne with as little effort as possible. The sounds of mice filled the land, with squeaks and chirrups echoing around constantly.

Mousebeard's hideout, known to the pirates as Giant Island, was inside the crater of an immense extinct volcano that towered out of the sea. Its mile-wide rim of sheer rock completely isolated the land from the outside world, and within its confines a whole new ecosystem had evolved, based on the warmth its geysers provided.

The giant stepped carefully along a well-trodden route, his enormous feet narrowly avoiding blossoming jungle and spiraling wooden buildings that broke through the canopy. Within a few strides, he'd reached the shimmering lagoon at the center of the island where a huge brooding fortress jutted out into the water. He bent down to place the *Silver Shark* on the water next to it.

Standing upon a gigantic platform stretching right out into the lagoon, the fortress was nearly a hundred meters wide at the base, and split into many smaller, spiky towers as it grew taller. Each of these leaned outward like the gnarled branches of a dying tree, with odd-shaped bones and mouseskulls hanging off them like leaves. Vines and chains draped from tower to tower, and each rooftop was home to a large cannon trained out over the cliffs.

"We're indebted to you once more, Ogruk!" bellowed Mousebeard from the top deck, relieved to be back in sight of his home.

The giant winked one of his bright hazel eyes then stood upright, sending a gust of air rippling over the treetops and across the lagoon. A flock of flying mice burst into the air, and with his head and shoulders high above the cliffs, he cast his eyes over the horizon and replied in his thunderous, ground-rumbling voice.

"The ships are massing like tadpoles again. I'll hang around to make sure you're okay."

"Excellent," shouted Mousebeard, patting his beard.

Mousebeard readied himself to leave the vessel. He pulled his jacket down and placed his black tricorn hat, with a jagged bite cut out of its edge, on his head. The little mice peeked out from his beard and squeaked excitedly at the prospect of coming home. Mousebeard had been at sea for over three months and, as ever, returning to Giant Island settled his nerves. He longed to see all the mice that lived on the island; he longed to find time for himself away from the pirates on his ship; and he longed to sleep without the waves rolling his bed beneath him.

His satisfaction at returning home was shattered in an instant by Miserley and Scragneck. They marched out onto deck and threw two raggedy children at the pirate's feet.

"Mousebeard!" cried Emiline, fear rippling down her back. Seeing the pirate so close was like being confronted by her worst nightmare. His eyes were dark brown, but hidden in the shadow of his bristling eyebrows they looked black and fierce. And because of his moving beard, it looked as though his face was possessed by another being. She scrabbled across the floor to escape, but found Miserley's foot firmly kicking into her ribs. Scratcher peered at her, but his mouth wouldn't open to speak.

The pirate turned his black gaze onto Scragneck.

"Who are they? Why are you bothering me with them now?" he growled, baring his yellow teeth.

"They escaped from the brig, cap'n. They want some punishment!" he replied.

Mousebeard looked back at the two mousekeepers. Emiline shrank back in spite of herself. He started to pace around them slowly.

"They escaped?"

Miserley jumped in. "They had trained mice that stole the keys."

With those words the pirate stopped and frowned. "Trained mice?" he said.

"They somehow managed to steal them from the guard," added Miserley.

"Where are these mice then?" asked Mousebeard.

Emiline shuffled uneasily on the floor, and Portly scurried out from around her neck. She tried to conceal him, but he rushed to the top of her head, and Mousebeard picked him up.

"A Grey . . . ," he said quietly, with the mouse looking minuscule within his bulging hand. "The commonest of mice is always going to be the one that surprises you."

Portly squeaked bravely at the pirate, and brought a brief, hidden smile to his face beneath the beard. Then he looked back at the mousekeepers and let out a growl.

"As far as I can see, these two are smarter mousekeepers than you, Miserley," he said. "Even so, I think I have the perfect punishment."

Emiline and Scratcher looked at each other nervously.

The thought of facing a pirate's punishment filled them with dread.

"Take them ashore," ordered the pirate, "and along with the other prisoners, put them to work in the Dung Mouse pen. That should give them something to do. It will keep them out of my way at least. Then send Drewshank to me in my quarters. I have some things I want to ask him."

"Aye, sir," said Scragneck, his tone less than happy. He didn't think it was anywhere near a suitable punishment for the mousekeepers. Miserley felt equally angry, and lifted Emiline to her feet, her fingers digging spitefully into Emiline's shoulders. Scratcher stood of his own accord, but soon found himself clasped in Scragneck's hands.

Mousebeard placed Portly on the floor and let him hurry back to the relative safety of Emiline's shoulder. He then walked casually to the bow of the ship, where some of his crew were readying the gangplanks. With a bang they landed on the platform, a loud high-pitched whistle blew, and the pirate walked down and out of view.

"Come on, Miserley," said Scragneck, "let's get off this ship."

They pushed the mousekeepers along the deck and Emiline looked upward for the first time. She froze at the sight. At least twice the height of the *Silver Shark,* the fortress looked fearful and commanding, while hundreds of eyeless skulls hanging from the towers were staring right at her.

"Yeah, yeah," said Miserley, pushing Emiline off the ship and onto the platform. Two pirates standing guard at the fortress gateway lowered their cutlasses and growled. Emiline heard Scratcher gasp behind her, and realized he'd just seen the fortress too.

"This way!" snarled Miserley, and kicked Emiline, making her walk toward the dense vegetation at the edge of the platform. As she stepped down onto the path around the edge of the lagoon, Emiline was struck by the warmth and lush green of the jungle. Miserley kept poking her to walk along the path faster, but Emiline looked around her as much as she could. It was unlike any place she'd been to. Instead of grass there was a mass of strange flowers and tendrils covering the ground, and to accompany them, shiny metallic-colored insects hovered from one plant to the next. To her left, dark green trees rose up from the jungle floor with leaves the size of handkerchiefs and bright fruit as big as cannon-balls hanging from their branches. The trees were strung with creepers and the plants were alive with all kinds of rustlings and squeaks.

Suddenly a tongue shot out from the undergrowth and caught an insect on its fat blobby end.

"A Flycatcher . . . ," muttered Emiline.

A small mouse with curly blue fur and massive ears darted out into Emiline's path, followed by three more in quick succession. They ran across extraordinarily fast, and then plopped into the lagoon with a tiny splash.

"What were those?" said Emiline, realizing she'd never seen that species before — not even in *The Mousehunter's Almanac.* She peered carefully into the bushes as she walked and spotted more weird and wonderful mice, momentarily forgetting the pirate girl behind. One was clinging to a tree, seemingly secured to the bark by its thick corkscrewed tail that wound into the very wood itself. She gasped as another swung before her out of the trees, hanging from a vine by its tail, its arms stretched out as if in a pose. Emiline wanted to tell Scratcher about it, but Miserley was right next to her and barging her at every opportunity.

"Right," barked Scragneck, bringing Emiline back to reality, "this way!"

They turned from the lagoon into the jungle, and the path quickly became damp and muddy, with the noise of the island's fauna growing in intensity. They walked farther along the shadowy path, and a smell so foul and horrible that it could turn milk sour wafted toward them.

"Blech!" spluttered Scratcher. "What on earth's that?"

Miserley smirked. "That's where you'll be spending the rest of your days — the Dung Mouse pen, clearing and packing mouse dung like good prisoners."

"Roarph!" choked Emiline, feeling Portly hide deeper into her hair.

"You'll soon get used to it," snarled Scragneck. "Thank your lucky stars I ain't in charge here, or else you'd already be dead."

Emiline turned and caught the pirate's eye. Scragneck was altogether different from Mousebeard. He wasn't inquisitive or particularly clever. His eyes burned only with fire and hatred, and she could tell he was rotten to the core.

They walked a few minutes more before they came to the Dung Mouse pen. It was built like an iron prison, with a thick wooden padlocked door, and through the barred windows she could see the herd of Dung Mice. They were quite large animals, almost as tall as Elephant Mice, but with shaggy coats and long tails.

A woman pirate stood on guard, with the longest sword Emiline had ever seen held at the ready. She greeted Scragneck and unlocked the door to the pen.

"There are shovels inside," said the woman. "Scoop up the dung and fling it into the hut at the back. They do their business at least thirty times daily, and with the eighty or so animals in there, it should give you more than enough to do. You'll find beds on the walls. They ain't that comfortable, but once you stink of mouse dung, you start not to care too much for luxuries."

Miserley shoved Emiline into the pen, and Scratcher was pushed in behind her. The smell was even worse inside, and the mice made no hesitation in investigating the new arrivals. The door slammed shut, and Scratcher sighed heavily as his legs were sniffed unceremoniously by a Dung Mouse.

"This is going to be horrible," he said, and put his hand over his nose to block the smell.

"Not even the Flaming Stink Mouse was as bad as this!" said Emiline, spluttering into her shirtsleeve. "How did we end up here?"

❧ ✳ ❧

Miserley and Scragneck walked back to the ship along the lagoon. The rest of the prisoners had been deposited in the Dung Mouse pen, and they were returning for some well-earned rest. They felt happier now that they'd been reminded how horrible life for the prisoners would be. Life as a pirate was always made better when you could inflict suffering on someone.

Miserley was about to speak, but her attention was

suddenly taken by a small flying mouse landing in front of them. It seemed rather directionless, and wandered around on the dirty floor without a purpose.

"That's a Messenger," she said. "What's it doing here?"

Scragneck picked it up and removed the note that was secured to its back. He unfurled it and read it quietly.

"It's from the navy," he said, looking at Miserley, his eyes bright. "They want Mousebeard, Lovelock's stolen mice, and any prisoners. If they get what they ask then the rest of us will be paid a fine ransom and set free."

"Are you kidding?"

"No, it's signed Lord Battersby, and gives his word as an officer of the Old Town Guard."

"Ouch!" yelped Miserley as another Messenger Mouse hit her on the head. She looked up to see at least twenty more flying over the lagoon. "It won't be long before everyone sees the note," she said, "including Mousebeard. It's got to be some sort of trick."

"Well I ain't gonna trust them navy types as far as I can throw 'em," said Scragneck. "But I reckon it's somethin' to bear in mind. Between you 'n' me, Miserley, I don't care much for that Mousebeard. Never 'ave done, and I don't think he cares much for us too."

"I hear that," she replied, "but it's too risky, and Mousebeard will surely see it coming?"

"If many of us see this note, though, somethin' might 'appen of its own accord — if you know what I mean. . . . Something to think about, eh? I mean, if there's a lot of us, there's nothin' he can do about it!"

Miserley fell quiet and let Scragneck plot and scheme to himself. Maybe she would play a part in a mutiny, but just for now she was keeping her allegiances secret.

The Howling Moon Mouse

THIS MOUSE IS THE BEST KNOWN OF ALL THE HOWLER MICE, CHOOSING TO *howl only on nights when there is a full moon. Found on the Plains of Albermarle, and on the remote islands of the Cold Sea, the Howling Moon Mouse lives a quiet life of solitude, and the only occasion when the species gather is on the first full moon of the year, when males will try and out-howl each other in order to win a mate.*

MOUSING NOTES
The Howling Moon Mouse is prohibited in residential areas (Mousing Regulation 567) because its howling can be deeply unsettling.

The Stolen Cargo

DREWSHANK WAS DRAGGED FROM THE BRIG ON THE *Silver Shark* and hustled over to Mousebeard's fortress. The rest of his crew had been taken to join Emiline and Scratcher. He surveyed the imposing structure before him and suddenly felt very alone. His eyes followed the rough walls, hewn from tree trunks, as they shot upward into looming, twisted towers. An unusually large and sinister mouse skull glared down at him from the wall above his head. The captain gulped and prepared for the worst.

He was pushed through a painted, bone-adorned gateway and directed up a twisting staircase by the pointed end of a spear, closely followed by a stinking pirate. He eventually came to a door with a mouse skull and cross-bones emblazoned on it in thick red paint, and he pushed it open cautiously.

The room was sparsely decorated, with a large window looking out over the lagoon and a finely knotted rug spread over the floor. There wasn't much furniture: a weathered wooden cabinet stood beside the window; a rounded driftwood table with a rare mousetusk candle-holder sitting on top near the door; at the far end of the room, a sturdy, metal-strung hammock stretching from one wall to the other. The room was chilly at best, despite the warmth of the island, and Drewshank thought of his own rather nice cabin and how this one could really do with a lick of paint.

Mousebeard was standing staring out over the water toward the jungle-covered land, his massive form almost filling the window.

"Ah, Drewshank, my unlikely adversary," said Mousebeard, without turning around.

Drewshank held his head up and took a few steps farther into the room without replying. He felt uncomfortable in his dirty clothes. He always preferred to face difficult people dressed as smartly as possible. Under the circumstances, however, he thought he'd try not to let it bother him.

"It was brave of you, captain — chasing after me like that. The fog encounter usually scares the life out of people."

"Well, when I saw your handiwork with a needle, I thought I had a chance, I must admit. You do a nice line in cloth mice."

Mousebeard jerked his head to the side and snarled. Drewshank stepped back quickly. He'd been pleased with his reply, but then realized that he should be less inflammatory.

"So you're a friend of Isiah Lovelock," said the pirate gruffly, turning around. "As you know, I hate him with every ounce of my flesh and every hair in my beard."

"I'm no friend of his. I was just doing some work for him."

"Ah yes," said the pirate. "You'd do anything for money. I know your type."

"I have some scruples, pirate, and though I do things for money, and dress as though I have plenty, I sail through life with a clean conscience. Unlike your-self . . ."

"Ha!" said Mousebeard. "You certainly know how to make yourself sound important!"

Drewshank clenched his fists. He didn't appreciate such a blatant slur on his character.

"Did you honestly think that aging ship of yours was capable of taking me on?" asked Mousebeard. "Did Lovelock really think I was that much of a pushover?"

"My reputation must surely precede me!" snapped Drewshank. "The *Flying Fox* was noted for her feats of daring!"

The pirate shook his head and laughed. "You are cer-tainly entertaining company, I'll give you that."

Drewshank was starting to fume. Never in all his life had someone spoken to him in this way.

"Just out of interest, why did Lovelock send you after me?" said Mousebeard, walking closer to Drewshank.

"Because you sank his ship and stole from him!"

"Of course!" boomed Mousebeard. Drewshank got the feeling that the pirate already knew full well why he had been sent after him. Mousebeard was playing with him, and it made him feel uneasy. He told himself to calm down.

The pirate suddenly strode over to the cabinet, his huge feet sending shudders around the room. He withdrew a mousebox with ornate metal edging, walked back toward Drewshank, and gently placed it on the table. The captain crept nearer.

"You should see this, Drewshank. If this is the reason you came this far — and it's a very good reason, I must admit — then it only seems fair to show it to you before we have you executed."

Drewshank swallowed sharply and grabbed the table to steady himself.

With the utmost care, the pirate unlocked the lid. It eased open and a bright shining golden light beamed out.

Drewshank gasped and bent closer. It was a pair of Golden Mice: the most sought-after and yet most dangerous creatures you could ever hope to find inside a mousebox.

"No, it can't be . . . ," muttered Drewshank. "They're a death warrant. . . ."

There were thought to be fewer than a hundred of

these mice left in the wild, and their fur was made of the purest gold. For centuries they had been the most desired of all species, but to be found in possession of them was punishable by death.

"Why would Isiah be after them? Every government and every army in the mousing world would come bearing down with full force on his doorstep."

"And now do you realize why he's been hunting me so ferociously?" replied Mousebeard.

"I can certainly understand why that navy is surrounding your island, but what could he do if he got them? Word would get out. He'd be brought to justice. There would be hell to pay. . . ."

Mousebeard growled, in a way that only a man with twenty years of seafaring under his belt could possibly do.

"Not if he found them by chance . . ."

"By chance?" asked Drewshank. "I don't understand."

"He set us both up from the beginning, captain."

Drewshank suddenly found himself growling too. When you spend time with pirates, maybe you start to act like one, he thought.

"So Lovelock planned all along for you to steal the Golden Mice from the *Lady Caroline*," he said. "He wanted you to take the blame when he recaptured them."

"Of course he wanted me to take the blame. If Lovelock had his way, then I'd take the blame for everything. He knew he'd be brought to task for stealing the mice, so what better way to get hold of them than to publicly 'save' them from me . . . pretend that *I* had seized them from Illyria! Then he could look after them in 'safe-keeping' for as long as he needs to fulfill his disgusting plans. The Mousehunting Federation already hold him under suspicion. What better way to prove his commitment to protecting mice?"

"Unbelievable . . . ," said Drewshank.

"Yes — that's Lovelock for you," said Mousebeard. "Every mouse on Illyria is counted and watched. If he'd taken and kept them without using me as a foil, they'd have discovered the truth eventually."

His huge dark eyes narrowed.

"So by sending someone so fancy and high profile as Devlin Drewshank after me, then he could be sure I would find out and set about spoiling his plans. I have a rather ridiculous obsession concerning pirate hunters, you see."

"He sent me out knowing I'd fail . . . ," said Drewshank.

Mousebeard let out another loud laugh.

"At last Isiah has got the better of me . . . who'd have thought?"

"So why did you take them?" Drewshank asked.

"At the time I hadn't a clue what he was up to, and I couldn't just let the Golden Mice perish at sea. I should have known something was up when there was just a skeleton crew and the hold was empty apart from this box and two Long-eared Mice running free. We'd already put holes in the side of her by the time I realized there were those damned creatures below the water level."

Drewshank's eyes lit up.

"So the Grak was your fault! It almost destroyed us!"

Mousebeard's eyes widened with rage. He leaned across the table and got so close that the tip of his beard was wriggling right under Drewshank's nose.

"Do you listen to nothing I say? You think I'd be stupid enough to do that?" he growled. His breath stank, and

Drewshank desperately tried not to inhale. "I didn't know they were there! You should know by now that Isiah plays by his own particularly sly rules. He would have seen the Grak as an ideal way of covering his tracks and completely destroying the *Lady Caroline*. That merchant boat was eventually smashed to pieces by the sea monsters. . . ."

"So you didn't destroy it on purpose?" asked Drewshank, still bemused.

Mousebeard huffed and stepped back, his cutlasses clattering. Drewshank remained silent for a moment. Was he being taken in by Mousebeard now, just as he had been by Lovelock? He didn't know what to believe.

"So this has all been a game of piggy mouse in the middle, with me in the middle?" said Drewshank. "A big setup from the start?"

"We're both fools in equal measure," replied the pirate. "They capture me and find the Golden Mice in my possession: I get the blame and the death sentence, Lovelock gets the mice and the glory of seizing Mousebeard, scourge of the Seventeen Seas. And Captain Drewshank is finally shown up as being rather useless."

"At least I'm only useless!" snapped Drewshank.

"How many people have died and are still going to die because of you both? There's no way this is going to end happily. . . ."

"I'm sorry about the men you lost, captain," said Mousebeard. "But you must realize that most of the stories that are peddled about me in Old Town are made up by Lovelock and his friends. It's all propaganda — lies . . . mostly . . . lies."

"Mostly?" questioned Drewshank, watching Mousebeard closely.

"Not even you are a saint, Drewshank. Besides, you know what Lovelock's like, and you also know of the deals and awful practices he's involved in. It's been my purpose for the past twenty years to stop him in any way I can."

"Hmmm," said Drewshank, his mind suddenly feeling worn out with all the thinking. "All I know is that we're now in deep trouble. What are you planning to do about it?"

"Nothing at present. I can't see a way past this navy that surrounds our island."

"What about that giant?"

"Ogruk? He won't hang around for long. He hates humans, and I don't blame him. He won't be enjoying all this, I can promise you."

"Oh," offered Drewshank.

"But eventually I'll take the Golden Mice back to where they belong. There's nothing else to do."

Drewshank paused for a minute, thinking about the strange man in front of him. Mousebeard had disposed of so many sailors, but every mouse he came across was infinitely precious to him.

"Can't you go after Lovelock at Old Town?"

"If only it were that simple."

"You found it so easy to destroy my ship, yet you can't attack the man that has so royally set you up?"

Mousebeard returned to the window and his broad shoulders almost completely blocked the light.

"You don't need to know why," he said, his voice solemn. "But I can't go after Lovelock himself either on land or at sea. And I destroyed your ship so that Lovelock would think you were dead. If you had really died in the process, then that would have been unfortunate, but I could have lived with it."

"Well, thank you!" exclaimed Drewshank.

"What fun is there bullying the ships of mere privateers? No fun at all."

"Why did you want Lovelock to think I was dead? What good would it do you?"

"None at all . . . but if I change my mind and let you live, Lovelock thinking you're dead might be the best thing for you."

Drewshank shook his head. "You've lost me," he said.

"Unless you're really stupid then you must have realized there's no way you can go back to your old life now. You've been implicated in this Golden Mice affair. You'll be hunted down by the authorities in Old Town — Isiah will make damn sure of that. He would never let you carry on as normal knowing what you know."

Mousebeard was right and Drewshank knew it. There really was no way back.

"For the time being, you're safe here anyway," said Mousebeard.

"So you're not going to kill me?"

Mousebeard shook his head. "I'm not inclined to

hurt people for the sake of it, captain. Threats are always a good way of making people open up, though."

Drewshank sighed with relief.

"And you could well be of use to me yet," added the pirate. "A captain who can survive a Grak attack is a good person to know."

"You heard about that?"

"I have some friends, Drewshank. Even so, for the time being, you'll have to return to your crew. There are things I have to do . . . Guards!" shouted the pirate.

Upon Mousebeard's calling, the door burst open, and two pirates promptly dragged Drewshank away.

"Lock him up with the rest of them," he ordered as they left. "I need time to think!"

❧ ✳ ❦

Inside the Dung Mouse pen, Emiline was scooping up steaming dung while desperately trying to keep her nose closed. Her crewmates were involved in much the same task, and it was making many of them feel sick.

"How long do we have to live with this?" said Scratcher, regretting the day he ever came to sea.

"The captain'll get us out," assured Fenwick. "He always has some sort of plan up his sleeve."

"I hope he gets us out soon," added Emiline, "or else I'm going to go mad."

She threw a huge dollop of dung into the hut at the back, and returned to look for more. The excrement of the Dung Mouse was used for fuel; its exceedingly potent smell made it incredibly flammable, and a very good replacement for coal. If you were to ask the people who collected it what they thought, however, they would much rather be doing something less smelly elsewhere.

Scratcher climbed up onto a bed and sat down to clear the dirt from his fingernails.

"This is rubbish," he said.

Before he could say anything more, a great flash of blinding light lit up the island, and a huge explosion shook the pen. The Dung Mice went crazy, rushing around with a demented look in their eyes, and the prisoners did their best to get out of their way.

Fenwick rushed to the window. Thin trails of fire rained slowly down onto the treetops from the sky.

"Firebrands," he said calmly. Another explosion

sounded overhead, and once more the ground shook violently. The sky was filled with even more fire bolts.

"What are they?" asked Emiline, gazing at the sky.

"They're the massive warships that shoot flaming missiles to burn things. They won't do much damage round here, as it's so lush, but they can burn down a wooden city if the weather's right," answered Fenwick.

"They're reminding Mousebeard that they're there," said Scratcher.

"But they want him alive, don't they?" asked Emiline, clinging to the bars.

"That's what I thought," replied Fenwick, curiously.

The guard outside slammed her sword against the window bars, causing the prisoners to jump.

"Get back to work!" she shouted as some of the fire bolts landed gently behind her and fizzled out on the forest floor.

"They ain't powerful ones," said Fenwick. "That navy is just sending out warning shots. Seems like Mousebeard's gonna have some decisions to make."

From the distance appeared three figures. They stopped briefly at the next onslaught of explosions, but soon reached the Dung Mouse pen. The door opened and Drewshank was thrown in unceremoniously.

"Captain!" cheered the crew.

Drewshank lifted himself up off the floor, narrowly avoiding placing his hands in a huge pile of dung. He was now so dirty that any last hope of maintaining a few vestiges of dignity had vanished.

"Good to see you all in one piece," he said happily, "but you really do smell!"

Fenwick greeted him and asked what happened.

"Are we in a whole heap of trouble!" said Drewshank. "That pirate's managed to steal two Golden Mice. . . ."

"Golden Mice?" exclaimed the prisoners.

"So I really don't see how he or we are going to get out of this. That Omen Mouse certainly knew how to pick the right people to fly by."

"Omen Mouse?" the prisoners echoed him for a second time. Emiline, Scratcher, and Fenwick looked at one another.

"So, quite frankly, I don't fancy our chances. However, Mousebeard has assured me that we'll be safe."

"The word of a pirate . . . ," muttered Fenwick. "But

it clears up why they haven't been attacking the island with any venom."

"Judging from what Mousebeard's told me, it's been a plan for Lovelock to get his hands on those Golden Mice."

"The sneaky so-and-so . . . ," said Emiline. "We were framed! And he let me come on this voyage knowing we'd be heading into trouble!"

"Ha!" laughed Drewshank. "What did you do to upset him?"

"Well, there was a Sharpclaw that escaped from my care. . . ."

"A Sharpclaw!" replied Drewshank. "The one on my ship?"

Emiline shrugged. "But I didn't think he knew about it."

"Well, here we are anyway," said Scratcher. "No point worrying about it now. We can just sit here, locked forever in an overgrown mouse toilet."

⇒ ✳ ⇐

"So then, cap'n," said Scragneck, his piercing eyes glistening, "what 'ave you got planned? This fire rain ain't up to much, but you know they're just playing with us. They'll be sending them mortars down on us soon."

Mousebeard continued to stare out of the window: "While we're here, we're safe. They won't do anything to harm those mice."

"Those mice!" snapped Scragneck, lunging forward. "As nice as they are, they're causin' trouble amongst the crew."

"Don't play this game with me, man!" growled Mousebeard, his beard twisting uncontrollably as his voice grew louder. "We don't go anywhere!"

"But, cap'n," said Scragneck forcefully, "the crew ain't so sure. Those letters they flew over 'ave got some of 'em thinking."

Scragneck moved farther into the room, and his slight form cast a long shadow across the floor. Mousebeard turned sharply and his eyes met his first mate's.

"Some of them?" snarled Mousebeard. "I know what you're up to, Scragneck, and it won't work."

"Me, cap'n?" he said falsely, bringing his hand to his chest. "I'd never do such a thing to you, cap'n."

"You're a pirate, man. I know exactly what you'd do given half a chance."

Scragneck reddened and his hand went to withdraw his sword.

"I'd snap you in two before it left your side," said Mousebeard calmly. Scragneck's thin lip twitched, and he lowered his hand.

"Well 'ear this, sir," he countered. "Some o' the crew think it's best we make speed and outrun 'em. The giant will give us a head start, at least enough to get us on our way."

"Have you no sense?" said Mousebeard angrily. "It will do us no good at all. They outnumber us in fire-power by a hundred to one. We might outrun the ships, but we would never beat the cannons."

Scragneck snapped once more. "Rubbish, captain! The *Shark*'s better than that."

Mousebeard's eyes bored into Scragneck's.

"We will not leave this island!" he shouted. "And you'll see to it that the rest of the crew understand that."

Scragneck scowled, and took a few paces backward.

"Your command over the *Shark* is not as strong as ya think, captain!"

"You think you'd do better?"

Scragneck stood in heated silence.

"I asked if you'd do better?" growled Mousebeard.

The men stared at each other. Each was tempted to move, but it was Scragneck whose will broke first. He stepped back farther and, knowing no other course of action, withdrew his sword and pointed it at Mousebeard.

"You'd better watch ya back!" Scragneck said savagely, and stormed out of the room.

Mousebeard slammed his hand down onto the table, which splintered and cracked along its width. He dragged his fingers along the broken wood, swearing under his breath.

After a few moments his breathing slowed, he sighed, and his shoulders dropped. Turning to look through the window, Mousebeard saw the huge far-off shape of Ogruk. His friend was peering out to sea over the side of the cliff, unperturbed by the raining droplets of fire.

The giant swatted them off his clothes like gnats, making a mockery of the navy's firepower.

"Oh, Ogruk," he said quietly. "What is happening to my island?"

Mousebeard knew that Ogruk wouldn't stay much longer. Even though they were friends, the giant hated human conflict and would do whatever he could to stay as far away from it as possible. The pirate feared his hand was going to be played too soon, and Scragneck would get his chance to strike.

The Golden Mouse

ONE OF THE MOST RECOGNIZED MICE IN THE WORLD, THE EXCEPTIONALLY *rare Golden Mouse has fur consisting of fine strands of pure gold. Found only in the forests of Illyria, this mouse is revered by the natives as an incarnation of their sun god. Its fur has been the subject of lengthy debate among governments, particularly over the terrible effect it would have on the price of the world's natural gold if anyone were effectively to harvest it as a sustainable source.*

MOUSING NOTES

The Golden Mouse is protected by international law and countless Mousing Regulations, and can never be traded, removed from Illyria, kept in captivity, or killed for its fur. To own or pursue ownership of a Golden Mouse is a crime punishable by death. The International Mousehunting Federation sets its strictest rules for this rodent, and defends its right to survival with every power at its disposal.

The Mutinous Crew

NIGHT FELL ON GIANT ISLAND, HERALDING THE HOWLS and whoops of nocturnal mice. The Dung Mouse pen was finally silent; the pirate crew of the *Silver Shark* were holed up on land, drinking the night away; and Mousebeard sat at his desk watching the Golden Mice. He was angry at finding himself in this position, and he was angry at not seeing to Scragneck while he had the chance. Mousebeard rarely slept more than a few hours a night. His mind was continually alive with thoughts and schemes, and he hated to waste time sleeping. Besides, as a pirate, it was always good to sleep with one eye open just in case someone took a dislike to you.

As well as the flaming missiles falling all around,

mortars were exploding on the volcano's rim. Lord Battersby's warships were destroying the cliffs, rock by rock, with the clear intention that no mortars should fall into the volcano itself for fear of hurting anyone or anything.

On top of the noise of the bombardment, the loud footsteps of Ogruk could be heard pacing around the island. He was becoming restless, and eventually Mousebeard heard him approaching the lagoon. His footsteps stopped, and the pirate leaned back in his chair as the walls of his room began to shake. The flat ceiling shuddered and tilted upward, and with a loud crunching noise it was lifted off to show the giant standing high above and the night sky stretching beyond. Holding the roof between two fingers, Ogruk crouched down and pushed his other fist into the lagoon to steady himself.

Ogruk's head, still a long way above the fortress, filled the open ceiling. Mousebeard could see warts and scars upon the giant's leathery skin, and with each breath Ogruk made, it was as though a hurricane had been unleashed in his room.

"Mousebeard," said the giant very loudly, his rounded

teeth and enormous tongue visible in the dark, "it's time I moved on. Those ships are destroying everything and, as you know, I choose not to fight."

"When will you leave?" shouted Mousebeard, knowing that the giant found it hard to hear him.

"Tonight," boomed Ogruk, his voice rattling the windows. "I'm fed up with all this."

Mousebeard twisted his beard. It was the worst news he could have had.

"I understand," he said. "Will you still take us out to sea?"

"Of course," replied the giant with little emotion. "I hold no hatred for you. One day we shall meet again under better circumstances."

"I'll get everyone ready then," said the pirate. "Thank you, Ogruk."

With a slow nod that sent his tousled hair spilling down over his face, Ogruk placed the roof down gently and walked off to the edge of the island.

"I'm an idiot," growled Mousebeard, looking around at his room and realizing he might never see it again. "All this is lost. . . ."

He collected his blunderbuss, pistols, and cutlass, letting out growls as the will took him. He pulled on his thick woolen jacket, strapped his belt across his chest, and grabbed the mousebox containing the Golden Mice. When the time came to face the navy, and he knew it would happen sooner rather than later, then he'd do it fully armed.

Mousebeard left his room and stepped cautiously down the staircase. It was a long walk to the ground floor, passing numerous entrances to other rooms and halls, all of which seemed quiet and unoccupied. Eventually he reached the bottom, where a worn-out pirate stood on guard. His upright spear rose and dipped as each nod of his head sent him closer to sleep. Mousebeard made a gruff reprimand, and the guard jumped to attention to unbolt the massive door in the gateway.

The cool evening welcomed Mousebeard with the sound of peaceful lapping water. He stood quietly for a moment, noting the respite in the navy's attack while watching the rippling lagoon through the cracks in the walkway. The gangplank onto the *Silver Shark* stretched out before him, and he made his way toward it. Mouse-beard felt something creeping up behind him, like a shadow falling over his heart. He turned around and saw Scragneck, and immediately drew himself up.

"I don't remember calling for you!" said Mousebeard angrily.

"So we're leavin', are we?" said Scragneck, tapping his sword menacingly in the palm of his hand. "He's not terrible discreet that giant of yours — havin' a mouth the size of a ship an' all!"

"You got what you wanted," replied Mousebeard, stepping toward Scragneck ominously, "so go and tell the men we're sailing in the next hour. Sober them up with a cold shower too; this journey ahead of us could well be our last."

"Ah, but cap'n, this journey ain't goin' to be our last. . . ."

Mousebeard heard shuffling behind him, and two pi-rates grabbed at his arms. He lashed out with anger as the Golden Mice were snatched from his grasp.

"You blasted fools," he growled. He managed to free a hand and reached for his cutlass.

"It ain't no good resisting, cap'n. I decided I didn't want to swing wiv ya after all." Scragneck's sword shot out and rested under Mousebeard's jaw.

The other pirates soon regained their nerve and raised their swords at his back and chest. Mousebeard could feel the sharp points pressing into him like the clutches of an iron maiden. He didn't care, though — he sensed his battle with Scragneck was going to be the least of his worries now.

"You'll send us to our death," growled Mousebeard, dropping his weapons to the ground, smoke still lifting from the blunderbuss. "The Old Town Guard will never let you go free. You're all walking into a trap the size of the Great Sea!"

"Ah, but, cap'n," said the scheming Scragneck, "you're forgetting that the *Shark* will be under my control!"

Mousebeard looked at the mutinous pirate, and cursed himself for ever keeping him in his crew. Scragneck's mind was clouded by his lust for power. Mousebeard breathed heavily, pushing his chest out forcefully, making the pirates' swords bend.

"Well, come on then . . . ," he said, his dark eyes still angry. "What are you waiting for?"

Scragneck smiled.

"Get 'im, boys!" he snarled.

Because of the sheer size and power of Mousebeard, it took five pirates to tie him up. They took his bulging arms and bound them three times over for security. His huge palms clenched and unclenched as the bonds constricted the feeling in his hands. His beard bristled.

"Stick 'im in the brig and clap 'im in irons. I'm the captain now." Scragneck turned. "Don't try anythin', Mousebeard!" he said, as the other pirates tried to jostle the big man up the gangplank with little success. Mousebeard was keen to walk as slowly and heavily as he could.

"Now's not the time," he replied caustically. "I'll need my strength for when the *Silver Shark* is sinking!"

Once Mousebeard had been taken aboard ship, Miserley strolled out of the boat with her head held high.

"I've sent a message to the navy. That Battersby's expecting us," she said.

"Good. Let's be prepared. Get as many guns as possible on top deck. And get that Drewshank on board; somethin' makes me think he'll be useful. Leave the others, particularly them kids, to rot in the mouse pen. That'll teach 'em!"

Miserley set off into the dark.

"Cap'n of the *Silver Shark!*" said Scragneck quietly. "Who'd 'a' thought?"

⇒ ✳ ⇐

Emiline lay awake on a hard and uncomfortable bunk. The Dung Mice were snoring loudly, as was Fenwick, and she was finding it impossible to sleep.

She'd heard the gunshot, but being used to the explosions from the navy, she hadn't thought anything of it. At least not until the door to the pen burst open.

There, on the threshold, was Miserley, standing confidently in her tight gray jacket with her hands on her hips. Her long hair swooped down over her eyes as she surveyed the bleary-eyed prisoners. Five pirates appeared from behind her and pulled Drewshank out into the jungle, scattering Dung Mice in the process. The prisoners jumped to their feet, and Emiline found herself charging through the door at Miserley. Emiline pushed her to the floor, but before Miserley had the chance to draw her daggers another pirate had kicked the prisoner back into the pen.

"Get away, girl," he barked.

Miserley lifted herself off the floor and shook dirt from her hair. Drewshank laughed, as did all the prisoners, but they soon fell quiet as the door slammed shut and the key turned in the lock.

"That's it for you lot," shouted Miserley, banging the door. "There's no way out now. We're leaving the island and letting you rot here with these disgusting mice."

Fenwick ran to the door and shoved it with his shoulder. "Captain!" he shouted through the bars.

Drewshank stumbled as his hands were grabbed and tied in front of him.

"Fenwick?" he shouted back bewildered. He looked back at the pen as he was pulled along. After the events of the past few weeks, he'd thought nothing could shock him anymore. But he was wrong.

"What's going on?" he said, wearily.

"You're being handed over to the navy. They want Mousebeard and the Golden Mice, and we thought we'd throw you in as well," said Miserley, sniggering.

"You really are most despicable," said Drewshank. "Don't you realize they'll either kill you or hang you high at Old Town?"

Miserley jabbed him in the ribs with her dagger handle.

"Lord Battersby has given us his word that we won't be harmed."

"Battersby!" exclaimed Drewshank. He suddenly stood still, causing the pirate in front to almost fall over. "Of course!"

"You know him?"

"Something like that . . . ," said Drewshank. "What have you gotten us all into?"

Miserley's temper exploded. "Shut up!" she shouted.

Drewshank fell silent, and resigned himself to whatever lay ahead. At least he now knew why he'd been chosen as bait for Mousebeard. There had never been any love lost between him and Battersby.

"Are you ready?" boomed Ogruk.

Scragneck stepped out onto deck and signaled his intentions. The giant looked down at the ship quizzically.

"Where's Mousebeard?" he boomed.

"Sortin' out a few things below deck!" replied the new captain. "He wanted you to carry us out of the volcano."

Ogruk frowned and looked at the tiny, insignificant Scragneck. He was utterly weary of the humans and their worthless battles, but his promise to Mousebeard still stood. The giant sighed, sending low waves rippling across the lagoon. Then he bent down and plucked the *Silver Shark* from the water.

In just a few long steps, Ogruk reached the rim of the volcano, and clambered up its side. The giant surveyed the flickering white lights onboard the many ships bobbing up and down on the surrounding sea. The navy was ready and waiting.

Scragneck looked out uneasily at the view.

"Put us down then!" he shouted.

Ogruk looked again across the sea, and raised the *Silver Shark* to one of his immense eyes. His flowing hair battered the hull like thousands of lashing whips, and as he spoke everyone struggled to keep on their feet for the force of his breath.

"Not here?" he rumbled. "Farther?"

"Yes, here! Put us down!" shouted Scragneck.

"But Mousebeard?" Ogruk said, taking a step down into the sea.

"This is what he wanted!" screamed the pirate, clutching hold of the ship's rail. "You can put us down now, Ogruk!"

The giant grumbled as though his throat were full of thunder, and lowered the *Silver Shark* to the sea far below. His grip loosened, and the water took hold of the vessel.

Flares went shooting into the sky, lighting the moonless night, and Ogruk made his way out into the deep, releasing large rolling waves in his wake. As his massive shape grew fainter and more distant, he never looked back. With a crackle of explosions, harpooned ropes fired out into the hull of the *Silver Shark* — even its metal sides couldn't withstand the brute force of the navy. Battersby had trained the guns of four huge warships onto the *Silver Shark*, their crews all ready for action. Bit by bit they drew in closer until the sailors were within shouting distance of the pirate ship.

On deck, Scragneck held his sword tightly, and ordered the rest of the pirates to draw their weapons.

"Are Mousebeard and Drewshank ready?" he shouted, turning to Miserley.

"They're chained up and ready," she replied. Her daggers, as ever, were primed for action, but she seemed restless. "I'll get them brought up."

Miserley went below deck and gave the signal to one of the pirates on guard. Mousebeard walked from the brig in silence, his wrists locked in irons behind his back. He proceeded up to the top deck with a grave look on his face, and every pirate he passed tried not to meet his eye. Drewshank was attached to him by a thick iron chain and struggled to shadow his steps.

Miserley watched them leave the lower deck, but

didn't follow. She walked to the empty stern of the ship and pushed aside a cabinet, which shunted as though on castors. Behind was a secret cupboard filled with weapons, food, and a barrel of fresh water. She took one look behind her to see that she hadn't been followed, and then crept inside, concealing the entrance once more.

Back on deck, Scragneck pushed his prisoners to the front of the deck so that they were in full view of the approaching warships. A crowd of excitable pirates joined him and withdrew their weapons in wait.

"You're giving yourself up," growled Mousebeard, watching the navy's ships come hull to hull with the *Silver Shark*. Behind the warships, the sea was filled with vessels big and small, lit up by the continuous stream of flares that were being fired into the sky.

"Shut up," snapped Scragneck; however, he couldn't help but eye the ships nervously.

From every side of the *Silver Shark*, sailors appeared and dropped onto the deck. Scragneck watched them intently, and they stared back without moving further — the sailors easily outnumbered the pirates. Finally, with a heavy thump, Lord Battersby landed aboard, a silver-butted pistol in his hand.

"Good evening," he said, catching the eye of Mousebeard. He approached him and looked him up and down.

In his chains, Mousebeard bristled, and his dark eyes held Battersby's gaze.

"How the mighty tumble," said Battersby. "And you, Drewshank . . . what a nice surprise. I thought you had gone down with your worthless ship. . . ."

"A small gesture for ya," said Scragneck.

"Well, that's much appreciated," added Battersby. "I shall enjoy watching him walk to the scaffold. He was just perfect for our little plan."

Battersby made a small gesture with his hand and sailors approached Mousebeard and Drewshank, seizing their chains. Even though the pirate was bound, the sailors clearly found his presence unnerving. He glowered at them as they tried to move him.

"Idiots," snarled Mousebeard, "thinking you can get the better of me!"

The pirate let his head fall back and whistled three short notes. Immediately, along the masts rushed tens of mice, who all started to wail. It was the same ear-piercing noise that Drewshank had heard when they were in the fog, and every sailor and pirate clutched their ears.

"Run!" shouted Mousebeard.

Drewshank was reeling from the noise, but found it didn't matter when he was being pulled along by the fearsome strength of Mousebeard. The pirate charged at Battersby and knocked him flying with his shoulder. Two sailors, struggling to deal with the wailing mice, managed to jump on Drewshank and drag him to the floor. The pirate pulled up sharply, but, giving a great tug, had his fellow prisoner back on his feet again.

"Get him!" ordered Battersby.

At least ten sailors released their ears and headed toward the pirate, who had barged to the edge of the ship. Mousebeard looked down into the choppy blackness of the sea, and his immediate thought was to jump, but he paused, and the wailing of the mice grew louder in a fresh chorus. With the weight of Drewshank hanging off him, he wouldn't stand a chance in the cold water. There was now nowhere to run.

The sailors eventually reached him, but first they bundled Drewshank to the floor. Mousebeard stood firm and felt his arms pull sharply with the chain. More sailors jumped onto him. He swung his body frantically, dispatching three sailors over the side and into the water before he was finally overcome in a torrent of punches. In a last gasp of strength, he let out a desperate cry of anguish, as his head smashed into his captors.

Battersby calmly found his feet and pointed the pistol at Mousebeard's neck.

"I'd finish this now if it was worth my while," he said.

"Do it," ordered Mousebeard.

Battersby smirked.

"Bringing you back to Old Town will make me the most famous man in Midena — and even the whole of the Great Sea. You're worth so much more alive. . . ."

Battersby turned his gun to where the mice were resting on the masts and pulled the trigger. Mousebeard's face paled as he watched three small mice drop like weights to the deck. Their wailing cries stopped briefly then started up again.

"Blow them away!" shouted Battersby to his troops, who were being driven mad by the noise. The sailors passed the order to the *Stonebreaker*, which unleashed a hail of shot at the offending mice, blowing the masts to pieces.

Mousebeard felt a hole widen in his heart at the sound of the gunfire.

"Take the prisoners away!" ordered Battersby exultantly, before he turned to face the pirates. "Who's in charge of this ship now?"

Scragneck stepped forward as the shapes of Mousebeard and Drewshank disappeared onto the *Stonebreaker*.

"Do you have the mice?" asked Battersby, slightly breathless.

"Do I 'ave your word?"

Battersby let his sailors surround him. "Of course you do."

A pirate carried over the ornate mousebox, passed it to Battersby, and then stepped back.

"Excellent," said Lord Battersby, his eyes glowing at the thought of the riches the mice would bring to Old Town. Before he stepped off the *Silver Shark*, he looked back and spoke.

"You have two choices," he said. "Either drop your weapons and surrender, or face our cannons and die like the scum you are!"

Then he turned and disappeared behind a freshly mustered line of sailors. Scragneck raised his sword.

"You lying, two-bit . . ."

Pistol shots rang out from behind him and his pirates fired through a row of Battersby's sailors.

"No surrender!" shouted Scragneck to his fellow pirates as he slashed with his sword. "Blast 'em back to Old Town!"

Safe onboard the *Stonebreaker*, Battersby watched the fighting from his cabin. He ordered more sailors to go onboard, knowing that before long the pirates would be completely overrun. When word eventually reached him of Scragneck's capture, he suppressed a smile. He relished the knowledge that his present for the Old Town gallows was going to be even greater than he'd hoped.

The Orange Mouse of Niladia

THE ORANGE MOUSE LIVES ITS LIFE IN PERMANENT DANGER BECAUSE OF *an unfortunate twist of evolution that's endowed it with bright orange fur. In most cases of such natural coloring, this would be an indication of the animal being bestowed with a deadly poison, but not the poor Orange Mouse. Instead, it is one of the most highly visible and hunted mice in existence, and is forever on the run from predators. When not fleeing from pursuit, the Orange Mouse is usually found rolling in mud to try and hide is coloring — a rather fruitless task.*

MOUSING NOTES

The Orange Mouse is, unsurprisingly, on the world's endangered list, but unlike many mice on the list, it is actively encouraged that collectors keep a pair in their collection. The mice seem to relish an unnatural habitat, and thrive in captivity.

The Return to Old Town

THE *STONEBREAKER* TORE THROUGH THE WATER ON ITS long journey back to Old Town. Chained up in a small prison cabin in its hull, with only shards of light to see by, Mousebeard and Drewshank looked totally defeated and battle-weary. Bruises were blossoming on their faces, and their outfits were dirty and damaged. And worst of all, not only were they still chained together at arm's length, but they had nothing to do other than talk to each other.

"I hate Lord Battersby," said Drewshank, leaning back uncomfortably.

The mice in Mousebeard's beard were fidgeting, and

the pirate was muttering under his breath. His dark brown eyes appeared pure black in the dingy conditions.

"Mutinous scum," he spat. "Just as I warned, they've got all of us killed."

"That's pirates for you," Drewshank replied. "But I must admit that I enjoyed your charge at Lord Battersby!"

"If the opportunity arises," Mousebeard said gruffly, "he'll get a lot worse. But my crew had turned, and in that situation it's each man for himself."

"You should have chosen your friends more wisely."

"Friends?" said Mousebeard angrily, leaning into Drewshank's face. "What would you know about my friends?"

Drewshank pulled back, trying to smooth his matted hair.

"Enough to know that most of them will be there to watch you plummet from the gallows," he said smartly.

Mousebeard frowned and closed his eyes.

"I won't make it that far, captain," he said. "I won't last that long."

"If there's anyone they'll keep alive for Old Town, it'll

be you," said Drewshank. "Your execution will draw all the crowds."

Mousebeard smiled grimly. His darkened eyes suddenly looked distant.

"If only staying alive was that easy."

"It's not like you've anything better to do," said Drewshank.

"You know nothing of what I face. I've lived under the shadow of death for many years, privateer. You'll understand things soon enough."

"It seems that we have plenty of time on our hands, so you might as well explain what you mean."

Mousebeard looked at him. "Sitting in silence would be far preferable," he said.

"Have it your way then," replied Drewshank.

He groaned and fell silent. In his boredom he started to pick at the manacles clamped tightly around his wrists. The cabin was hot and airless, and sweat was dripping down his forehead. He stopped thinking about Mousebeard and his secrets, and instead thought of the horrific prospect of returning to Old Town with heavy chains clanking around his feet and wrists.

An armored sailing vessel slipped silently into Old Town harbor at the dead of night, unseen by the other ships navigating the channel. Its sails slackened and it pulled up smoothly at the quayside. The harbor was relatively quiet, just the odd sailor and usual drunks, but as Beatrice Pettifogger disembarked with four armed bodyguards to protect her, a cloaked figure approached.

"Aah, Lady Pettifogger," exclaimed Spires, striding toward her, "your carriage is waiting for you!"

Spires looked more tired than usual. Isiah Lovelock had been sending him on errands round the clock of late.

"I take it all is well," said Beatrice Pettifogger as she walked alongside the butler, her cloak skimming the floor.

"Yes, ma'am. Mr. Lovelock is waiting in great anticipation of your news."

Lady Pettifogger touched his arm very lightly.

"And he won't be disappointed. I received word this morning that everything has gone to plan."

"Excellent," replied the butler, ushering Lady Pettifogger to her carriage, waiting by the Old Town Gate.

Spires followed the lady onboard and gave the order to move on. With a jolt they set off, and sped through the streets of Old Town.

When they reached the heights of Grandview, Isiah Lovelock was standing at the roadside, taking in the air outside his mansion. He was lit by the glowing lamp nearby, and his long shadow stretched out over the cobblestones. It was a most unusual sight, and Spires hastened to jump down from the carriage.

"Is everything well, sir?" he asked.

"Yes, of course! You made good time," said Lovelock with a faint smile. Spires opened the other side of the carriage and Lady Pettifogger stepped down, pulling her cloak across so her feet hit the ground first. She took Lovelock's cold hand.

"Isiah!" she exclaimed warmly, "how wonderful to meet again, and in such marvelous circumstances."

These words brought a tiny sparkle to his eye.

"We have them?" he asked hopefully, leading her into

the hallway. The dim lights along the walls caught the whites of Lovelock's eyes as he stopped and waited for her reply. Lady Pettifogger glanced around, drew nearer, and whispered to Lovelock.

"Each and every one, Isiah," she said. "The pirates gave up their captain and the Golden Mice without so much as a sneeze. And we have the *Silver Shark* intact but for a few scratches. What better trophy is there? It will prove a great draw for the young mousekeepers of Old Town."

"Lord Battersby will be rewarded with the highest honors, Beatrice," said Lovelock. "This is the most fabulous news I could have received!"

"And the fleet will return within the next week or so, all being well. I believe a celebration will be in order."

"I'll send word to the Mayor of Old Town," said Lovelock. "The scaffold will have to be erected on Pirate's Wharf — and the gibbet readied for Mousebeard. He still has supporters around the Great Sea, so we should make an example of him."

"We shall be in the history books, Isiah!" exclaimed Beatrice.

"And the Golden Mice will herald a new dawn for this land. Old Town will once again become the richest city in the world. We'll put the fire back into the people — get them thirsty for wealth and glory. Old Town will soon be unstoppable. . . ."

➤ ✳ ➤

After news reached Old Town of Mousebeard's capture, rumors spread like wildfire. In the taverns it was said that Mousebeard could command giants and sea monsters, and word had got out about Battersby's return and his notorious cargo. No one knew what to believe for sure, but everyone felt it was a major event in the history of Midena. On the streets, rows of mousebunting were hung from building to building, and effigies of the captured pirate were staked on the end of tall pikes in celebration.

In Merchants' Square, outside the Town Hall, boys and girls distributed the daily papers with the breaking news. With every day that passed there was a new artist's impression of the pirate's scowling face blown up large on the front pages. It was impossible to escape: even the walls of the docks were plastered with posters proclaiming the virtues of Lord Battersby and the Old Town Guard, and how the menace of Mousebeard would soon be extinguished for good.

Within the confines of the hallowed Hall of Mousetrading, dealers discussed the impact that Mousebeard's capture would have on their fortunes. There was quite a buzz around the city, and the price of lucrative Angel-eyed Mice — Old Town's most recent mousing discovery — rocketed. In the space of just a few days, the city was once again the talk of Midena.

For all the young mousekeepers of Old Town who had grown up listening to horrifying stories of Mousebeard the pirate, it was almost too exciting to bear. Hearing of his capture and knowing that he was being brought to their city was the most amazing thing ever to happen to them, and the pirate's arrival couldn't come too soon. Even in Old Rodent's Academy, there was much talk among the professors and students, and the day of the pirate's arrival was made a holiday so that everyone could visit the harbor and catch a glimpse of the prisoner.

So when the navy's ships eventually appeared on the horizon, it didn't take long for everyone to hear about it. Every viewpoint in the city grew congested with on-lookers gazing out to sea, and those able to make the journey through the marshes to the harbor did so.

The *Stonebreaker* was the first to reach the docks, its flags flying high and snapping in the wind, with, behind it, the pirate ship in tow. Every sailor lined the deck; their faces were stern but triumphant. The tailing war-ships slipped quietly into the harbor and formed an im-penetrable wall between Old Town and the sea, making it impossible for any sort of escape.

The cobbled quayside was cluttered with cheering supporters, all trying to outstretch each other for the best view of the ships. It had been almost a century since an arrival had brought this much excitement to the harbor. As a loud whistle sounded, the crowd retreated slightly, and a wide gangplank fell to the ground with a clatter. "Where is he?" shouted an old lady, struggling to see the events unfold. Her cry was echoed by the rest-less crowd, and a chorus of "String 'im up! String 'im up!" belted out.

Suddenly, armed sailors marched out and drove a corridor through the crowd to the Old Town Gate. The rabble grew louder and louder, waiting for Mousebeard, until eventually Lord Battersby walked into view in full uniform. He carried a mousebox, and as he stepped out a huge cheer rang out. Behind him came more sailors, and then the crowd went quiet at the sight everyone was waiting for. Mousebeard stood tall on deck, his immense size gradually revealed by the dispersing crew. But his face was drained of color, and he looked tired — certainly not the fearsome presence that people were expecting. A guard shoved his back to make him move.

He stumbled at the top of the gangplank. His wrists and ankles were shackled, allowing him little movement, but he slowly shuffled onto the flagstones, heralding wild cheering from the crowd. Stones were thrown at him, and clumps of dirt flew into his face, but he was unfazed, instead feeling a sense of bewilderment at the solid ground beneath his feet. Sailors rushed to form a barrier between him and the crowd, twisting their pikes sideways in unison to stop anyone pushing through.

Mousebeard hesitantly took a few steps forward —

something that briefly warmed every part of his soul —
but the crowd's attention quickly focused on his face,
which was contorting. It suddenly lost all its color and
his dark eyes scrunched shut. He tumbled to the floor,
his huge body clattering down, and he started to twist
and writhe in agony. Sailors kicked him and demanded
he rise, but the pirate couldn't move. His chest had
seized up as if an iron hand were squeezing his heart. It
had been years since Mousebeard had felt the pain.

Lord Battersby rushed over.

"Get up, man!" he ordered. "Pick him up!"

Four sailors lifted Mousebeard — his weight was
such that it needed that many — and it was immediately apparent that all was not well.

"I can't walk," he muttered, breathing heavily. The
crowd around started to jeer.

"We'll drag you along the roads if we have to," said
Battersby sharply. "Keep him coming." Lord Battersby
walked on through the crowds at a faster pace, with
Mousebeard being pulled behind.

Drewshank was the next onto the gangplank, and the
response of the crowd turned to one of confusion. He

looked at the faces around him, searching vainly for friends. Everyone knew of Drewshank's attempt to capture the pirate, but they had no idea why he was now a prisoner. As the rest of the pirates emerged onto the gangplank, a single cheer lifted the people again, and soon Drewshank was amid the roaring jeers just like Mousebeard.

Drewshank focused on the route ahead and saw Mousebeard struggling along the cobblestones, his arms clenched by soldiers. His immediate reaction was to walk on faster, to try and help the man who had shown him mercy, but as he neared, three soldiers stuck out their pikes and halted him. Something was wrong with the pirate, and he wished he'd understood more of what Mousebeard had been speaking of while chained in the prison.

Battersby led the pirates through the Old Town Gate and out onto the marshes. The crowds thinned slightly, but people still stood cheering along the route. The crowds followed to the point where the snaking line of prisoners veered from the road onto a less-used, muddy, pot-holed track. Not even for a glimpse of the pirate would any sane human venture onto that path. Its narrow course wound slightly upward toward the western reaches of the city, and prisoners trudged for nearly half an hour before they saw their destination. Everyone but Mousebeard tilted their heads up, and a sense of dread filled their hearts. Like a fallen tombstone in a graveyard, a stone-walled fortress lifted above the surrounding woodland and scrub. It was Dire Street Prison: the darkest, dingiest, and best-guarded prison in the land. If you were ever to leave, it would only be to Pirate's Wharf, where the gallows awaited you.

Upon reaching the perimeter wall, they halted before a set of rusty iron gates, and Battersby called out to the guards on the other side. The gates opened with a squeal and soldiers marched out. Mousebeard and Drewshank were taken inside first. Drewshank felt wretched but he was more worried about Mousebeard. Looking back, the captain could see that the pirate had been weakening minute by minute. He had always seen Mousebeard as a terrible figure, to be hated and not pitied, but he couldn't help but feel saddened by seeing such a strong man brought so low.

The prison governor, a ginger-haired stocky woman, dressed in a tight military-style dress, greeted Lord Battersby just inside the gates.

"Well done, sir," she said, shaking his hand and smiling proudly. "Anything you need me to do?"

"Get the mice from his beard," said Battersby, "and have them delivered to me."

"Certainly, sir. What about his treatment? Shall we rough him up a bit?"

"No, definitely not. Make sure he's treated well — we need him on top form to face the gallows."

Lord Battersby bade her farewell and walked from the prison with a frown. He too was puzzled by the pirate's condition, and he too was concerned — it was imperative that Mousebeard live long enough to face the executioner.

⇒ ❋ ⇐

Lord Battersby dusted down his broad chest and tweaked his coat. He wanted to make an entrance worthy of the occasion, and he scratched his chin to check that stubble hadn't grown in any great measure. He smiled to himself, ran his hand across his hair, and finally rapped on the door at the Old Town Gentlemen's Club.

Situated on the edge of Grandview, where the mansions became crowded by townhouses, it was a rarefied venue, with rich and influential figures as members. The Club was a tall gray brick building, regrettably built on weak foundations, which meant it required an immense, meter-wide iron chain to be joined between its top floor and the ground to stop it from falling over. Three chimneys rose high into the sky from its roof, and each was adorned by aging chimney pots. Out of keeping with the rest of the Club's appearance, one of these was home to a large stork's nest, which the manager — a meticulous man — had never managed to banish.

The door opened immediately and Battersby walked in, his appearance creating a great stir among the smartly dressed doormen and waitresses standing in the hallway.

"Isiah Lovelock?" asked Battersby.

A waitress nodded.

"This way, sir," she said. "Can I take the mousebox and your jacket for you, sir?"

"Oh, no, no! That won't be necessary," he said briskly as he followed her.

They walked up a wide staircase, past paintings of former members and their favorite mice, until they reached a door with a green glass handle. Spires stood nearby and gave a formal nod of greeting.

"Mr. Lovelock and his guests are in here, sir," said the waitress, before taking her leave.

"Good to see you back safely, sir," said Spires plainly.

"It's good to be back," replied Battersby. He knocked firmly on the door then strode in, a feeling of great accomplishment welling within.

"Alexander!" cheered Lady Pettifogger, jumping up to greet him, a beaming smile across her face. Lovelock lifted himself from his chair, his eyes wide.

The room was modestly sized but exquisitely furnished, with big antique pots and vases at its edges. Landscape paintings adorned the walls below the red velvet drapes, and everything was lit by the dreary glow of oil lamps. A half-full bottle of wine sat on the table, and Beatrice Pettifogger filled an empty glass for Battersby.

"Good afternoon," said Battersby, sitting himself down in a leather armchair. "I think it's safe to say that all is well in Old Town this fine day!"

Lovelock received the mousebox and placed it on the table. His thin pale hands were shaking with excitement.

"These are the Golden Mice?"

"Indeed, Isiah. . . ."

A glint of light in his eyes, Lovelock unlatched the lid and raised it effortlessly. The radiant glow of the Golden Mice gushed out, bathing his cold face with luxurious yellow light.

"You have given me the greatest gift, Alexander — and a wonderful prize for the people of Old Town. I don't believe there is any way I can repay you."

"Honestly, Isiah, it proved easier than even I could have hoped," said Battersby, flushed from the wine.

"And Mousebeard?" asked Lovelock wryly. "How is he coping?"

"He's safely locked up in Dire Street Prison, under

the watchful eye of the Old Town Guard. He seems most unwell though, ever since we reached Old Town."

"I expected as much," said Lovelock, his eyes returning to the Golden Mice.

"You did?" asked Lady Pettifogger.

Lovelock paused slightly. "He's just trying to make people feel sorry for his plight. He'll make the scaffold for dawn tomorrow, though?"

"I've given the governor the duty of making sure of it . . . ," replied Battersby. "And the mice in his beard will be delivered to us in due course, too."

"Excellent," replied Lovelock. "But it really would be a travesty if he died before he had the chance to swing."

"I couldn't agree more. We even have that idiot Drewshank in irons too. It seems the pirate took kindly to him," said Battersby.

"What will happen to Devlin?" asked Lady Pettifogger with a slight catch in her throat. She looked genuinely concerned and clutched her hands together. Battersby shook his head.

"Your affection for him is very sweet," said Battersby slowly.

"You can't start worrying about that privateer," said Lovelock. "I'm surprised he made it this far! His fate's sealed. Besides, by now he knows too much about our plans. I'm certain Mousebeard would have informed him of the Golden Mice."

Battersby agreed.

"He'll take the drop with Mousebeard," he said. "I'm afraid he's only getting what he deserves."

"I suppose you're right," said Lady Pettifogger quietly, continuing to grip her hands tightly together.

"We even have another vile character called Scragneck to hang too," said Battersby, changing the subject, "along with at least twenty other pirates."

"It'll be quite a show tomorrow morning then!" added Lovelock, his face warming slightly at the thought. "It will be a major celebration. We need to see to it that posters and newspapers are distributed around town announcing Mousebeard's imminent execution. Can you deal with that, Beatrice?"

"Of course," she said, "but we should announce the rescue of the Golden Mice at the same time. We are sure to face some pressure from the Mousehunting

Federation, and most likely the Illyrians, in time, will demand their return. But if we declare that we have them safe, we should buy ourselves enough weeks to start breeding them."

"My feelings exactly," said Lovelock.

He sat quietly for a moment, and then called out for his butler, who promptly arrived at the door. Lovelock was looking almost longingly at the Golden Mice before him, and ran a finger along one of the shimmering coats, before reluctantly closing the mousebox.

"We shall be inviting the Old Town Guard to station a post within my mansion. In the meantime, can you take these mice to the Mousery and tell that young mousekeeper it will be more than his life's worth if he damages them in any way. Don't let any strangers in either. We have to be absolutely secure — even more so than usual."

Lovelock lifted up the mousebox, clutching it for a few more seconds before dropping it into the butler's hands.

"Yes, sir," said the butler. "Very good."

As he was leaving the room, Lovelock called him back.

"Can you also do something else for me . . . ," he said. "I'm worried about Mousebeard's health. Can you head to Dire Street Prison at some point this evening and report back to me on his condition. I'm sure you'd appreciate the air."

"V-very good, sir," stuttered the butler. Just hearing the name of the prison was enough to chill the soul.

The Methuselah Mouse

A MOUSE SO RARE THAT IT IS OFTEN CONSIDERED TO BE A MYTHICAL *creature, the Methuselah Mouse is thought to be the longest living of all mice. The only evidence of its existence is the priceless specimen kept in the museum of Old Town's Mousetrading Hall, although its color has faded and its ears are slightly worn with age. Unfortunately this creature passed away seventy-two years ago and is now stuffed and residing in a glass cabinet. Because of this Methuselah Mouse, we can say for sure that it is a relatively hairless creature, with wizened whiskers and a very slight build, but an understanding of its habits and characteristics is lost to us now.*

On that note, however, there is one person alive who saw this mouse while it was still in the land of the living, but unfortunately he has declined to speak to the Almanac for fear of being inundated by aspiring young mousehunters.

MOUSING NOTES
We can only guess at how the Methuselah Mouse would live its life, but scientists and breeders alike believe it would prefer peace and quiet to a hectic mousery.

A Secret Past

EMILINE WAS SITTING AT THE BARRED WINDOW OF THE Dung Mouse pen, attempting to identify the different calls of the nocturnal mice that were ringing out over Giant Island. The hours had passed slowly since the pirates had left, and life with the Dung Mice had become worse than tiresome. The smell was unbearable, as was the thirst and hunger of living without supplies.

"What was that one?" asked Scratcher, responding to a weird *ecky-ecky* sound.

"Could be a Bilge Mouse?" she said, peering into the darkness.

"A Silurian or a Congurese?" quipped Scratcher.

Emiline shrugged. "I don't know! How can you tell?"

"They like different types of bilge to lie in," said Scratcher. "All depends on what part of the world they come from."

"Oh, of course . . ."

Emiline had never cared much for Bilge Mice, and for once in her life she hadn't felt it necessary to learn all there was to know about them.

As another mouse call rang out, something caught her attention in the dark jungle. Two faint flickering blue lights were hovering a few hundred meters from the mouse pen. They seemed to be nearing, and with them came a sound not unlike the creaking of metal joints.

Scratcher soon realized Emiline had seen something and joined her.

"Look at the lights," she said.

"They don't look human," he added, tapping Fenwick to get his attention. Before long every prisoner was staring at the lights as they approached.

"Are they some sort of flying Night-light Mice?" asked Scratcher.

The noise grew louder, and the lights intensified.

"They're coming toward us," whispered Emiline as the two lights jumped a little and stopped dead a few meters in front of them. They shone right into the mouse pen.

"And looking at us," said Scratcher.

"Hello!" shouted Fenwick. "Who's that?"

The lights dimmed a little and then a flare sparked up to their side, illuminating the strange creature. It was holding the flare in a pincerlike hand, and the glow shimmered over its bulging metallic body.

"Who is it?" asked Emiline. "What are you?" she shouted.

Suddenly the creature jerked backward and dropped the flare. Its beaming eyes looked downward, and then twisted sideways before tilting upward into the air and vanishing. The flare then moved again, lighting the creature once more. It was a face that everyone recognized.

"Algernon!" cheered Emiline and Scratcher excitedly. Behind him followed Chervil and a procession of the ship's mice that had been hiding since the arrival on Giant Island.

"Emiline? What are you doing in there?" he exclaimed. Algernon stomped forward and peered into the mouse pen. His suit was a metal full-body diving apparatus, with buttons and dials twinkling all over. The helmet now removed, his small face was bathed in the blue light issuing from a line of bulbs around his neck.

"We've been locked in," she said. "Can you get us out?"

Algernon lifted the right arm of his suit to reveal a small drill on its end. It started to spin noisily, and in a few seconds he'd drilled right through the lock. With a heavy push the door swung open, and all the sailors cheered a cry of relief.

"How come you're here, Algernon?" asked Scratcher, rushing to freedom.

Algernon's face screwed up into a tiny ball.

"Ooh, you all stink!" he said, trying not to breathe. "I came to find Mousebeard, but everywhere's deserted! What's going on?"

"You came to find Mousebeard?"

"Yes, yes, it's a long story. I'll explain later, but where has he gone to?"

"The pirates have left and they've taken Drewshank and the Golden Mice."

Algernon looked puzzled. All the prisoners had now

escaped the pen and were standing before him, relishing the fresh but still stinky air.

"You know about the mice?" He stopped and thought for a moment. "Ah, I suppose it's a good thing. . . . But why have they taken Drewshank? What would Mousebeard want with him?"

"No, that's not all!" exclaimed Emiline. "As they were taking Drewshank I heard one of the pirates say that they were handing Mousebeard over to the navy!"

Algernon didn't understand. "What do you mean?" he asked.

"They're handing Mousebeard over to the navy along with Drewshank and the mice in return for a ransom and their safety."

"But that can't be so. No, that can't be." Algernon was clearly shocked.

"We have to get them back!"

"But how?" asked Fenwick. "We've no way off the island."

"Well, I have a way," said Algernon, "but most of you will have to stay here. I only have room for a couple of short people."

"Short people?" exclaimed Emiline and Scratcher together.

"Yes! I have a small submarine, and we have no time to lose. Are you two coming?"

Algernon was looking at the two mousekeepers.

"A submarine?" said Fenwick.

"Yes! How else do you think I got here? But I have to leave right away — well, as soon as you two have had a bit of a wash. . . ."

Algernon walked off as fast as his suit would let him.

"Are you coming?" he shouted once more to a bewildered Emiline and Scratcher.

"But, Algernon!" shouted Fenwick, who chased after him. "You'll need more than these mousekeepers to get our captain back."

Algernon turned to Fenwick, his dials flashing urgently.

"Sir, I appreciate your concern, but there's just no space for you, Mousebeard, *and* Drewshank, should we be successful. You'll be safest here. There's food in the fortress, which will keep you alive. Please understand. . . ."

"You're right," said Fenwick reluctantly, and he

clasped Emiline and Scratcher in each of his arms. Portly jumped from his shoulder to Emiline's, and swiftly disappeared under her hair.

"So then, the captain's fate rests in your hands. I ain't happy, but that can't be helped. You're no use to any of us, nor the captain, if you're dead, so make sure you stay alive. I don't fancy living off Dung Mouse meat for the rest of my days. . . ."

Emiline jumped up and hugged the man. She smiled as broadly as she could and then ran off after Algernon.

"We'll get Captain Drewshank back, Mr. Fenwick. I promise!" she shouted, "and then we'll come back for you!"

Fenwick watched them disappear into the darkness before heading off with the rest of the crew. Each man picked up his mouse on the way and gave Chervil a rough stroke.

"There's bound to be some food 'ere somewhere, men," he said, grateful to be away from the Dung Mice. "I'm starving."

❧ ✳ ☙

The submarine powered swiftly through the underwater tunnels out of Giant Island like a copper bullet. The small window afforded little view to Emiline, but the tiny particles that zoomed by reminded her of sailing through a snowstorm. She moved away from the cockpit and sat down on the floor with Scratcher. The submarine was so small that that there was just the pilot's chair to sit on, and the curved hull gave only a minimal amount of leg room when one was resting on the floor.

Portly emerged from under Emiline's hair and ran over to the dashboard. Three of Algernon's Boffin Mice were sitting staring out of the window, and Portly promptly introduced himself.

"What a thing to happen," muttered Algernon. "If only I'd found out about this earlier."

His hand gripped the control stick tightly, and he steered the sub through the twisting, water-filled tunnels under the volcano with great skill.

"I should probably have been more honest with you both when we first met . . . ," he added.

"I still don't understand," said Scratcher. "Why did you come to the island to find Mousebeard?"

"Ah yes," replied Algernon, "Mousebeard . . . oh, hang on!"

Suddenly the submarine sped up, and the tunnel burst out into the sea. Algernon tapped a button and a small panel lit up; he looked quickly at a tatty chart pinned to the wall and made a few calculations. Once they were through Winter Vale it would be plain sailing to Old Town.

"Hold tight," he said, before pulling back on a gear stick. The submarine shook violently and zoomed off even faster. He pressed a number of buttons and a blue light flicked on.

"Right then," he announced, swiveling his chair so that he faced his passengers.

"Are you not going to drive?" asked Scratcher, worriedly.

"Oh I have autopilot, of course!" he replied, pointing to a dial that clicked and jerked every second. "My submarine has done this journey so many times I think it knows exactly where it's going by now. But still, it's time for some details. . . ."

Emiline and Scratcher sat upright excitedly.

"Mousebeard . . ."

"I've been helping Mousebeard for a long time now . . . ," said Algernon.

"You?" Emiline said, with shock. "Why would you work for a murdering pirate like him? Algernon?"

Scratcher frowned and crossed his arms. "People died on the *Flying Fox* because of him. We're lucky to be alive. . . ."

Algernon raised his hand to calm them and looked grave. "I'm not saying I support everything Mousebeard does — there are things about him I will never know or understand," he said regretfully. "But things aren't as everyone in Old Town and Hamlyn would have you believe. Mousebeard and I go back a very long way — way before he was a pirate."

"But you're an innkeeper!" said Scratcher.

"An innkeeper and an inventor — might I remind you! How do you think Mousebeard came across such a wonderful ship? Or a fog machine, or even learned how to harness the power of Dung Mice?"

"The fog!" exclaimed Scratcher and Emiline.

"Yes, just a simple little machine."

"But what was the wailing? Was that your doing too?" asked Emiline.

"Oh no. Mousebeard is terribly good at training mice. I think you'll find that was the sound of his Wailing Spirit Mice that live on the masts of his ship. They do make quite a racket, though. Blooming nuisance much of the time!"

He took his hat off and breathed into his goggles before continuing.

"And who better to keep a pirate informed of the goings-on in the sailing and mousing world than an innkeeper, anyway?" he said. "Drunk people say an awful lot of things that should remain secret!"

"But how do you know him?" asked Emiline.

"From the Old Rodents' Academy — it's a very long time ago now, as you can imagine. We were mousers of the first order, winning awards and trophies the world over for mice we found."

"The photo in your workshop!" said Emiline excitedly. "But that was Isiah Lovelock in that picture!"

"Ah! Yes, yes. Well remembered! That really was a special Triplehorn Mouse I caught . . . ," he said dreamily.

"So the other one was Mousebeard?" said Scratcher.

"Precisely. Isiah Lovelock, Jonathan Harworth, and Algernon Mountjack: Team Mousing Trophy winners three times in a row. Of course, Isiah took all those trophies after our friendship ended, the cad. He always was a determined so-and-so. . . ."

"But what went wrong?" asked Emiline.

"I don't know the precise details, but it happened on a mousehunting voyage years ago."

"Were you there?" she asked.

Algernon had completely forgotten about his goggles. He breathed into them once more and wiped them clean.

"Oh yes . . . that trip to Stormcloud Island will stay with me forever."

"Well, what happened?" pleaded Scratcher.

"Through our professor at the Academy, we'd heard that an old lady who lived on Stormcloud Island owned a Methuselah Mouse. As you probably know, these creatures are so rare that you have more chance of spitting a grape seed to the moon than finding one. And so Isiah, being the rich and determined young man he was, decided to visit the island in order to persuade the owner to let him buy the mouse. It took four weeks to sail there, and when we reached the island it certainly lived up to its name. We didn't see the sun once, for the whole island was shrouded in thunderclouds.

"We sailed round it many times looking for signs of habitation, and found there was only one building. It was built of huge white stone blocks and perched gloomily, and a little precariously, atop a rocky hill. I reluctantly remained in the boat while they went off — the storms were so strong that we feared it might break its moorings. I wish I'd gone with them, for all I know is that while they were there some horrible deed took place that turned them against one another. I watched Jonathan walk back alone down the rocky outcrops and winding paths, and I could see he was in agonizing pain. He clutched his chest and clambered weakly onto the boat.

"'For as long as we live, Isiah is no friend of ours,' he growled, his eyes pale and distant. He picked up an oar and pushed us out into the sea. I tried to stop him, but he was so much stronger than me that I couldn't fight against it. When I turned back to the island I saw the silhouette of Isiah on the hilltop. He just stood there silently, like a rock alone in the wilderness.

"The moment our boat had left the shore, Jonathan's pain subsided, and he breathed normally again. Despite my protestations, he wouldn't return for Isiah, and he defiantly refused to explain anything. When we returned to Old Rodents', Jonathan fell ill again. Unbearable chest pains struck him down, and he weakened hour by hour. I endeavored to take him across the sea to one of the best hospitals I knew of and, unbelievably, while we were on the boat his pain eased. We realized there and then that solid ground had become poisonous to him. Anytime he tried to set foot on land he was stricken with that same intense pain. . . ."

"A curse?" whispered Scratcher, shuffling his legs in the excitement.

"Of the worst kind," replied Algernon. "From that day on he turned away from all we knew and sailed the Seventeen Seas. I soon lost track of him completely, and it was only ten years ago that I received word of the course his life had taken. It came as quite a surprise to learn he was the pirate Mousebeard. He told me of

Isiah's dealings, his horrendous Mouse Trading Centers and horrifying breeding programs. The man was single-handedly turning mice into a commodity; sucking them dry for everything they're worth. Isiah had become everything we used to rally against at the Academy."

"But what about *The Mousehunter's Almanac?*" asked Emiline. "That's done more for the welfare of mice than anything."

"True," replied Algernon, "but it also feeds the desire for collecting mice. Isiah's a canny old soul — he knows what he's doing all right. Think of the Wide-eyed Sand Mouse that's amazing at catching sand fleas — up until a few years ago they were as rare as blue moons, but now you can find them in every Trading Center. And how many are left in the wild? None. All captured and living in people's collections to keep mites and other creepy-crawlies at bay. Mousebeard believes, as do I, in fiercely protecting the Mousetrading Regulations."

"There are so many to remember, though," said Emiline.

"But of course there are! The history books tell us exactly what it was like without them: mousehunters would remove whole populations from lands with little thought; unscrupulous collectors would breed fancy mice without any knowledge of what they were doing; and the conditions that mice were kept in were often appalling. It was a shocking state of affairs."

"Old Town has a lot to answer for," said Emiline sadly.

"It's true, much of its wealth did originally stem from the exploitation of mice, although it did create the first laws governing mouse protection, don't forget. Sometimes good things can happen if the people ask for it. However, it would seem that our friend Isiah Lovelock is attempting to benefit from our furry friends once more. And that's exactly why Mousebeard and I must continue to fight back."

"So Mousebeard became a pirate because of Lovelock?" asked Scratcher.

"It was a good part of it. When you can't set foot on land, the life of a pirate is all there is, especially if you seek to trouble Lovelock. Jonathan was never a bad man, though he could always scare you with a glance. But years at sea, in exile, have done strange things to him.

He's the fiercest protector of mice I've ever come across. Men like Lovelock drive him wild. Through all these years, despite what you may have read, Mousebeard's only ever sought revenge against him. Every ship he sank, every mouse he captured, all had something to do with Isiah's underhanded dealings, and he's mostly tried not to kill. There's a lot more to that old rogue Lovelock than most people know — and he's done a good job of spreading lies about Jonathan. . . . Although Jonathan himself hasn't helped his image in any way."

Emiline was transfixed. She would never have guessed that Isiah had once been a friend of Mousebeard. No wonder he kept it secret, she thought.

"So where are we going now?" asked Scratcher.

"To Old Town," said Algernon.

"We're going home?" exclaimed Emiline.

"That's where they'll be taking Drewshank and Mousebeard. I still have one acquaintance there that might be able to help us. I just hope that we can get to him in time."

⇒ ✷ ⇐

Almost a week after leaving Giant Island, the submarine surfaced just a few hundred meters from Old Town harbor, with only a few frothing bubbles announcing its arrival. They'd waited for nightfall so as not to alert any keen-eyed soldiers, but they were desperate to get on with the task in hand.

With the moonlight rippling across the swelling waves, the hatch flipped open and Emiline sneaked a look out toward the wall of warships blocking the docks.

"Is it as we expected?" asked Algernon quietly.

"Ships everywhere," she replied. "We'll have to carry on to the river estuary. They'll have ships there no doubt, but we'll just have to go under them, then sneak up the river into the city."

With a firm tug the hatch closed once more and the sub sank quietly to the seabed. It moved off gently and traveled in amongst the reeds and shoals of fish that filled the bottom of the sea.

Using the dim front lights of the sub, Algernon traced the edge of the docks and eventually came to the river. Once again, navy hulls littered the underwater path inland, obliging Algernon to navigate with extreme care around them. He calmly motored on, keeping steady as the river narrowed and grew shallower. The water was by now a horrible murky brown, full of dirt and the sort of rubbish you'd normally find in a junk shop.

At the point where he could proceed no farther due to the flood defenses snaking up from the riverbed, he drew alongside the bank and eased the submarine to the surface. Once again, Emiline opened the hatch and peered out carefully.

The first thing that struck her was the darkness. Short jetties poked out into the river, boats, and lobster traps tied to their sides. Rickety, toppling buildings rose up only a short distance from where they were, blocking out all the night-time sky. It felt like an age since she'd run away from Lovelock's mansion, and all the grim reality of the city returned to her like a stray dog.

Her eyes wandered down the narrow path that followed the river until she saw a streetlight flickering at the water's edge. It was the lamp at Pirate's Wharf, and she could see men constructing a large wooden platform out into the river. The scaffold was built on a platform that fully crossed the river, giving full view to the towns-people that lived on both sides.

Suddenly Emiline felt a pull on her trouser leg.

"Where are we?" whispered Scratcher.

"We're safe for the moment," she whispered, "just a few minutes upstream of Pirate's Wharf."

Algernon heard Emiline's words and rose from his seat. He called for them both to sit down, and as they appeared he unlocked a cabinet.

"Now, I doubt," he said seriously, "that either of you ever had any intention of partaking in this sort of trouble, but things often turn out how you least expect them. I just need to ask you if you're willing to risk everything to rescue not only your captain, but Mousebeard too."

"Do you believe him?" asked Scratcher to Emiline, nervously.

"Of course," said Emiline. "I've never really taken to Lovelock anyway."

Scratcher didn't feel quite so sure, but his friend was usually right.

"All right then," he said shakily.

"You, Emiline?" asked Algernon.

"I'm still not sure how I feel about Mousebeard . . . but for your sake, I'll help."

Algernon looked at them for a second and then withdrew a wooden box from the cabinet and passed it to Scratcher.

"This is the only weapon I have!" he said. "I'm afraid it's the best I have here, as I had to leave Hamlyn in something of a rush."

Scratcher opened the box and found a beautiful ornate knife, which Emiline immediately recognized.

"But that's just like the knife Mr. Spires gave me!" she said.

"Horatio gave you his Mothma Mousebone knife?" said a puzzled Algernon.

"Horatio?" exclaimed Emiline. "Are we both talking about Mr. Spires here? Lovelock's butler?"

"But of course! Why else do you think I brought you along? Only someone with insider knowledge could get into Lovelock's mansion!" replied Algernon.

"But Mr. Spires is so stuffy and boring!" said Emiline, struggling to come to terms with things. "Is Mr. Spires really your friend that we've come to see?"

"He most certainly is. . . ."

"But he told me to use it if I ever came face to face with Mousebeard. I just didn't get the chance before the pirates took it off me."

"Ah!" said Algernon. "Now that makes sense. Mr. Spires was trying to look after you."

"He did try to stop me from going on the voyage," added Emiline.

"He's a clever sort is Horatio, and a very good judge of character. If Mousebeard had seen you with that knife he would have wanted to know exactly where you got it from. There are only four like it in the world. You would have been safe."

"So is Mr. Spires Mousebeard's spy?" asked Emiline.

"Most definitely, and a very good one. Why else would I know to persuade Devlin Drewshank to bring his injured mousekeeper to my inn? I had to find out as much as I could about the course of his mission. As soon as I heard Lord Battersby was involved though, I knew something worse was afoot, but by that time it was too late to notify Mousebeard."

Algernon started to scratch the stubble forming on his chin. He would never have made a decent pirate as his beard was patchy at best, but a few weeks of living in a submarine brings out all sorts of hidden growths.

"We have to get to Horatio as soon as possible," he said. "He'll know exactly what's going on."

"There are all sorts of ways into Lovelock's mansion," replied Emiline. "Getting to Mr. Spires will be easy."

"Then what are we waiting for?" said Scratcher, desperate to add something to the conversation.

"Right then," said Algernon. "You two head for the mansion, and I'll wait on the river bed. When you return, get my attention by throwing three stones into the water so that they hit the sub. When I hear them, I'll rise to the surface."

"You're on," replied Scratcher.

"We'll try not to be longer than a few hours," said Emiline.

"Excellent!" he replied. "Just enough time for a short think and a long nap."

The Comet Mouse

THE FASTEST LAND-BASED MOUSE IN EXISTENCE: BLINK AND YOU'LL MISS IT. *With slick, short white fur, Comet Mice are regarded as a particularly stylish breed, and are a favorite with fancy-mouse breeders. These mice are something of a prize among collectors, mainly due to their incredible speed and agility, which make them very hard to catch. In fact, these mice are relative newcomers to the scene: the first known Comet Mouse was brought to Old Town by Guidolfo Jones, an extremely talented mousehunter, nearly sixty years ago. Up until that point they were thought to be flights of fancy and had a near mythical status among collectors.*

MOUSING NOTES

A large cage is essential. The Comet Mouse also requires a good water supply to quench its thirst, and comfortable bedding to soothe its weary legs and restore its energy.

The Old Town Spy

EMILINE DRAGGED SCRATCHER BY THE HAND PAST Pirate's Wharf. Soldiers were everywhere; some were hammering and banging nails into the wooden execution platform, others were starting work on tall structures at every edge of the wharf. When Old Town was set to hold an execution, the townspeople were hungry for the best view, and grandstands were built up for paying guests.

Unusually for Old Town, the night was free of mist or fog. Stones were visible in walls, faces could be seen on passers-by, and the unearthly glow that regularly surrounded the streetlamps had vanished. The mousekeepers turned left at the wharf, past Mr. Droob's hut, and made their way up a road of twisting townhouses.

Scratcher caught sight of a fresh poster nailed to a billboard and halted in his tracks.

"Emiline," he said, "look!"

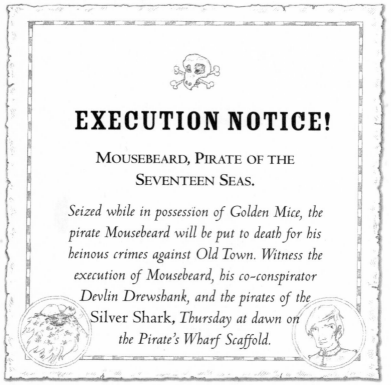

EXECUTION NOTICE!

MOUSEBEARD, PIRATE OF THE SEVENTEEN SEAS.

Seized while in possession of Golden Mice, the pirate Mousebeard will be put to death for his heinous crimes against Old Town. Witness the execution of Mousebeard, his co-conspirator Devlin Drewshank, and the pirates of the Silver Shark, Thursday at dawn on the Pirate's Wharf Scaffold.

"Co-conspirator Devlin Drewshank?" whispered Emiline, dumbfounded.

"Thursday at dawn?" added Scratcher. "That's to-morrow!"

"We've got to run!"

Emiline grabbed Scratcher's arm once more and charged off up the street. When they reached Grand-view, Emiline slowed down. She could see Lovelock's mansion in the distance, but something was going on in front. There were soldiers everywhere.

"Why are there soldiers?" she said. "We're never going to get through them!"

They stepped into a shadow beside one of the im-mense buidings lining the road, and Emiline tried hard to think of what to do. While they stood there a car-riage came traveling up the road with two small lamps at its front. Led by two black stallions, it was decked out in the colors of Old Town. It stopped outside Love-lock's mansion, and Mr. Gumpino, the city's potbellied mayor, leisurely stepped down, his numerous golden chains catching the lamplight. Emiline saw the butler come out of the building and take in the mayor, who was followed by three assistants.

"There's Mr. Spires," she said. "At least he's there!"

"Why don't I distract the soldiers?" said Scratcher, "Maybe get them to run after me. Would that help?"

"If I could get around to the Messenger Mice pens behind the mansion, I should be able to find a way in."

Scratcher nodded and smiled. "That's our plan then. You ready?"

"I'm ready," replied Emiline. "But where are we going to meet up? Back at the submarine?"

"If we don't meet up before, then the sub it is!" said Scratcher, and with that he took off, tailed closely by Emiline.

Scratcher charged up the hill as though he were chasing after a Comet Mouse. He stayed to the path, running in and out of shadows. Because of the noise of his footsteps, the soldiers had seen him and were watching him closely. They withdrew their swords and formed a wall. Scratcher ducked down awkwardly and picked up a handful of the stones off the road. The soldiers stamped their feet, called out to him to stop, but he slid to a halt and threw the stones right at them.

"Oi!" shouted one of the guards. "Come back 'ere, you blighter!"

The sight of four soldiers pelting after him gave him enough energy to run faster than he'd ever done before. He felt as though the wind were in his heels, and he closed his eyes, hoping for a good escape.

Emiline watched Scratcher disappear into the darkness. Two other soldiers ran after him, and the rest muttered to each other, their attention on the road diverted. Emiline thought fast. She slipped through the shadows and crept down beside Lovelock's mansion. Right in front of her was the Messenger Mouse pen. The only light around was that emanating from the stairwell winding up inside the house, but Emiline used it as well as she could to search for an unlocked window.

She scaled the pen and dropped down on the other side. A dim light shone out from the back of the mansion, and Emiline shuffled carefully around to its side. She found a smashed window; its glass was broken into daggerlike shards jutting up like shark's teeth.

Emiline carefully climbed in and dropped to the floor. The room was lit up by a glow from the corridor beyond, and she could see wet muddy footprints leading from the window. She wasn't the first to break in that night.

She headed toward the corridor and eased the door open further. The way was clear, and the wall lamps guided her out and up into the main hallway. Noises and shuffling feet could be heard moving around in the direction of the kitchens, and Emiline quickly hid in the unlit reception room. She waited and waited, and eventually two people came walking past. One of the voices was Mr. Spires, and Emiline's heart skipped a beat.

The voices soon joined the sound of footsteps as they climbed the stairs, and Emiline darted from her hideout to follow them. It was a very strange feeling to have returned to her old home. Her views on all its inhabitants had changed so much since she left.

She tiptoed up the stairs, aware of each little noise around her. The shadow of Mr. Spires trailed on the wall a few floors above and came to a halt on the floor with Lovelock's office. Emiline hoped that he would turn round and return, but he didn't. He entered the room along with the other person, and Emiline's hope of a fast exit quickly faded. The only option left to her was to return to the old haunt of her secret passageway, and find out what was happening inside.

"We've had a break-in, sir," said the soldier. "We got distracted by some boy, and it must have been then that someone sneaked round the back."

Lovelock stood up angrily.

"Are the mice safe?"

"Yes, sir!" replied the soldier. "And I've ordered a complete search of the mansion from the ground up. Whoever's here won't get very far."

"This is not good news, Spires!" snapped Lovelock.

It was obvious that the Mayor, whose balding head was shining brightly, was none too impressed either. The Mayor looked an odd sort of man: nearing old age, his enormous body told of a life of opulence and overindulgence, yet his balding, shiny forehead and pudgy, rosy face made him look like a baby. He sat with his hands crossed over his fat waist, tutting at everything the soldier said.

"I've asked for a guard to be placed outside your office, sir, just to be safe," added the butler.

"Excellent, Spires. At least there's someone here whom I can trust."

From the inside of the passage Emiline smiled. She would never have guessed that Mr. Spires was a spy, but now it made perfect sense. She remembered all the messages he used to send out, and how they must have been going to Algernon at Hamlyn.

Suddenly Battersby spoke up.

"Isiah, we do know that there is still one of Mousebeard's accomplices in Old Town. Despite our best efforts to capture the innkeeper in Hamlyn, we know he was receiving word from here."

"Well then, butler, you'd better make it *several* guards," declared the Mayor.

"Yes, sir!" said Spires, who then continued, "I shall be gone for a while to the prison upon your orders, Mr. Lovelock. Do you wish me to wait around?"

"No, Spires. That won't be necessary. I have Lord Battersby here."

"Very good, sir," replied the butler, and he promptly left the room.

Emiline rushed out of hiding. The corridor opened out and she could see Spires making his way down the stairs. She hurried down each step, and eventually, three floors down, she quietly called out.

"Mr. Spires!"

The butler stopped dead in his tracks and turned around. Astonishment spread all over his face. Then he frowned.

"Emiline!" he said frustratedly.

He grabbed her by the arm and pushed her against the wall into shadow.

"What are you doing here? It's not safe!" he whispered.

"I'm here with Algernon. We need to talk."

"Algernon?"

"He's told me all about you. We're here to save Drewshank and Mousebeard. We need your help!"

The butler's eyes darted up the stairwell as if he'd heard something.

"Fine, but we have to go elsewhere. Where is Algernon?"

"Along the river past Pirate's Wharf."

"Right then," he said, touching his brow. "Meet me at Pirate's Wharf in twenty minutes. Can you manage that?"

Emiline nodded.

"Excellent," said Spires, "I'd like to be sure you escape, but my hands are tied, Emiline. Keep safe. . . ."

The butler hurried downstairs without further ado.

Doors started to bang shut on the lower floors, and Emiline peered over the staircase to see soldiers milling about, checking every room. She found herself not knowing what to do. She glanced around, looking for a way out. Her only chance would be through a window, and she opened the first she saw.

She climbed up onto the stone windowsill and saw the long drop below. There was a drainpipe running all the way down a short way off, and when she heard the soldiers inside working their way up the stairs, she knew there was no other option. Emiline stretched out and caught hold of the metal pipe with one hand, and with the other she pulled the window closed. With a deep breath she leaped out and secured herself with both her hands and feet. Then, after quickly checking the route down, she started to slide: at first gracefully, but then as fast as she could manage safely. It was simply important to make it to the ground in one piece.

Emiline jumped the final few feet and landed safely. She was at the side of the mansion, and could see soldiers lined up at the roadside. Everything was still and surprisingly peaceful. She took a few steps forward, stopped to catch her breath, and then suddenly felt a heavy weight smash into her back.

She fell to the floor and was immediately jumped upon, a dagger positioned at her neck. The pain in her back was intense, and her arm throbbed from the fall.

"Always in my way," said Miserley, kneeling on her spine. "You had to come barging in here, didn't you, Blonde!"

"It's you!" said Emiline. "Why are you here?"

"That would be none of your business," said Miserley.

"It's the mice, isn't it?"

"What?"

"The Golden Mice! You came to get the Golden Mice back!"

Miserley pressed down harder with her knee. Emiline struggled to breathe.

"Let me go," implored Emiline. "I have to go."

"Why should I do what you ask, Blonde?"

Miserley grabbed Emiline's arm, bent it behind her back, and lifted her up.

"What do you want?" pleaded Emiline, feeling Miserley's breath at the side of her face.

"You're going to get those mice for me. . . ."

"I'm what?"

"Like you said, I've come to get the Golden Mice, but I had to get away when the soldiers came. And obviously, now that you're here you can do it for me."

Miserley saw Emiline's hair twitch, shoved her hand in, and grabbed Portly.

"And if you don't," she said, holding the mouse aloft, "your mouse is going to lose some limbs, starting with the tail." Pulling her dagger out, Miserley grabbed the mouse's tail, holding the knife to it as if she were about to peel an apple.

"No!" cried Emiline. Miserley shoved her away roughly and stood holding Portly by the tip of his tail, his body squirming. Mice hate being held by their tails, and Portly squeaked with pain. Weazle sat up on Miserley's shoulder, gleefully watching the events unfold.

"Put him down! He hasn't done anything," said Emiline angrily.

"Aw, poor little Blonde, this upset you? I'll tell you what, you can have him back once you go inside and get those mice."

"It's teeming with soldiers; there's no way I could get them . . . ," whispered Emiline urgently.

"Save it, Blonde, this is getting boring," said Miserley, pushing her dagger against Portly's tail, whose ears shot back against his body.

Emiline tightened her fists.

"Oi! You!" shouted a soldier from a window. "Right, men! Here they are!"

Miserley's eyes flicked from left to right. She opened the mousebox that hung at her belt and threw Portly inside.

"Looks like we'll have to postpone our little girly chat for now. This isn't the end, Blonde. Mark my words!" Emiline watched as Miserley turned and charged off through the undergrowth.

"Come back!" she said desperately. She could hear

soldiers shouting and doors banging. There was nothing else to do — she had to run.

⇒ ❋ ⇐

Emiline ran down the cobbled streets and caught her breath in a disused doorway not far from Pirate's Wharf. Portly was gone, and she'd only just avoided the soldiers at Lovelock's mansion. Her heart was torn in two — she knew she had to meet the butler, but all she really wanted was to rescue her mouse.

She let out a long sigh, and looked up and down the street. The butler's carriage sailed past, bumping up and down as each stone rocked its wheels.

"Come on," she said, lifting herself. Emiline continued down the street, hanging close to the sides of buildings. She reached the wharf and saw the carriage stop beside Mr. Droob's hut, which was now sitting under the beginnings of one of the viewing stands, with woodworkers crawling over it. Spires called out something about checking that all was good with the scaffold, and then stepped carefully to the ground.

The butler was fully wrapped in a black cloak, and he

walked over to the soldiers, who greeted him warily. Normally it would take three days' work to put up such a giant scaffold, but they'd been given such a small amount of time that double the number of troops had been put on the job. After a close inspection, the butler was assured that the execution platform was almost finished, with six oiled-up and working trapdoors nearing completion and ready for the condemned.

Emiline left her cover but kept to the shadows and navigated the wharf to the riverside. Spires was glancing around himself and eventually caught sight of Emiline. He casually made his leave with the soldiers and strode off along the water's edge. Within a short time he was covered by shadow, having stepped out of the reach of any oil lamp, and Emiline approached.

"Mr. Spires," she said, looking around uneasily, "follow me."

Emiline led him to the river path. She looked along the river, ready to point out where Algernon's submarine would be, but there was no way to get to it. Marching slowly toward them, partly concealed by the darkness, was a battalion of soldiers. Emiline dropped her hand.

"I have to hurry, as I'm certain you appreciate," said the butler, anxiously.

"I know," she replied, "but look!"

"Damn," he muttered, spotting the men. "Old Town is crawling with soldiers!"

The soldiers' footsteps were coming closer, and eventually the group of men halted only meters in front.

The leading soldier pushed his hat up and eyed them suspiciously.

"Your papers!" he ordered, as the other troops massed behind.

"Yes, sir, certainly," replied Spires. He withdrew a small piece of paper from his suit pocket, which outlined his name and position. As soon as the soldier saw the name Isiah Lovelock, he waved and apologized for the inconvenience. He then looked at Emiline, noticing how dirty her clothes were.

"And this is his mousekeeper," said the butler promptly. Emiline tried to smile.

The soldier waited a few moments, looking closely at her face, but then looked back to Spires.

"Right you are, sir!" he said gruffly. "Carry on, men!"

Emiline sighed with relief as the soldiers walked past, but as the last two men walked in front of her, Emiline gripped the butler's arm. Before she could cry out, Spires grabbed her, placing his hand over her mouth.

Walking behind the battalion, arms tied and joined to the soldiers in front by an iron chain, was Scratcher. His head hung low, and blood was dripping from a cut on his forehead. He struggled to walk, and didn't notice Emiline as he passed by.

"Scratcher," she muttered as the butler's hand lowered.

"Your friend?" asked Spires.

"Yes," she replied, tears welling in her eyes. She suddenly felt that she was on the brink of losing everything.

"We have even less time to lose now, then," he said bravely. "I did try and warn you about all this, Emiline. . . ."

"I know, I know. . . ."

The butler placed his hand on her shoulder kindly.

"Take me to Algernon, Emiline. We need to sort out this mess."

Emiline watched Scratcher walk out of view past Pirate's Wharf, and then she started to run.

"Quick, Mr. Spires," she said, heading off down the path.

She reached the spot where she'd left the submarine, and threw a handful of stones into the water. They both looked cautiously around, making sure the way was clear. Within seconds, bubbles were popping at the surface, and the submarine broke the water. With a *click* and a *whirr*, the circular door on its roof kicked back.

"Horatio!" exclaimed Algernon happily. "So good to see you! Come on in!"

The Miramus

A VERY UNUSUAL AND RATHER CREEPY MOUSE THAT'S RARELY SEEN IN THE wild. *The Miramus wanders the land until it finds a mouse it likes (never one of the same species, however) and then becomes its doppelgänger, mimicking its every movement and actions.*

Many mice go insane once they've been ensnared by a Miramus, and because of this it is seen as a harbinger of madness: "He's been spotted by the Miramus" is a phrase often said of someone who appears slightly unhinged.

MOUSING NOTES

Miramus have been kept by collectors, but never very successfully. Many a collector has lost prize species to the Miramus, despite their being caged at a great distance. It's not a banned mouse, but it's not one to be kept without proper supervision.

The Shadow of Pirate's Wharf

"I T'S LOOKING PRETTY GRIM," SAID SPIRES IN A FLASH, quashing his friend's enthusiasm. He clambered awkwardly into the small opening, with Emiline following. She pulled the hatch closed and the lock whirled and clicked shut.

"We're in a rather grave situation," continued Spires.

"They've got Scratcher and Portly," said Emiline, her voice breaking when she heard the words come from her mouth.

Algernon took off his glasses and sat down slowly. Spires was shocked.

"You didn't mention your mouse!" he said.

"Oh, my!" said Algernon. "This is worse than we could ever have thought possible."

"Mousebeard's mousekeeper attacked me," said Emiline. "She was after the Golden Mice."

"That girl is a bundle of trouble," he said angrily. "And where's she gone?"

"I've no idea . . . but there was no way I was going to give her the Golden Mice!"

"If she's after those creatures," said Spires, "the best chance she'll get will be at the execution tomorrow. They're going to be on display — shown to the crowds to let them know what an amazing thing Battersby's achieved."

"They are?" said Algernon. "Then we'll have to keep our eyes open. We'll have to do our best to make sure she doesn't get away. . . ."

Algernon whistled loudly, his mice rushed to the dashboard, and soon the submarine was sinking to the river floor.

"Oh, I've made such a mess of it all," said Spires, ducking in the cramped interior in a manner most unlike a butler. "They kept so much from me, Algernon. It was all that Battersby's doing. There was so much I didn't know about. And now Emiline's friend and mouse are involved too. . . ."

"These things happen, Horatio," said Algernon calmly. "Do you think he suspects you?"

"I think Battersby must have some doubts, but nothing to go on as yet. Besides, the past ten years will all have been for nothing if Jonathan dies tomorrow. What can we do about it though? My hands are tied."

"I've been thinking about this a lot, my friend. Can you break them out of the prison? With your connections?"

"Impossible," replied the butler. "I'm going to visit them now, but they'll be so heavily guarded. No inmate in the prison's two-hundred-year history has ever escaped, so I think it highly unlikely we would succeed anyway."

"I suppose we shall have to wait for the morning then," said Algernon.

"When they bring them out ready for the execution?" asked Spires.

"I think that will be the only opportunity. Just like it

will be the only chance to rescue our small friend Portly."

"But we have to rescue Scratcher too," pleaded Emiline.

"Has he been taken to Dire Street as well?" asked Algernon.

"I don't know," she said. "They were dragging him up the road as we came to see you."

Her eyes started to well up with tears as the words left her lips, and Spires tried to ease things. "I doubt there would be space for him in Dire Street, what with all the pirates. They'd probably take him to the barracks first for questioning anyway. They'd want to find out what he knows. I doubt he'll be caught up in all the events tomorrow."

"Oh, most definitely not," added Algernon.

"Well, what are we going to do then?" she said, desperately.

"I have an idea!" said Algernon, his eyes opening wide. He started to rummage about under his chair, and open assorted boxes and cases. "You mentioned you were going to visit them?"

"Isiah wants me to check on Mousebeard's health," said Spires. "I fear the curse has already taken him."

"Well, this could be our best and only chance to put our plans in place, Horatio."

"But I cannot be seen to set them free — it would ruin all our hard work," Spires argued.

"Oh no, no, nothing of the sort," replied Algernon, deep in thought. "I think we should utilize all that we have at our disposal. And I need a few things in particular. . . ."

⇒ ✳ ⇐

"So you say these Golden Mice could provide us with an unlimited supply of gold?" asked the Mayor, fidgeting slightly in his red velvet gown.

"If we can keep the authorities away from us for a few months — maybe while we slowly negotiate the mice's safe return to Illyria," replied Lovelock, watching a smile of approval from Old Town's leader, "then we should have a large enough base to maintain a sustainable supply of gold fur from. It can be spun into thread with the greatest of ease, and so there should be no trouble in concealing our plans."

"This is excellent news indeed, Lovelock."

The Mayor's cheeks grew rosier as the scale of what they'd achieved sank in.

"And with the capture of Mousebeard, there's little anyone would do to stop us."

"It is perfect," added Battersby.

The Mayor was greatly impressed.

"I hear tomorrow's execution will draw quite a crowd," he said. "News has spread fast, and I've been informed that people from towns the length and breadth of Midena are traveling as we speak to catch a glimpse of both the Golden Mice and Mousebeard before his death."

"And all this only serves to raise our standing in people's minds," added Lovelock.

"Brilliant, just brilliant. And tomorrow, I take it I shall receive you in the mayoral box?"

"As much as that would be an honor," said Lovelock, "I have specifically asked the guard who will be conducting the execution if I might have a minute to speak with the great Mousebeard himself before he dies. They have agreed, of course, and that means I will be on quite the wrong side of the wharf to enjoy your company."

The Mayor tapped his pudgy fingers together and made a slight shrug before continuing.

"Lord Battersby? Would you and the delightful Lady Pettifogger grace me with your presence? We shall be serving only the finest Château de la Souris!"

"I could think of nothing better!" replied Battersby courteously.

"Ah! Wonderful," said the Mayor joyously. "What a fine morning it shall be, and with such an early rise I must take my leave. You have done a terrific service to Old Town, Mr. Lovelock. I take it you would not be averse to a lordship, like Battersby here?"

Lovelock allowed himself a dry smile.

"If you believe it necessary. . . ."

"Oh, I do!" he replied.

"I'll show you to the door," said Battersby, rising from his chair.

"Thank you once again, gentlemen," said the Mayor, and promptly left.

Alone once more in his office, Lovelock withdrew a tightly bound bundle of papers from his desk and placed them in front of him. He flicked through the yellowing pages, each one describing a few details of a different mouse accompanied by a roughly scribbled drawing. He'd never shown anyone these papers. They were from the building on Stormcloud Island that changed the course of his life, and were no one's business but his own.

Each mouse that adorned the pages was a mystery, and quite possibly had never existed: at least he'd never seen a note about any of them in any mouse book anywhere. The old hag that he stole the pages from assured him they were of no worth, but he didn't believe her. There was something about a series of markings at the bottom of each page that intrigued him. He had no idea what they meant, but they meant something, he was sure of it. And after all, if he'd never seen the pages he'd never have thought to write *The Mousehunter's Almanac.*

Suddenly a knock came on his door, and Battersby returned.

"They've finished the search, Isiah. A number of soldiers ran after a boy, but we've no news of that yet. Whoever broke in seems to have left as quickly as they came. Everything is intact," he said.

Lovelock felt enormous relief at the news. "That's wonderful, Alexander," he replied. "These mice will change our future — of that there can be no doubt."

"Do you need me for anything else, Isiah? I probably should be going myself. . . ."

Lovelock paused for a moment.

"As a matter of fact, there is a small thing," he said. "I've never shown anybody these papers before, but I wondered whether you might be kind enough to take a look."

Battersby walked to the desk and flicked through the pages.

"Mice?" he said.

"Most unusual ones, and I wondered if you had any idea what these inscriptions are at the bottom?"

"That's some sort of code, Isiah. I'm not the best at these things, though, but back at the barracks I have some friends who work on these sorts of ciphers. Smedley's particularly useful — I could get him to take a look?"

"Yes, that would be excellent," Lovelock said. "Hearing news of Mousebeard in Old Town made me remember them again."

"Mousebeard?"

"Oh it's ancient history now, you understand, but I never did get to the bottom of these pages. Probably best to keep them as much of a secret as possible."

"I'll do my best for you, Isiah. Secrecy is what I'm good at after all. . . ."

The two men finally shook hands, and Lord Battersby departed, leaving Isiah Lovelock alone with his thoughts of Mousebeard.

➣ ✻ ❧

It was still a few hours before dawn and the Old Town Guard were amassing at Pirate's Wharf. The extensive wooden scaffold, erected on the water's edge, was being inspected for the last time, with every screw tightened, and each rope secured. The gibbet stood empty, waiting for its next occupant — the great pirate Mousebeard. Not even a breeze was riding the river, which flowed slowly on its way out to sea.

While preparations were made for their execution, Mousebeard and Drewshank were huddled awkwardly in their prison cell. The pirate could feel his life ebbing away as the curse fulfilled its deadly promise. His once bulging body was thin and gnarled, and he was continuing to lose weight; his skin drawing closer to every bone. As he rested, his breathing was forced and irregular, and with each exhalation the blackness of his beard faded a little bit more to gray.

A key turned slowly in the prison door, and Drewshank stirred. Through the drift of greasy lank hair that dropped over his eyes, he watched a cloaked man walk in, his polished shoes clomping on the floor. He remained quiet and still.

Mousebeard moved a little, moaning in pain as he shifted along the floor. "I thought everyone had forgotten about me," he whispered, his voice hoarse and broken. "Left me with only rats for company. Not a mouse anywhere."

The man knelt down and placed his hand on the pirate's shoulder. He withdrew a small rum bottle from his cloak and held it so that Mousebeard could swallow every last drop.

"You'll last until the execution, won't you?" asked the man quietly.

"Don't worry, you'll see me hang. . . ."

"Excellent," said the man, "then things will surely go as planned."

The pirate raised himself slightly and took hold of the man's cloak.

"You've come to help me?" he asked wearily, his mind clouded with tiredness.

"Jonathan, has this curse eaten your memory too?" The man bent lower and whispered directly into Mousebeard's ear. "It's Horatio Spires. . . ."

Mousebeard tugged the cloak tighter, and a weak smile brightened his haunted face.

". . . Of course I've come to help, and before the hour's out, you'll be free once more. As long as this damned curse doesn't consume you first."

"They've taken my mice," said the pirate.

"I know they're in safe hands, but for the time being they'll have to stay where they are."

Drewshank finally broke from his silence. He sat upright, tugged at his chains, and motioned to the man. Spires saw him stir and raised a finger to his lips to stop him from speaking. He crept over to Drewshank and whispered to him.

"Keep Mousebeard alive. He's your ticket out of here. I'm sorry about this mess, but your friends have come to help you escape. It's not going to be easy. Stay calm to the last. . . ."

Spires quickly retreated to the door, and before he left placed something on the floor. Drewshank was certain he saw movement, but it was so dark he thought it was probably his overactive imagination. And no matter what Spires had said, he couldn't shake the fear of the scaffold from his mind.

The Nosferatu Mouse

A FOUL AND EVIL LITTLE CREATURE, THE NOSFERATU MOUSE IS LIGHT *gray in color with bright red eyes. Having a strong craving for blood, the Nosferatu Mouse is nocturnal and will sneak around in the dark recesses of alleyways, attacking vagrants and defenseless animals. The Nosferatu Mouse waits until its prey falls asleep, then bites deep with its fangs, sucking enough blood to double its body weight with each session.*

You can sleep soundly, though, as the Nosferatu Mouse is found only outside on the streets, and will never live in your home. Unless you invite it in, of course, and no one should be foolish enough to do that.

MOUSING NOTES

This mouse requires a licence to own, due to the danger it poses to all living creatures.

The Day of Execution

"WAKE UP, YOU LOUSY PIRATES!" SHOUTED A SOLDIER, banging on the cell door violently before opening it wide to the wall. The iron door chimed like a mourning bell and woke Drewshank with a start.

"Get to your feet!"

Drewshank stretched out and touched Mousebeard on the shoulder. The pirate was almost unrecognizable, but his beard, now gray, remained huge and consumed nearly his whole face.

"It's time," said Drewshank quietly.

Mousebeard was barely conscious, but he opened his eyes to the captain.

"Thank you," he croaked. "When we come through this,

captain . . ." He stopped to catch his breath. ". . . We will need to talk."

The pirate tried to move his chained arms, but his strength was at its lowest.

"What is wrong with you?" asked Drewshank. He placed his hands under Mousebeard's arms and tried to help lift him. His body was cold.

"It's a curse. . . ."

Drewshank wasn't usually one for believing such things, but now anything seemed possible.

"A curse? Why?"

Mousebeard tried to gather the energy to move, but he failed dismally.

"I'm cursed to sail the waves for ever . . . land is death to me. . . ."

"So that's why you couldn't attack Lovelock!"

"Blast that man," growled Mousebeard.

Drewshank helped to lift the pirate slightly higher. It was a start at least.

"I can't believe I'm here helping you," laughed Drewshank absurdly. "Only weeks ago we were trying to kill each other. . . ."

Mousebeard fell silent, but for the tortured breathing.

"Oi! I said get up!" shouted the soldier who had returned to their door. Five other soldiers barged into the cell and pulled Drewshank and Mousebeard to their feet. One of them proceeded to unlock them and join their chains together.

"Carry him," said a soldier to Drewshank, who propped his shoulder under the pirate's arm and took his much-diminished weight along with his own.

Drewshank was jabbed in the back and made to walk through the door and out into the corridor. A procession of manacled pirates was led out through the prison, with Drewshank struggling with Mousebeard on his shoulder at its very end.

The prison was steadily being lit by the glowing pre-morning sky. The sun was about to rise, its light allowing the prisoners to see the atrocious state of their cells as they passed. Black mold covered the walls, the floor was littered with straw and dirt, and rats were scurrying from door to door checking to see if the prisoners were still alive, looking out for their next meal.

The column of pirates wound out into the open

courtyard, where soldiers lined the route out toward Old Town. The pirates filed along silently, their eyes half closed, squinting at the light.

In front of Drewshank and Mousebeard trudged Scragneck. He occasionally glimpsed back and caught sight of them, but Drewshank evaded his glare.

"You'll swing wiv all of us, Drewshank, you scumbag!" shouted Scragneck, finally finding within himself a piece of bile he considered good enough to throw out.

A soldier at the side of the road swung his pike at him and hit him on the back. It failed to cause Scragneck much discomfort, but it at least shut him up.

"Is that Scragneck ahead?" wheezed Mousebeard, the fresh air reviving him a little.

"It is," replied Drewshank.

"That makes me happy . . . I'll get to see him die . . . One more reason to keep alive a little bit longer . . ."

"I could think of better reasons . . . ," muttered Drewshank.

Mousebeard coughed a dry laugh.

"When revenge is the only thing keeping you going for years . . . captain . . . it becomes your lifeblood. . . ."

"Revenge against Lovelock?" asked Drewshank.

Mousebeard took a short breath.

"Of course. It's only my will that's stopped me going mad all these years. . . . Each strike against Lovelock's empire was like an antidote to this curse. . . . I'm sorry for all the deaths that came about because of this, but I promise you, captain, Isiah would have done more damage to the world. These pirates . . ."

Mousebeard groaned as the pain increased throughout his body. Drewshank pulled him further onto his shoulder to take more of the weight from his legs.

"If we come through this," said Drewshank determinedly, "you can explain it better then. Just try to keep breathing for now."

The road and procession wound on, eventually reaching Old Town and the more recognizable streets lined with towering houses. Mousebeard stared at the townspeople filling the streets — they were there for him, after all. Heckling and cheering rang out from the windows and pavements as they passed.

The pirates were led through denser winding streets, and then eventually arrived at the river and Pirate's

Wharf. Drewshank had never seen so many people in one place before. The cobbled wharf front was rammed; rooftops were crowded, and the finished towers and viewing stands filled to bursting. Only a small square by the river edge was left clear for the prisoners. As they walked along the cobbles with the whole town's eyes upon them from both sides of the river, the blue horizon opened up into a bright pink sky. Light came flooding down onto the wharf, and if there hadn't been a scaffold and gibbet awaiting the prisoners, they would have all thought it the most beautiful sight.

"Quite a morning," murmured Mousebeard.

"Even the sun has come out to watch us die," said Drewshank morbidly, eyeing the scaffold.

The wooden platform rose up from the wharf and jutted out directly over the river to the other side like a wide, flat bridge. Two thick wooden posts stood upright at its edges, with a long joist running between their highest points. Six rope nooses hung down ready for the condemned.

Drumming drilled out from the assembled soldiers, and the prisoners were made to sit down in clusters on the cobblestones, just meters from the river. An armed guard, five men thick, surrounded them, and the first six prisoners were unceremoniously dragged out and pushed toward the scaffold.

"People of Old Town!" shouted the Town Crier, standing on the gallows platform. He looked at least seven feet tall, with a thin wispy beard. His dark green jacket was buttoned tight around his neck, and its coattails flicked back and forth with his gestures. The crowds started chattering excitedly in anticipation. The Town Crier let out a loud cough to regain everyone's attention, and his voice rang out to both sides of the river.

"There are two reasons why we're all here. . . ."

The crowd clung to his every word.

"First . . . to see these little golden beauties!"

The Town Crier pointed to the center of the crowd on Pirate's Wharf to where a cage containing the Golden Mice was suspended above their heads. The mice twinkled in the morning sun as though they were covered in dew. A band of soldiers and Lovelock's butler stood uneasily on guard below the cage.

The crowd hushed in awe. Everyone's eyes turned to

the cage. Judging the moment perfectly, the Town Crier started up again, his arms shooting out and waving wildly.

"Two perfectly formed Golden Mice! A rarer sight you won't see, and if it wasn't for the brilliance of the Old Town Guard, they would have met a grisly and untimely death. . . ."

The cheers thundered out again.

"And this brings me neatly to the second reason why you're all here. . . ."

The Town Crier puffed out his chest and strode to the edge of the platform.

"Let me present to you . . . the great . . . the magnificent . . . the soon-to-be-executed . . ."

The crowd shrieked as he pointed to the huddle of prisoners with his long arm.

". . . MOUSEBEARD!"

The whole of Pirate's Wharf erupted with devilish joy.

⇒ ❋ ⇐

Emiline was engulfed by the noise of the crowd as she slid through the back streets, dodging deftly from left to right to avoid the people. She was alert to everything around her, her eyes wide open and on the lookout for Miserley. Nothing would stop her from getting Portly back.

"Get out of the way!" shouted a man as Emiline hurried past. She elbowed him and rushed on, amazed at how many people had come to see the executions. Just past the entrance to the wharf, all the viewing stands loomed high. They were full of rich people dressed in fine clothes — all people that should have known better, she thought.

She avoided any soldiers on the way, ducking low and using her short height as an advantage to avoid prying eyes. When she first caught a glimpse of the completed scaffold through a gap in the crowd, she was overwhelmed. The Town Crier held everyone's attention as he paced back and forth, working his audience. When she spotted the cage of the Golden Mice she headed straight for them, squeezing into the tiniest gaps so that she could get closer.

The crowd suddenly erupted around her and started shouting "Mousebeard" over and over in a deafening chant. She carried on, finding it easier to move now that people had their arms raised and their attention focused on something. Eventually she saw Spires, looking awkward amongst the mob of people and soldiers, and she moved closer. Luckily no soldier knew who she was, so when she approached, they thought she was out to watch the executions like everyone else.

"Mr. Spires," she said cautiously, tugging at his jacket sleeve. "Any sign?"

Spires looked down and shook his head. He was trying to maintain an air of authority, and was partially succeeding.

"Nothing, I'm afraid," he said, his eyes fixed firmly on the crowd and not Emiline. "But Battersby isn't here yet. His seat is empty, and it's not like him to miss his moment of glory."

Emiline's attention was taken by the Town Crier, who had succeeded in dampening the noise of the crowd a little. She struggled to see over the crowd.

"And so we come to the purpose of this morning. Let me introduce the first of our condemned prisoners from the *Silver Shark*!"

The crowd roared again, and the six pirates were herded up through the crowds onto the wooden platform. The executioner was dressed in loose black garb, with a hood pulled down over his head. Through small eyeholes his beady eyes surveyed the prisoners as they walked past. Mr. Droob stood quietly next to him and made notes in his little book.

Emiline struggled to see the men walking onto the platform, and stretched up to try and see if it was Drewshank.

"Don't worry yet," said Spires, who had a much better view. "You won't miss Mousebeard or Drewshank. They'll be executed last. I'll make sure you get a good look."

Emiline realized that he was letting her know the situation without giving any secrets away to the soldiers next to him. It didn't do anything to stop her from worrying though.

"Any news on Scratcher?" she asked desperately as the drums got louder and more ferocious. Each pirate was being taken to a position above a trapdoor.

"Nothing. . . ."

Suddenly the drums stopped dead. Emiline looked to Spires as the trapdoors clunked down and the crowd roared. The deafening noise made the moment even more horrific.

Emiline grew steadily more scared as time passed with still no sight of Miserley. Group by group, the pirates took their turns on the scaffold. The crowd's cheering grew ever louder as the morning progressed, everyone awaiting the main event: the execution of Mousebeard.

⇒ ✳ ⇐

"Come on, boy!" shouted Battersby as he dragged Scratcher through the crowds toward Pirate's Wharf. An armed guard cleared the path ahead.

"There are more of them — they must be here," said Miserley, who was walking behind. Her eyes surveyed every face she passed.

"You're lucky you aren't going to hang too," said Battersby.

"I'm too useful," said the girl knowingly.

"For now, at least," he added. "I've been waiting for this day for years, and I'm sure not going to miss it because of those scum. I'll have my soldiers informed of your worries. No one will rescue Mousebeard. . . ."

"I wouldn't be so sure. I told you, I'll find them myself," she said.

"I don't care!" he shouted back, pulling Scratcher against his will. "The Old Town Guard will do a better job!"

The crowd started to react to this odd stumbling group. A ripple of acknowledgment spread through the people. When they realized it was Lord Battersby, his name was soon echoing around the wharf.

The Town Crier raised his hand to stop the executioner, and left six pirates standing helplessly over the trapdoors.

"And what is this surprise?" he shouted joyfully. "None other than Lord Battersby! What an entrance!"

Battersby basked in the adulation before reaching the base of the scaffold. Miserley stood close by.

"I've got another pirate to hang," he said proudly, and with these words the crowd cheered even louder.

Scratcher was thoroughly worn out and finished. His eyes were bruised and his face bloodied. It looked as though he'd been beaten and received no rest since his capture. He slouched behind Battersby, his arms tied.

"One more criminal for the gallows!" bellowed the Town Crier.

Emiline's face paled. She'd heard the chanting of Battersby's name, but she had no idea what had been going on. The crowd roared.

Spires gripped his hands and scratched his palms.

"They've got a boy they plan to execute, Emiline," he said plainly, trying not to let the worry show in his voice. "He looks about your age. . . ."

Emiline felt her hope vanish.

"But there's also a girl with Battersby. They're talking. . . ."

"Long dark hair?" asked Emiline.

"And a mousebox . . ."

"It's Miserley!" said Emiline.

"It would seem so," replied the butler.

Emiline took a deep breath.

"Don't worry, Emiline. I'll see what I can do."

Spires said a few words to the soldiers guarding the

Golden Mice and then pushed through the crowd, leaving Emiline alone.

⇒ ✳ ⇐

As the trapdoors dropped for the penultimate time, Scratcher was taken to the last huddle of prisoners. He was pushed to the floor next to his captain and Mousebeard.

"Scratcher!" said Drewshank.

"Hello," he replied sadly. "We tried to help. I don't know what happened to Emiline, but Battersby's men got me."

"I hate him," muttered Drewshank.

"His time will come soon," said Mousebeard, the color returning slightly to his white face. The fresh salty air that drifted out from the sea-bound river had revived his spirits a little. "Be strong, boy. This won't be your last morning. . . ."

Scratcher looked beyond the line of guards that surrounded them and was suddenly awed by the sight of rows of people seated high up in the stands. It was as if he were center stage in some nightmarish drama, and he felt indescribably scared and exposed. The scaffold was only meters away, and he trembled beneath its shadow. The crowd cheered again as the Town Crier returned to the execution platform.

"And now, the final part of the show — it's what you've all been waiting for!" he shouted.

Scratcher felt his leg being kicked, and a soldier arrived at his side.

"Your turn!" said the man gruffly, and prodded Mousebeard and Drewshank with his pike.

"Remember," whispered Mousebeard as Drewshank helped him find a footing on the stones, "you have friends, and in this world that's the most important thing. When you have friends, there's always hope. Don't give up yet."

Scragneck and two other pirates were also told to get up and pushed toward the scaffold. As the first of the pirates reached the platform, the crowd fell silent in wait for the great Mousebeard. Scragneck stepped up, looking out for any onlooker who dared to make eye contact. Drewshank followed them up the wooden steps, nerves shaking every muscle in his body. Nothing could have prepared him for such a feeling. The crowd let out a gasp as Mousebeard appeared on the steps, and a cheer burst out that almost lifted the roofs from their buildings.

As soon as Mousebeard stepped off land and onto the platform over the river, his breathing loosened, his eyes cleared, and he felt strength seeping back into his legs. The water coursing below his feet gave him power and the strength to stand on his own — if a little shakily. No matter how much he hated being tied to the sea, the feeling of being back on water filled his soul with determination, and a vengeful light appeared in his eyes. The executioner hurried him along to a noose and stood him alongside Drewshank, and the crowds roared their loudest.

Scratcher felt disoriented as he walked the length of the platform to the final empty noose. The noise and sights muddied his thoughts. He spied the crowd, but as hard as he tried he couldn't see Emiline. He was confident she'd tried everything she could to save them, but what could she do now? As he reached his position, the executioner draped the rough rope noose over his head. Mr.

Droob shouted out angrily, and he rushed along the platform, his hands waving in the air with frustration. "Nobody mentioned that a child would be up here!" he said. He tugged Scratcher's rope and started measuring it.

"Oh, but it's not going to be right!" he cursed, looking around for his assistant. Mr. Droob had to get everything right.

The executioner glowered at him.

"I didn't plan for this," he muttered. "You'll have to wait!"

≫ ❋ ≪

"Lord Battersby, sir," said Spires, catching up with the man on his way to join Lady Pettifogger and the Mayor in the grandest box on the tallest of the viewing stands. Miserley was walking alongside with a member of the Old Town Guard. She noted the butler's arrival with a look of disdain.

"Ah, Spires," said Battersby, "it's all going well, eh?"

"Absolutely, sir. Have you seen Mr. Lovelock at all?"

Lord Battersby smiled. "He's due to make his entrance any moment now."

"Good, good," said the butler.

Battersby reached the base of the stand, where two soldiers stood guarding the stairs to the seating.

"Well, I must leave you all," he said to Miserley and the guard as he made his way up. "Keep me informed of any findings!"

With that, the guard walked off, his rifle over his shoulder, and Miserley stood staring at Spires.

"What?" she said firmly.

"You look like a mousekeeper," he said, listening to the crowd cheer wildly in the background.

"And what of it?"

"I knew a girl your age who was a terrific mousekeeper, with blond hair and a little Grey Mouse. I just wondered if you knew her?"

Miserley sensed something odd in the butler's tone.

"What?" she asked with feigned confusion.

Since Battersby had left, the crowd had swelled into the area, trying to get a better view in what limited space there was. Spires stood motionless, but his face was stern.

"I don't know who you're talking about," she said, swaying slightly with the bustle of the crowd.

"You don't know Emiline?" he asked, moving a step closer to the girl. Spires knew it was now or never. "Are you sure?"

As soon as they'd been totally consumed by the crowd, Spires grabbed the girl. His hands squeezed hold of her wrists and he twisted her sharply around before she could clutch her weapons. He took hold of her mousing belt and tugged sharply, breaking the metal clasp and tearing it from her as she attempted to kick out. The mousebox attached to it came away freely, and he pushed her forward into the surging crowd — her cries of frustration smothered by moving bodies.

Making sure no one had seen his actions, Spires turned and tore off toward the scaffold and to where Emiline stood waiting.

⇒ ❋ ⇐

Mr. Droob continued measuring Scratcher's rope as the executioner freed the chains on all the other prisoners' legs. A soldier stood next to Mousebeard and made sure he was upright. Nooses were looped over their heads, and the crowd's chanting of "Mousebeard" grew ever louder.

"Havin' to die next to a worthless privateer," spat Scragneck, hissing under his breath, "is worse than having yer eyes poked out wiv mouse horns!"

"Shut up!" growled Drewshank, looking to the sky. He breathed in and found his mouth felt like sandpaper.

"Leave him to die angry," said Mousebeard gruffly.

Drewshank glanced at the pirate and noticed his beard twitching. He hadn't seen it do that since his mice had been taken away.

Once again, the Town Crier returned to the platform and marched along in front of the condemned.

"And so here we are, and here he is in his last moments . . . the pirate Mousebeard."

The crowd went wild.

"Shhh!" he said noisily, bouncing his hands up and down to quiet the crowd.

"But we've one more surprise for all you patient onlookers. . . ."

He paused for effect and then pointed to a carriage moving through the densely packed wharf.

"Let me welcome the world-famous mouse collector, Isiah Lovelock!"

The crowd fell silent with reverence. Most of them had never seen the man out in public before. The carriage stopped at the base of the scaffold, and Lovelock stepped cautiously down. He looked along the river and hesitated before walking onto the platform. He seemed to be breathing lightly, as though the salty air that flew down from the sea was not to his liking.

Mousebeard saw the man and let out a stifled laugh.

"Finally, we get to meet . . . ," said the pirate.

⇒ ✳ ⇐

"You have to go," said Spires, moving easily through the silenced crowd toward Emiline.

"What?" she said. "But Miserley, Scratcher . . ."

The butler pushed the mousebox into Emiline's hand, and she heard a bright squeak from its inside.

"Spires!" she said happily. "You did it!"

"I did, but she's still out there and will be intent on getting her own back. You must leave now. Go back to Algernon, otherwise everything could fail."

Emiline prized open the mousebox, and a sprightly

Portly rushed up her arm and came to rest under her hair.

"Go, Emiline! What are you waiting for?"

The butler's tone was insistent. Emiline wanted to hug the man, but he was looking at her sternly.

"Go!"

"Thank you, Mr. Spires," she said, running away as fast as she could.

⇒ ✳ ⇐

With Lovelock's first step onto the platform he felt his chest ache. He stopped and clutched his heart before proceeding further. It was as though his blood were freezing. He stumbled slightly, but then righted himself, and took a few short breaths. Mousebeard watched keenly as the man struggled over the decking toward him.

Both of them felt a buzzing within their bodies: a tingling from the toes to the top of their heads. It was as though sparks of electricity were gathering between and around them. Drewshank looked from left to right, watching both men with amazement. A blue light was now forming around the platform, emanating from the mortal enemies and getting brighter as they grew closer.

The crowd began chattering in excitement — they weren't exactly sure what they were witnessing. It was clear that there was something unearthly about the two men. As Lovelock walked farther along, passing the vile Scragneck, the executioner approached him.

"You all right, sir?" he asked.

"I'm fine! Yes!" he said, waving the man away. Lovelock was in control of the pain in his body, but it was growing stronger and stronger with every second.

"Jonathan," said Lovelock, his face fading from its usual gray color to white, "I'm glad to see you're finally in the place where you belong."

Mousebeard shifted his neck to move the noose slightly then looked straight into Lovelock's eyes.

"I'm glad to see the curse still affects you too," he said. "Your breathing is heavy. Your chest hurts. As we speak your life is seeping away. Just being this far from land clearly makes you feel as bad as it makes me feel good."

"But I had to see you one last time, old friend," Lovelock said bitterly. "I can cope with a small amount of pain just to enjoy your downfall. That old witch thought she could separate us for ever, but how wrong she was. And with you dead, the curse must die too."

"You'll never be free of me, Isiah, whether in this world or the next."

"You're a dead man, Jonathan. You're of no bother to me now."

As he finished speaking, Lovelock staggered slightly, and a ripple ran through the crowd. He pulled himself together and walked away from Mousebeard.

"And thanks for your help, Drewshank," he added breathlessly before stepping down. "You've been most helpful — I'm just so sorry it had to end in this way."

Drewshank growled like a true pirate.

Lovelock left the platform and raised his hand for the execution to resume. The drums started up again, rolling faster and faster. The soldier at Mousebeard's side walked away.

"Don't forget the boy," said Mousebeard firmly. His beard rustled and then fell completely still.

The soldier looked back at the pirate. "What?" he said.

"Don't forget the boy!" he barked again. Mousebeard's voice was terrifying, and suddenly Mr. Droob arrived, hot and bothered, with a replacement rope. He threw it over the scaffold with the soldier's help, and looped it over Scratcher's head. The executioner approached and hurried him along, as he made sure everything was correct.

"Look, it's got to be right!" snapped Mr. Droob.

"Just hurry up!" shouted the executioner.

Suddenly all Scratcher could hear were the drums rolling. Eventually Mr. Droob stopped his work and motioned to the executioner.

"It's done," he said, grateful to leave the platform.

Drewshank clenched his fists behind his back and gritted his teeth. He looked at all the faces in the crowd baying for his blood. He'd been to executions before but never fully understood how violent and horrible they were.

"They really want to kill us," he muttered.

"That's humans for you . . . ," said Mousebeard, his voice reaching its usual volume and depth.

The crowd was shrieking.

Drewshank took one last look at the beautiful blue sky. The sun had risen past the tops of the buildings and cast strong shadows across the whole of Old Town. He breathed one final, fulfilling breath that reached the bottom of his lungs.

The drum roll stopped.

The trapdoors unlocked.

The prisoners dropped.

The Cadaver Mouse

A BEASTLY MOUSE THAT THRIVES ON ROTTING MATTER — WHETHER *human, animal, or plant-based* — *you are more likely to smell the Cadaver Mouse before you see it. Often mistaken for a rat, the Cadaver Mouse enjoys the dark and roams around in packs, hunting for the next meal. These animals are rarely kept in collections, though it has been known for certain, darker sections of society to breed them and keep them in their cellars. The famous murderer, Obern Crown, was even said to have asked for his corpse to be thrown to his Cadaver Mice after his execution.*

There really are nicer mice to keep.

MOUSING NOTES

It's wise to stay as far away from these creatures as you can, as they mainly spread disease.

The Tail End

EMILINE HAD LEFT THE PACKED STREETS AND REACHED the deserted riverside downstream of Pirate's Wharf with little time to spare. The chants of the crowd carried down the river. The view of the scaffold was now partially blocked by a wooden barricade on the river path intended to restrict movement so close to the site of execution. Emiline knew that just on the other side were armed soldiers, but they would be far more interested in the hangings than the goings-on along the river.

At the inside curve of the river, Emiline saw the copper dome of Algernon's submarine breaking the surface. He'd cunningly covered it with a few pieces of scrubby

bush that had fallen in the river, and it was well concealed a short way out from the river bank.

"Algernon and his submarine . . . ," said a voice from
behind Emiline. "I figured there had to be some way you
escaped the island."

Emiline span round and saw Miserley.

"You're not going get away this time!" said Miserley,
two daggers held at the ready. Emiline sighed.

"Emiline? Is that you?" said Algernon, his head and
arms appearing from the hatch. He shoved all the green-
ery out of the way.

"You keep out of this, little freak man," said Miserley,
pointing the dagger in his direction. "It's between me
and Blonde here!"

"Stop calling me that!" said Emiline. Miserley just
looked at her with a sneer. Portly rushed onto Emiline's
shoulder and squeaked as angrily as he could.

Miserley leaped forward and lunged with her daggers
outstretched. One pierced Emiline's jacket as she twisted
to avoid the attack: it caught her between arm and
body, and she clamped her elbow tight to trap Miserley.
Sensing blood, Weazle couldn't hold himself back. He

rushed onto Emiline's shoulder and snapped at Portly with his dirty teeth. The Grey Mouse swiped his small paw in defense before running under Emiline's hair. Weazle followed, biting hard at the smaller mouse's tail. Emiline heard a loud squeak of distress close to her ear and, still holding onto Miserley's arm, kicked out, knocking the other dagger to the ground.

Emiline kicked out again, her anger rising, and this time aimed hard into Miserley's stomach. Her attacker crumpled in two, and Emiline released her arm and pushed her back. She felt the other mouse move under her hair and grabbed it, bringing it out for Miserley to see swinging from her fingers. Portly continued to squeak sadly, and appeared at Emiline's shoulder; the end of his tail was completely bitten off and a small trail of blood was running down Emiline's jacket.

"You want me to kill it!" said Emiline, filled with rage. "You want your mouse to die? I'll kill it!"

Miserley snarled and flicked her hair to the side in a gesture of defiance.

"Do it, Blonde!" she said, trying to call Emiline's bluff. "Go on, I dare you! You don't have the guts."

Weazle twisted his body and stared at Emiline with his jet-black eyes. She faltered, and Miserley sneered in disgust.

"Emiline!" shouted Algernon, who had brought his submarine directly behind her. Its engine was chugging along contentedly. "It's Spires . . . the sign!"

Emiline looked up to see a lone Messenger Mouse fly into the sky over the river.

Seizing her chance, Miserley charged and rammed Emiline with her shoulder. Weazle was catapulted into the air and Emiline screamed as she tumbled helplessly backward. She grabbed Miserley's jacket in a last-ditch attempt to right herself, and held it with all her might as they both careered head-first into the river with a great messy splash.

"Emiline!" shouted Algernon, grabbing his head in exasperation. He leaned farther out of the submarine and peered into the dirty river, but he could see nothing. Suddenly, Portly appeared at the surface with a burst of bubbles, struggling frantically against the current. Algernon swept him up and saw the horrible mess of his tail.

"Oh, what can I do? What can I do?" he muttered, using his other hand to clear dirt from the surface of the water. Each second that passed gave him less time to save his friends.

"Emiline! Where are you?"

The water started to bubble, then jitter. A shadow started to form below the surface, and then it broke and Emiline burst out, inhaling a massive gulp of air.

"Oh, thank heavens," cried Algernon, stretching out both hands and pulling her up and then hauling her into the little submarine. He pushed her down into the hull and slammed the hatch shut.

Emiline caught hold of the metal side and struggled for breath.

"Are we too late?" she asked, her heart thumping and water dripping from her jacket.

"We might be," he said grimly.

Algernon pushed the gear stick to send them powering through the water just a few feet below the surface to Pirate's Wharf. It was then that Emiline saw Portly and his poor tail.

"Portly!" she cried, picking him up and stroking him tenderly.

"He'll be fine with a bit of love and care," said Algernon. "But we're here now, Emiline. There's more to do yet!"

With all the commotion going on at the riverside no one noticed the submarine's tiny bubble trail popping on top of the water. They surfaced directly under the large execution platform, where they were hidden in shadow. Emiline quietly unlocked the hatch and looked up anxiously. She felt her heartbeat quicken. The trapdoors were still in place but she could hear the drums rolling.

"We made it!" she said, poking her head back into the submarine. She hoped that Algernon's mice had done their work. She clambered out onto the top of the submarine, conscious of her fingers twitching nervously.

The drums stopped. Emiline held her breath.

The Boffin Mouse

CONSIDERED THE MOST INTELLECTUALLY EVOLVED OF ALL MICE, THE *Boffin Mouse is capable of learning simple tasks and procedures. First discovered on the beaches of Endwyn, digging small Bumpworms out of the sand, Boffin Mice rarely take rest. It is thought that they thrive on being busy, and while they do have incredible concentration, they are also very sociable animals. With their happy and well-balanced temperament, Boffins make excellent companions for humans; they've even been known to take active roles in the workplace, where they excel.*

MOUSING NOTES

Teaching your Boffin Mouse is simple, but don't forget to reward excellence with treats. Their favorites are Jumbly Flies, but if these are hard to come by, try some delicious Brain Beans.

The Bond of Friendship

WITH A LOUD *CLUNK* THE TRAPDOORS DROPPED down, casting shards of bright light onto the river.

Two of the pirates came plummeting through to the river, but one remained suspended. Emiline was horrified by the sight of Scratcher hanging halfway through the trapdoor.

Drewshank and Mousebeard hit the water and struggled to remain afloat. Drewshank saw the submarine and shouted at Mousebeard. With their hands bound it was difficult to swim, but they struggled to the submarine's side. Emiline, still watching Scratcher's feet anxiously, grabbed Drewshank and pulled him closer with all the strength that she had.

"Scratcher!" she screamed.

"Oh no," muttered Drewshank as he clambered to safety, his eyes falling on the terrible sight.

Scratcher's body had dropped a few inches, but no farther, and his movements were getting slower.

On top of the scaffold, the three Boffin Mice were feverishly biting through Scratcher's rope. At the pirate's signal they had scurried from his beard, darted up his rope to the scaffold, and chewed through the prisoners' nooses — but the third had proved difficult. Mr. Droob had replaced it with a particularly strong kind. They gnawed away with immense determination at each separate strand of twine, every second seeming to last an eternity. But then, with the very last thread, the rope snapped, and Scratcher dropped like a stone into the water.

All three squeaked triumphantly. Algernon's training had taught them to be pleased with success, and their ears were bolt upright soaking in the pleasure and relief of finally saving Scratcher. But their time was short. The executioner had noticed that something odd had happened on top of the scaffold and was staring up at them.

The mice rushed along the long joist and scampered down to the platform, where they ran out unnoticed through the soldiers charging back and forth. They made their way to the cobblestones, scuttled along the riverside, and disappeared into the crowds.

The cheering suddenly stopped as the crowd inhaled in unison. Soldiers hurried to the river's edge and focused their rifles on the river. Battersby jumped up from his seat in the stands and pushed past Lady Pettifogger, who let slip a brief, wry smile. Isiah Lovelock yelled out as though a knife had been driven into his heart.

As Scratcher hit the water, Emiline cried with joy. She jumped into the river and caught hold of her friend as he sank below the surface. Then they both popped up, coughing. Scratcher could hardly breathe, his windpipe constricted by the rope around his neck, but he was alive at least. He struggled to speak. And then gunshots blasted out from the riverside. The Old Town Guard had opened fire on them. Bullets whizzed overhead and popped as they shot into the river.

Algernon reached out from the submarine and mustered enough strength to pull Scratcher in. The boy managed a delighted cry as he realized he was safe.

Emiline then turned for Mousebeard. His strength was returning rapidly, but he still needed help and was struggling to keep on the surface. Both Algernon and Emiline caught hold of his jacket. Emiline pushed and Algernon tugged as hard as they could. Thin as he'd become, the pirate was still incredibly heavy, but together they managed to get him to the hatch where he could pull himself in. Mousebeard looked up quickly to see Scragneck's body hanging limply below the scaffold.

"Thank you," he said, before squeezing into the submarine. "Your mice were unbelievable. . . ."

"They are a clever bunch," said Algernon. "They'll be all right out there. I'm sure of it."

Emiline let the pirate and Algernon drop down and then followed them. Soldiers had jumped into the water and were closing in. She lowered her head and secured the hatch.

"Get a move on!" she shouted — a call that was echoed by everyone inside.

The submarine's engine kicked in louder than ever, and they sped off, leaving Old Town to become a dark and hated memory.

➤ ✳ ⬅

"No!" shouted Battersby, charging down from the viewing platform. "Where's that girl? Where's that Miserley girl?"

Isiah Lovelock and his butler met him at the bottom of the stand.

"Alexander," said Lovelock calmly. Inside he was fuming. "We have the mice and Mousebeard's ship. The pirate can do us no harm in the foreseeable future."

"They've made a laughingstock of us. And that girl knew it all along. Where's she gone?"

"We caught Mousebeard once, Alexander; we'll catch him again. He now has no crew — he can't do a thing. In two months' time we'll have piles of golden fur and enough money to buy an even larger army and navy. He won't get away. . . ."

Battersby's red, angry face gradually lost some of its fire.

"Well, for now we'll let them run, Isiah. But they know too much of our plans. It will come back to haunt us if we're not careful."

"I'm always careful, Alexander."

Battersby nodded. "But just to make me feel happier, I'm going to find out who among the Old Town Guard let this happen, then make them pay with their lives."

"If it makes you happier," said Lovelock. "Maybe you'll find our spy that way!"

"I will find that traitor if it's the last thing I do," Battersby said angrily, and marched off.

Spires stood quietly, looking along the river to where the estuary panned out into the sea. He knew all too well that his time in Old Town would soon have to come to an end.

"Spires!" called Lady Pettifogger. Ever poised, she arrived beside them, seemingly unruffled by the recent drama. "Is our carriage ready?"

"Yes, ma'am," he said, his mind elsewhere. "Sir?"

Lovelock looked at him.

"We should be going. The streets will prove a horror to travel in with this crowd, sir."

"You're right, Spires, of course. What would I do without you?"

The butler smiled.

"Thank you, sir," he said.

⇒ ✳ ⇐

Once the submarine had passed the navy blockade of the harbor, Algernon set it motoring of its own accord and breathed a sigh of relief. Despite having lost his mice to Old Town, he was sure they could look after themselves. He swiveled the pilot's chair and flicked a small switch, turning on a thin blue line of lights that traveled around the interior. Algernon looked back into the rather cramped submarine and couldn't help but laugh. Mousebeard was taking up an unfair amount of room, with his legs turning at an awkward angle to avoid Drewshank, who was contorted around the submarine's curved side — it wasn't built for men of their stature. Emiline and Scratcher were sitting right at the far end, with even less room. No one was particularly comfortable, but it was definitely preferable to standing under the gallows.

"Algernon," said Mousebeard, "I owe you my life."

"It's these mousekeepers you should thank," he said honestly. "A braver pair I've never known."

The pirate twisted his heavy head around to look at them, sitting at the back. Scratcher was holding his neck. He was still in great pain and could hardly talk. Emiline was simply exhausted. She looked back at Mousebeard nervously. The pirate, though much thinner, was still a sizable man and his brooding face continued to fill her and Scratcher with a certain amount of dread.

"I knew there was something about you two when we first met. Accept my apologies for any pain I caused."

Emiline thought back to the moment she and Scratcher had been flung at Mousebeard's feet onboard the *Silver Shark*. It seemed strange they were now sharing Algernon's submarine with him.

"It's fine," she said bravely. Scratcher rubbed his neck and tried to form a smile.

"I shall make up for it, I give you my word," said the pirate solemnly.

"But my, you're looking thinner, Jonathan!" laughed Algernon. "You look like you did fresh out of Mousing Academy — apart from the gray hair, of course."

"Gray hair?" said Mousebeard, shuffling around to make his body fit the small space better. He grabbed his soaking beard, wrung it out like a wet cloth, and lifted it to his eyes.

"It's gray! No!" he said, panic rising within him. Throughout all the time that the curse ate into his being, he hadn't realized his black beard had been losing all its color, while his clothes now looked as though they had space for six of him.

"This is ridiculous!" he said, pulling at the saggy folds of his shirt. "That damned Isiah Lovelock! How will anyone take me seriously looking like this?"

"You'll need a ship first, Mousebeard!" said Drewshank wearily. He felt utterly bedraggled and couldn't even bring himself to look at the state of his clothes.

"The *Shark!*" proclaimed Mousebeard, jumping to his

feet. The submarine rocked and faltered in the water. Its engine started to roar unhappily.

"Jonathan!" yelled Algernon, stretching to the controls and steadying the ship. "This sub isn't made for big oafs like you!"

Mousebeard froze and held his arms out to find a balance.

"Don't worry, it's all right," added Algernon finally, after tweaking the controls.

Mousebeard slowly returned to the floor, and avoided the sprawl of everyone's legs.

"But they stole my ship!"

"Don't worry about it," said Drewshank, "at least they didn't destroy her as you did mine."

"Ah, yes," growled Mousebeard, "but you were asking for it. . . ."

"Hey!" said Algernon, looking at the pirate sternly.

"You're right," said Mousebeard moodily. He turned to Drewshank, his face tightening as he attempted not to frown. "I think we should let all that's happened in the past be forgotten, captain. You've made up for your bad judgments."

"Those words," said Drewshank sarcastically. "From a pirate like you they mean the world."

Mousebeard lifted one of his bushy eyebrows. Behind them Emiline and Scratcher held their breath.

"You need me as much as I need you now, Drewshank. Lovelock won't let us get away with this. He's going to come after us harder than ever before, and don't be surprised if we find we now have even more enemies."

"Ah, yes," said Algernon. "The Mousing Federation will rally the nations of the world to seek us out. We'll be cutthroat fugitives!"

He looked rather excited.

"Battersby will never let us rest," added Drewshank bitterly.

"So what are we going to do?" asked Emiline, who was nursing Portly's wounded tail. The mouse hadn't been right since Weazle's attack.

"We're going to strike back," boomed Mousebeard, making Emiline shrink back against the submarine wall. "We'll start afresh. There's fight left in me yet. We can't let Lovelock turn all the mice in the world into his slaves!"

"What about my crew on your island?" asked Drewshank.

"Your friends? They'll be good for a while. The volcano — if it's still standing — is the best defense there is. Once we have a ship, it'll be our first port of call. We can send them a message to let them know our plans; I'm sure I can spare some of the Rodent Rum in my cellar. . . ."

Mousebeard's left eye almost trembled into a wink.

"I guess they're old enough now to look after themselves for a while," Drewshank concluded. "Fenwick will see to it that they're all right."

Mousebeard scrunched his beard in his hand. "And how will they feel when I ask them to join us, Drewshank?"

"Us?" he said, slightly shocked.

"Of course," exclaimed Mousebeard. "I'll need a first mate, and I'll be needing a new crew. . . ."

"Well, I don't know about being first mate!" spluttered Drewshank.

"How about Captain of Land-based Adventures?"

Drewshank shrugged in acceptance. That sounded

quite grand, he thought, trying to persuade himself. He was finding it difficult to picture himself on a ship full of fugitives, after his rather dazzling career as captain.

"And we'll be requiring some mousers too . . . ," said Mousebeard.

Emiline and Scratcher sat up.

"You want us too?" said Emiline.

Mousebeard eyed them thoughtfully.

"You saved my life. At some point I want to repay that debt. I can teach you a lot about the mousehunting world, as long as you're prepared to live the life of a wanted pirate?"

Scratcher looked nervous, but despite everything she knew about Mousebeard, Emiline was starting to feel some excitement as well as trepidation. She still wasn't sure if Mousebeard was more bad than good, and he was definitely the most terrifying man she had ever met, but she could understand a bit more about why he had become that way. The world of mice was a much darker and more dangerous place than she'd ever imagined, but that only made her want to see more.

The excitement of the day had taken quite a toll on

Portly and, against Emiline's wishes, he crawled down her arm and scampered off to stand on Mousebeard's stomach. The pirate had always been popular with mice, and he knew full well what Portly wanted. He bent over slightly, allowing the Grey Mouse to scurry up his body and find a warm nest right in the heart of his damp beard. Mousebeard let out a growl of a sigh. Even though Portly wasn't like his own mice, it was comforting to have him there, and it made him feel like himself again — so much so that the feeling of revenge started to bubble deep inside him.

"Algernon," he said darkly. "It's time . . . ," His voice trailed off.

"Time for what?" Algernon replied, looking at him with puzzlement.

"To break the curse that lies within me. I am ready. . . ."

Mr. DROOB PACED PIRATE'S WHARF, SURVEYING THE
last remaining soldiers as they dismantled the
huge scaffold over the river. Bodies had recently stopped
washing ashore, possibly due to the high presence of
soldiers in Old Town guarding against any wrongdoing.
Over the past few weeks, his assistant had had next to
nothing to do, and spent many hours wandering along
the riverside with his hook and lamp, dragging his heels.
Today had changed their fortunes, however.

It was a dark and misty night yet again, and a cold
breeze — enough to chill the tips of your fingers in
your fingerless gloves — blew across the wharf. Despite
the lack of recent rich pickings washing up from the

river, Mr. Droob's pockets were bulging with money, and while keeping his hands warm he flicked through the dollars.

He was pleased with his work and had been paid a lot to see to all the pirate bodies. He would have liked the chance to deal with Mousebeard, but even without the captain he couldn't argue with what he'd been given. There was no body in the world as colorful as a pirate's, and he took a last look at the cage of the gibbet, swinging gently. It was his masterpiece, and he took great effort to make it as imposing as possible.

The ironwork trapped the pirate perfectly, with only one arm falling limply through the bars. Apparently, the pirate had been called Scragneck, and Mr. Droob thought the name most apt. He was an excellent warning to any would-be pirates.

Mr. Droob called to his assistant to come out of the cold, and then headed back to his hut, where a warm fire was burning away. The night was going to be a long one.

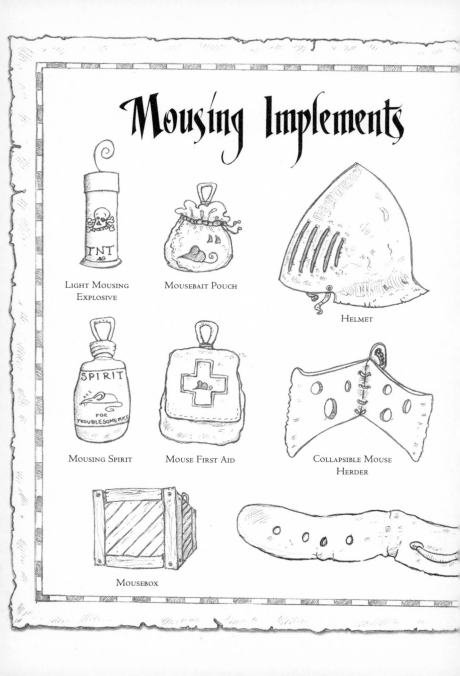

Mousing Implements

Light Mousing Explosive

Mousebait Pouch

Helmet

Mousing Spirit

Mouse First Aid

Collapsible Mouse Herder

Mousebox

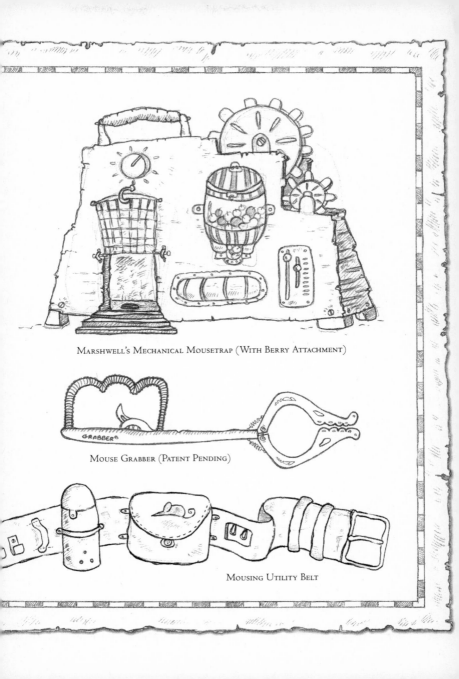

MARSHWELL'S MECHANICAL MOUSETRAP (WITH BERRY ATTACHMENT)

MOUSE GRABBER (PATENT PENDING)

MOUSING UTILITY BELT

Algernon's Workshop
& Submarine

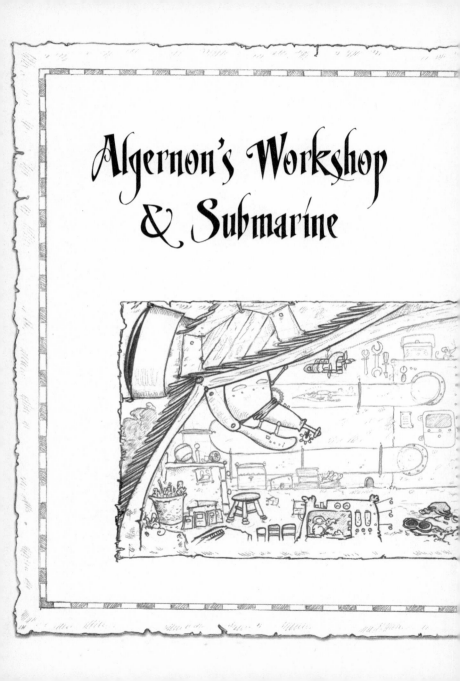

Acknowledgments

OVER THE COURSE OF WRITING THIS BOOK, SO MANY people have given me so much, but there are a select few who deserve a special thanks:

Mum, Dad, Rob, Gran, Nan, and Granddad — your support has always been there, and I couldn't have asked for more.

John, Lia, Caroline, and Oli — you gave so much more to The Mousehunter than just your names.

Richard, Patrick, and Billy Gibson — your encouragement really helped me get to the end.

Everyone at PC Pro magazine — never before has a group of people endured such incessant musings, ramblings, and drawings on the theme of mice.

Emma Snow and Catherine Daly — one chance meeting turned a dream into a reality. Thank you.

Laura Cecil — your confidence and support have been incredible.

Roisin Heycock — your enthusiasm from the outset made this little book so much more than it was.

Katie Lee — the love of my life and my best friend. This book was written for you.